THE CAPTAIN'S LADY

A MARRIAGE OF CONVENIENCE HISTORICAL ROMANCE

ROBECCA AUSTIN

COLORFUL PEN PRESS

EXCERPT FROM THE CAPTAIN'S LADY

"Are you drowning, Lady Isabella?" His Scottish accent was a bath in hot springs. His thumb brushed the tip of her nose. Lingered. Her nostrils flared and the scent of him invaded her senses. His hands snaked around her waist, guiding her closer.

"You," Isabella whispered.

"Aye, me." He kissed her cheek. "Is your nose still covered in freckles, lass?"

"No!"

"Liar." He brushed the tip of her nose with his. "Did he kiss you?" His lids lowered to watch her mouth. "I'll be damned if I kiss you after him."

"No." She shivered, the sensation curling her toes in anticipation. "Emsley didn't kiss me." The man holding her in strong arms was something old, from her past, something forgotten. Isabella relaxed, molding against the captain. Oh, but she needed this, to feel like a woman again, alive and desired. His tongue brushed against her lips, not once but twice, tracing the outline of her mouth—a delightful distraction from her recent episode.

"Let me in, lass."

His warm breath fanned her face. She had dreamed of this, years ago, when she was young and thought the world not full of danger but adventure. His gaze moved from her mouth, wet from the tantalizing brushes of his tongue, to her eyes. In the darkness of the night, his eyes were black fire. Hot. Wicked.

"What a bonnie reward for my second rescue."

"You've botched your count, sir."

"A new tally is in order, then."

"Brilliant."

He smiled. His lips descended in slow torture, groaning his approval when his tongue brushed hers. All rational thoughts scattered. He explored her mouth. Heat pooled. Fanned out. The shudder that shook her was not from anger, but fear and desire.

The sea, that's what he was. Raging waves that didn't settle in the wee hours of dawn.

ALSO BY ROBECCA AUSTIN

Ladies in Scandal Series

THE CAPTAIN'S LADY
HER RUNAWAY EARL
HER WICKED VISCOUNT

Robecca Austin is a truly gifted writer. She knows how to set a scene, subtly develop a character, and build tension as the story unfolds. She evokes time and place in elegant strokes, and creates vividly realized, emotionally rich people. Her first book is a cause for celebration!

    —Kate Cayley, Trillium Book Award Winner, How You Were Born

I adored every single thing about this book! From the characters jumping off the page to the perfect plot, I loved this story.

    —Goodreads reviewer

Robecca Austin has created a compellingly romantic and adventurous story set in the vibrantly-portrayed Regency period, *The Captain's Lady* is rich with vividly-drawn characters in captivating and smouldering scenes of surprise and intrigue. Who could resist?

—Gary Barwin, author of *Yiddish for Pirates,* shortlisted for the Governor General's Literary Award and the Giller Prize

THE CAPTAIN'S LADY

Print edition ISBN: 978-1-9990032-3-4
E-book edition ISBN: 978-1-9990032-4-1
First Edition: August 2020
Cover Designer: Erin Dameron-Hill
Edited by: Enterprise Book Services
Formatted by: Colorful Pen Press

Colorful Pen Press
www.colorfulpen.com

Thank you for buying a copy of this book and for supporting independent creative works.

To receive advance information, news, and exclusive offers online, please visit www.robeccaaustin.com.

ACKNOWLEDGMENTS

My husband, who shows faith and patience while I create stories.

My children, for their company, though often filled with distractions.

The Wordsilly crew for your support.

Meghan Mazzaferro, for your thoughts and insight.

Mom, your encouragement has been second to none.

Uncle Frank, for reading my first drafts. Hugs.

For everyone who has and continues to believe in Robecca Austin.

To you, my loudest cheerleaders. Thanks for reading my stories.

CHAPTER 1

London, England
The start of the Social Season

*C*aptain Nicholas Ferguson walked through the dining room as the china was being laid out for the evening meal. Two hours into the festivities and he was convinced his solicitor, Tom, had misled him. Tonight presented no opportunity to align himself with the upper echelon of London. He scowled at a small group of young ladies whispering behind their fans as he passed. Their giggling and gossiping was another reminder that he did not belong among the elite. He was as far apart from them as a goat was to a stallion—no doubt they thought him the goat— yet he needed their wealth and connections. It was the one reason he'd worn this damnable attire instead of sporting his kilt. They already considered him a barbarian—his lips twitched—and Tom insisted he not add to the flames. Near the end of the large room, he loosened his necktie, intent on slipping away unnoticed.

"Good evening, Lady Isabella." The footman's voice rose above the noise coming from the ballroom.

"I prefer not to be announced."

He'd never forget the sound of a voice he'd heard years ago calling out for help. Nicholas's steps faltered. He stopped behind a large potted plant. He moved closer to the absurd palm a few feet from the foyer. From his position, he assessed Lady Isabella from her beaded slippers to the top of her pinned hair. Her dress, though not the latest French fashion, cupped curves matured by womanhood. Arched stiffly, her shoulders were held in a tutored position and her eyes looked guarded. Full lips stretched into a wisp of a smile that did not reach her eyes.

The fire-cat he remembered now looked subdued. The previous time he'd seen her, five years earlier, she had been standing in an old rowboat that was twice the size of a hip-bath and flaked with red paint. On a lake that separated two properties, she had drifted toward the whitewashed eight-foot marker. He had handed the last case of liquor he'd been holding to the kitchen lad to stow, then leaned against a post to watch. A gust of wind swept her umbrella into the air, and she began to hop from foot to foot.

"You think she's in trouble?" the lad asked.

"I trust she's getting her stockings wet," Nicholas said.

The boat rocked from one side to the other, and she tried to gather handfuls of lace and frills. The higher she lifted the silly frock, the more her calf and knee were exposed.

"Might be she aims to have a wee swim." The lad chuckled. "There be a damsel, Captain, if I ever saw one."

"Impertinent…"

Her arms flapped. The boat tipped, and she was thrown overboard.

Her loud splash drew gasps from the onlookers. Her flurry of fabric disappeared beneath the darkened waters. He hesitated at first, partly because he wanted to see what would happen next and partly because he knew his efforts would be unrewarded. Seconds later, when she didn't resurface, Nicholas ran to the end of the boat dock. He unbuttoned his tailcoat and dropped it onto the green grass. The heel of his boot in hand, he dragged one then the other off, tossing them against the wooden platform. At the end of the dock, he arched his shoulders, arms shooting outward. He took a breath, then plunged into the dark water.

His hands circled her slender waist, and he swam towards the capsized boat. The small vessel provided some cover and a place to allow her some composure before she confronted her friends. Face flushed, she took labored breaths. Each indrawn breath brought the fabric of her gown straining against her chest, but it was her flushed cheeks and tilted chin that drew his attention, sending a whisper of awareness seeping through his wet clothing. She looked at him for a measured moment, then squeezed her eyes shut as if the sight of him stung her eyes. In that instant he knew the woman in his arms was not helpless. That she had expected to be rescued long before the hem of her expensive silk gown swept the bed of the river. She just did not expect her rescuer to be him.

"How dare you? Unhand me!"

He did as she ordered, but she began to sink. He pulled her upward; she choked and slapped the water in an effort to float. "Your dress is too heavy," he said, and held her against his chest.

Her cheeks pinkened. Her fingers shook and she pushed wet strands of hair from her face. She looked ridiculously adorable not hidden behind social conventions. Her racing heart echoed his through their wet clothes. She looked to him again, her freckles dancing beneath the droplets of water. Bedraggled and beautiful.

"Who are you?"

"Relax. I'm trying to save you."

"Where is Emsley?"

"Who?"

"Oh, take me back. You've ruined everything."

He watched her chin quiver, eyes glossed with unshed tears. She was embarrassed and disappointed.

"Why are you not picnicking with your friends, enjoying the sun?" he asked.

She blushed and turned away to avoid meeting his eyes.

"Aye." He shook his head. "This Emsley fellow? He didn't rescue his lady. He's no gentleman."

Her lips thinned. "Neither are you, sir."

"Ah, but I'm the one that's wet," he said. "Let's get you back to him, then." His right hand circled then tightened around her waist, ready to take her back to shore.

"Wait!" she hissed.

Nicholas paused, the panic he heard in her strained voice making him curious and too interested in her plight for his own good. He didn't know why he was tempted to soothe her nervousness, but he found himself wanting to reassure her. He clenched his teeth against squeezing her slender waist in comfort and kept his hands as they were.

"Can we have another moment?"

The color dusting her cheek and her lowered lashes told him that she was embarrassed.

"To rattle your fellow?"

She was bold and daring, he mused, yet her eyes revealed a hint of vulnerability that contradicted everything he thought he knew of high society. Her cocktail of courage and innocence tugged at his soul. She had attempted to gain her gentleman's attention by drifting off into the lake. Her plan might have worked, too, if she'd checked the boat for holes and her gentleman didn't lack the courage this lady possessed. Now that her plan had failed, Nicholas mused, she was trying her hand at jealousy.

"A man can always tell when his lass has been kissed."

"But we… I did no such thing."

At least her frustration did not stem from the disgust so many English ladies showed at being in the presence of a Scot. There was hope yet. Or perhaps it was their hidden position that made her bold.

His knuckles brushed the side of her face, then tucked a wayward strand of hair behind her ear. Her eyes closed when the pad of his thumb touched her nose, and he felt her swift intake of air on his finger before her breath held. He spread the fat droplets of moisture along her nose, over her parted lips, and wished he had time and the lineage of a peer to explore each freckle. "You're thinking of it," he said, and to his satisfaction, she reddened. "Don't let go," he warned before encircling her waist.

She had clung to him that day.

Now, Lady Isabella left the foyer and descended the stairs. No, he hadn't forgotten the fire-cat, and neither had his body. Since the scandal, the changes in her were subtle, but he noticed. She was not floating around the room, enchanting each gentleman with her bewitching smile. He was no gentleman, no English peer, but a Scottish Captain intent on marrying Lady Isabella, even if that meant exploiting the scandal surrounding her broken engagement. However, he did hope to restore her confidence.

He walked along the edge of the ballroom, careful to avoid people as he moved through the crowded space. The host of the party took Isabella's arm, and she threw back her head and laughed at some scandalous nugget the host whispered in her ear. He doubted she noticed the curious glances she received and, as he watched her, his hope flared that she'd not completely buried her true nature or turned cold.

The hall stood still. He stopped when she turned in his direction. Her eyes lifted, met his gaze. He watched color creep up her neck, transfixed. The flush dusting her cheeks grew bright, and, for a brief moment, he saw a glimpse of recognition in her eyes before she turned away.

CHAPTER 2

etermined not to cower, Lady Isabella Pennington stepped through the high arched entryway that led to the ballroom. If she turned around now, no one would notice. No one would recall she had been here. The tips of her fingers tingled. No matter what she told herself, she couldn't dispel the trickle of cold fear lining her veins. It was the same fear that told her the upper class did not forget scandal.

Her breath caught on the scent of buttered pastries. The fragrance perfumed the air. Jeweled and leather-tailored slippers filled the floor. The center of the room was lit by a fueled chandelier that hung from the high ceiling. Mounted lamps with glass chimneys were fastened along the walls. Ladies of fashion wore the latest styles: rich silks and lowered bodices that would have created a scandal if worn two Seasons ago. Now beaded tailoring was the rage of London. Her fingers touched her own dress: a deep yellow she had commissioned from the dressmaker last year. Though simple in comparison to the fashion of her peers, her foresight in removing the laced trim from her undergarments and adding the material to the bodice and skirt worked in her favor.

"Isabella, is that you?"

Isabella turned and stared at Lady April Godric. They had attended finishing school together and made their debut the same year. April, however, had found a husband her first Season and, from her growing abdomen, it appeared she was also with child. They smiled at one another and she'd never been more grateful to see a friend.

"I hoped to find you here," April said and hugged her. It was an awkward embrace, but they were too happy to care.

They had tried to remain friends after her scandalous broken engagement. April had been kind enough to send word offering private support, but that had also proved impossible with April's husband, Lord Richard, battling scandal of his own—being accused of killing his first wife. Her other friendships had crumbled like old plaster beneath the weight of impropriety; they sought husbands of their own and couldn't afford a tarnished reputation. She understood. She did not blame them for their lack of loyalty. After months on her own, she knew their fears.

"You must know I didn't believe any of it, not for a moment," April said. She leaned close. "All of London knows you were in love and wouldn't have risked it over an affair. Least not until you were well married."

Isabella wrinkled her nose. Lord James Emsley, her former fiancé, had planted seeds of doubt among his friends regarding her supposedly less-than-chaste character—though she had no proof of his involvement, those whispers were enough to avert potential suitors. It was not until after she confronted her father that she learned she no longer had a dowry and guessed at the real reason Emsley called off their engagement.

"And your father, surely he must see reason."

"It's not so dreadful, renting an apartment. I have the freedom of a spinster. Another year on the shelf and no one will raise a brow," she said, patting April's hand. Over April's shoulder Isabella saw three of Emsley's friends heading towards them. She shifted deeper into the shadows where the light did not quite meet the corner. Old hurt and humiliation rose to choke her. She should not have attended the ball regardless of her intentions.

April rose to the tips of her toes and looked over Isabella's shoulder. Isabella's fingers tightened on her friend's hand, willing her to still her movements and not draw attention, but April's brief glance was enough to note who had captured Isabella's attention.

"How's your husband, Lord Richard?" Isabella quickly blurted in an attempt to regain her friend's attention. She could have pinched April. The last thing she needed was for Emsley's friends to note April's strained gaze focused on them.

"Richard's embarrassingly attentive," April said. She unfolded a handkerchief before blotting the perspiration pooling around her neck. "We both know you're not the least bit interested in my husband."

Isabella looked at her friend, her lips parting in objection, then closing when April giggled.

"I haven't seen Emsley, if that's what you're wondering. I did, however, hear he was in London," April whispered. "Not much of a honeymoon if you ask me, and I can't imagine he'll show here."

The first ball of the Season, of course he'll show, Isabella thought. Lord Emsley never missed an opportunity to be noticed. A small part of her, however, wished April was right. "Why wouldn't he attend? He lost nothing."

April frowned. "He lost you."

Isabella swallowed, waved away April's words. "Nothing of consequence, I mean. What of his wife; do you know who she is?"

"I haven't met her myself," April said and gave Isabella one last assessment before facing the room again. "She was born and raised here with her mother. That's where her title comes from. The girl's father, however, is an American who made his fortune in the coal mines."

"Oh." There was something intriguing about earning one's wealth and being able to replicate it, not to be dependent on or begging aid.

"And from her swiftness in luring Emsley, I'd say she does not give a fig for rules of propriety."

She agreed with April: Lady Emsley's actions mirrored a woman who knew the power of money on not one continent but two—not a spoiled girl.

"I insisted my husband seek his friends' company, but I'm afraid I must find him now," April said, "before he gambles a year's income over a hand of cards. If you need anything, Isabella, you have only to ask."

April opened her fan and left her side. Isabella watched her move deeper into the room until the crowd swallowed the smallest glimpse of her. With no lady companion, Isabella intended to stand among the wallflowers but then decided against it. They were looking for husbands and would pounce at an opportunity to be cruel.

Isabella searched the crowd of women with their pinned hair twisted in exotic fashion. She looked for faces of dwindling wealth to whom inexpensive music lessons might appeal. Her choices of income were tutoring or becoming a governess. She shuddered at the thought of becoming a governess for ladies she once considered her peers. Ladies who would remind her at every turn her new lot in life. No, tutoring was her only option—the post paid better and she could tolerate the parents in small doses.

She did not notice Lady Jane, Duchess of Kenningsly Estate, step into her path. The older woman was her mother's childhood friend. The last time they had seen each other was at her mother's funeral years ago.

Isabella's heart raced. She hoped the woman remembered sending an invitation and that she'd accepted before the scandal broke. Would the duchess have her escorted out? Isabella felt numerous eyes in the room and knew she was not the only one awaiting the older woman's verdict. No, she decided, this woman was her mother's friend; she would not create a to-do at her own party.

"Lady Isabella." The duchess's smile emphasized her high cheeks and straight nose.

She curtsied. "Duchess, what a grand event to start the Season."

"I am delighted you were able to attend." The duchess's eyes twinkled. Eyes that mirrored the color of her dark green dress.

Isabella raised a brow. "Are you?"

The older woman threw back her head and laughed. She linked her arm through Isabella's and steered them in a new direction. At least she was not being led to the door. "Of course, dear. After all, I did request your presence."

"So you did."

"Could you imagine, my ball, the talk of the ton for weeks? Ladies will be asking my recommendations before sending a single invitation."

"I am happy for you."

The duchess's eyes sparkled with mischief, and she laughed again. It was a rich sound, as if used often. Her bosom swelled with merriment to the top of her dark green gown. Isabella had mistaken the lines on the older woman's face to be those from age, but the lines deepened each time the duchess laughed. Those wrinkles were caused from much happiness and high spirit. Isabella wondered if she would ever be so lucky.

"Since your success in planning balls is linked to my embarrassment, you are sure to be remembered forever and a day."

"Come now, your slip will be forgotten by then."

Isabella groaned. "My apologies, I didn't mean to suggest you did not turn me away for your own benefit." The woman had not caused her disgrace and, so far, had shown Isabella more kindness than her own father. She had also given Isabella comfort in the weeks that followed her mother's death.

The duchess waved away her apology. "I see fire in you, and if this gaggle of…" she extended her hand to include the room, "bores don't see that, they can all go hang. What do you say we even the odds, dear?" The duchess stopped and turned until they were facing the dance floor. "Do you see the two ladies across the room, dressed in lavender and sage? Have you noticed how their husbands keep refilling their glasses?"

Isabella nodded.

"I happen to know they often partake in naughty adventures."

"All four of them?"

"In the same bedchamber, dear."

Isabella flushed, then giggled. The duchess continued to feed her tidbits of gossip as they circled the room, each more scandalous than the last. She forgot the crowd, forgot her reasons for attending the ball. She floated, arm in arm with the host of the ball. The duchess had saved her with this show of kindness.

For a moment her woes became a distant echo, until unease nipped at the fine hairs along the back of her neck. This particular sensation, however, was distinct. It was a never forgotten feeling of awareness. One she'd only experienced once, years ago, under the gaze of her dark-eyed rescuer. She was being watched, and the suspicion both frightened her and sent her blood racing.

She was searching the sea of people when her eyes settled across the room. A gentleman turned from the hallway where she guessed housed the gentlemen's card game and library. He towered over most of the men. Thick strands of raven hair inches above the high collar of his white shirt were fastened by a black ribbon. His frock coat, the color of his impudently bunched hair, hugged his shoulders. And from across the room, she suspected his frock coat needed no padding to help fill the broad planes of his chest.

His skin was dark, sun kissed. An unbidden image of nibbling his strong dark jaw rushed to mind, and with it curled awareness low in her stomach. Only she had no desire to feel anything, nor could she afford to. Not when her emotions led to trouble. Hadn't scandal proven desire was naught but trouble? But, even as she tried to still the wayward fluttering in her stomach, it refused to heed her commands.

His very presence demanded attention, and he entered the room as if he belonged wherever he chose. Her gaze moved lower to his tailored breeches hugging his trim waist.

"That rogue, dear child, is Captain Nicholas Ferguson."

He inched through the crowd, moving closer, and she spied high black leather boots—an impractical choice for dancing—on his feet, instead of the heeled shoes the other gentlemen wore. The rascal dashed any notions of dancing. Her heart rolled in her chest as her eyes slowly made their way back to his face. His clenched jaw held determination as he surveyed the crowd, and she suddenly remembered what it was like to be under his scrutiny. Did he remember her? She shivered at the thought, hoping he did not. But as her eyes raked him once more, she decided he was not a man who likely forgot anyone. Especially a woman he was convinced he had rescued. No, she decided, the man was more likely to remind her of her folly than forget.

"Handsome devil, isn't he?"

She watched as he slowed to a stop. Their eyes locked. Isabella sucked in a breath as awareness curled her fingers.

"Oh my," the duchess whispered.

Oh my, indeed. Isabella blushed. He had caught her staring. A gentleman would have nodded and turned away, but not him. Instead, his bold gaze held hers. The air grew thick, each breath heavier than the last. She looked away.

"…both Jack and Daniel will be delighted to have a turn with you," the older woman was saying. "Jack's a brilliant partner."

When Isabella glanced back, Nicholas was gone. A smile touched her lips then faltered as she tried to focus on threads of the duchess's introductions, but she'd only heard their Christian names. Dear heavens.

Jack bowed. "May I have the first dance, Lady Isabella, unless you've promised it to another?"

The duchess huffed. "Of course she hasn't, Jack. I wouldn't match you with someone already taken."

"I don't have a dance card," Isabella said, turning over her wrists to reveal them naked of strings.

"Good. Silly things, really." Jack took her fingers into his firm grip and led them towards the center of the dance floor. "I believe the music is about to start."

"And I shall have the next," Daniel said. "A waltz, I believe."

Isabella glanced at Daniel and the duchess over her shoulder. They both smiled and nodded. The evening had taken quite a turn. She didn't think she'd have a single dance partner all night, and now she had two. Surely this was not the way to tame gossip.

Their dance was delightful. Jack turned out to be a splendid partner, every bit as impressive as the duchess had suggested. He held her perfectly, never too close, and showed the right amount of interest to make her feel she was the only woman in the room. She knew he took in all the innocent, affectionate eyes staring back at him and would never ask for a second dance.

"My mother is fond of you."

Of course, Jack was the duchess's son. How had she forgotten his deep blue eyes and the way a honey-colored lock of hair fell over his eyebrow? She wasn't sure how to respond to his question. Did he think she came to take advantage of his mother?

He squeezed her hand. "And I can certainly see why."

A second gesture of approval. The duchess had rallied in her favor, first by walking her about the room, then by having her son do the same. They twirled a final time and, as the song ended and a new one began, Isabella found herself in Daniel's arms. The duchess had also introduced him while she'd been distracted by the captain's appearance in the ballroom. Now, if she could get him to reveal his rank...

His hands were warm, sliding against her lower back as they drifted in the midst of other dancers. The tune played and she searched her mind, anything to distract herself from how scandalously close he held her. "My...lord?" She blushed.

"Call me Daniel."

"I will not." The music called for them to separate.

"And I shall call you Isabella." Together again, his hold on her lower back tightened. He grinned, the scoundrel. "It's only reasonable." His face dropped an inch. "Since you don't recall my rank. You haven't tried earl; I've always fancied that title." The mischievous twinkle in his eyes took the sting out of his reprimand. Another gentleman would have huffed, his chest swelling with indignation. And at another time, when she'd made her entry into society, she would have gushed at such an introduction from the duchess. Isabella sighed; she would have also taken note of a gentleman's rank, property, and lineage.

Isabella straightened her back. Her past life scarcely mattered, except acquiring students to support herself financially. That meant she needed the ton.

She eyed him warily; he was right, of course. Why had she not paid attention instead of allowing herself to be distracted by Captain Nicholas's presence? "You don't intend on telling me, do you?"

"Absolutely not."

She sighed. They moved to the side of the dance floor as the band started another tune. New dancers filled the space, shouldering them farther into the room. "What is it you want?"

"To be your friend. To call on you." He smiled, raised his elbow, and waited for Isabella to place her hand on the sleeve of his coat.

"Why would you endure such inconvenience?" she asked warily, lacing her arm through his.

"On the contrary, I consider myself an excellent judge of character, my lady, and you're delightful." He stopped, pausing their stride through the crowd for a breath, and looked at her. "My aunt thinks highly of you."

"Your aunt..."

He chuckled, reminding Isabella of a boy caught in

mischief. It was also a lighthearted sound that wrapped around her heart. But she couldn't afford such luxury, nor another slip, not when she was sorely in need of funds. So she strengthened her resolve against Daniel's easy charm. "The duchess is generous. Do you always accept your aunt's judgment in character?"

"Only when she insists."

She briefly toyed with the idea of keeping silent and accepting his offer of friendship, then dismissed the notion. "I'm not at all the sort of friend you need." They turned towards a more private hallway.

"Nonsense, you're exactly what I need, and by all accounts, you could use a friend."

Isabella's brows arched. "I've been called rebellious..." Her steps slowed, and she looked at him. "Disobedient for not following my father's wishes."

"I prefer my friends not to be simpering cowards." He smiled, revealing a pair of handsome dimples resting below proud cheekbones. "And you should know...I've been called naughty."

Isabella blinked, resisting the urge to rub the back of her neck. Surely her nape was on fire from his brash words. She quickly looked around and noted with relief that no one paid them heed. It has been a long time since she'd bantered so freely with anyone from high society, least a gentleman who offered friendship. She could no more resist the possibility that he understood her circumstance than if he'd offered fresh cream. Tilting her head slightly closer, Isabella dropped her voice to a whisper. "Is that true? Are you naughty?"

He covered the hand that rested on his sleeve. "Only if one believes rumors." They took a few steps in silence before his gaze met hers. "Are you alright? You seem...distracted."

The hallway seemed longer. The walls stood at her back as if they had moved closer. Her smile fell, replaced by a nervous tingle at the corners of her lips. "I need a moment. It's been a time since I've enjoyed so much attention."

"Only a touch of excitement, then?" he asked, and, when she nodded, Daniel left her at the door of the powder room, promising to return with refreshments.

CHAPTER 3

*F*our years ago, Nicholas would have given little thought to Isabella's reputation. Of course, that was a different time. He'd been restless and young, had held no particular affection for the ton, and still didn't. This time, however, he had more than himself to consider. There was Cassie, his daughter.

Over the years, no woman had distracted him for any great amount of time, and he often found himself thinking about the girl in the lake—wet, with mussed hair, trembling against him as she tried not to drown. He would not have released her to a fate beneath the water, and he had no intention of releasing her now. Lord help him, but he was going to make her a proposition, and he hoped she'd grown into the reasonable sort.

"The night is full of surprises, wouldn't you say?" Viscount Greystone, a rival ship owner, stood at Nicholas's side. "The captain at a party far outside his circle, for one."

The smile wavered from the corners of Nicholas's mouth. He never trusted a man who proclaimed to own the best cargo vessel but never ventured to sea once. He'd seen the man turn green from simply attempting an inspection. It was as if the waters Nicholas treasured had turned up its nose each time the viscount ventured near its depths, recognizing an imposter.

"What is a man like you doing here?" Greystone asked. They locked eyes for an instant before Nicholas shrugged. "Don't bother denying it; you seldom do anything without reason."

"Don't wrinkle your collar," Nicholas said.

The viscount sipped the contents in his half-empty glass. "I'll make introductions, can't imagine anyone else has offered." Of course he'd wave his title, even one of viscount, and effectively remind Nicholas of his lack of peerage.

Just as the sea rejected the viscount, Nicholas declined his offer. "Generous, but I've already met the butler."

"Even I believe you're a notch above that." The viscount stared at Isabella about the rim of his glass. "My mother assured me Lady Isabella would not show. I've just lost fifty pounds."

"I hope it wasn't part of your payment to me. Mayhap you shouldn't bet on the certainty of a lady."

The man swallowed his drink, then thrust his empty glass onto the tray of a passing waiter. "Your man is holding my shipment hostage."

"Only until you pay your debt," Nicholas said, reminding the man of his trip to the coast of Africa, a place he knew the viscount was not brave enough to venture. The muscles at the side of the viscount's neck twitched before he faced the dancers again.

"You think Lord Emsley knows of Lady Isabella's presence? His wife is in tow tonight."

Nicholas froze. He hadn't thought Isabella might

encounter Lord Emsley and wondered if *she* knew Emsley attended the party. "Why not ask him?"

"I'm in no spirit for his foul temper."

Nicholas wished the viscount would move on and find another ear to torment. Lady Isabella was now into her second set, this time in the arms of Lord Daniel.

The viscount followed Nicholas's gaze and frowned. "What the devil is she wearing? Bollocks, man. She looks like a peeled banana." The words were said in a huff, as if trying to convince himself of them.

Was the man blind? "Gold," he said, without looking at the viscount. Golden flecks, he thought more precisely. "Her skirt isn't so outrageous that it hides her curves." She looked as beautiful as he remembered and, just then, when she laughed, he saw her spirit. A lock of raven hair fell from its cage at the top of her head to brush against the curve of her neck, and he wished to be closer to see the soft strands wisp against her pale skin. Her cheeks were flushed pink from dancing and laughing, and he was delighted she did not paint her face as was the custom with ladies past their prime. The light from the gas lamps and her golden dress made the freckles along her nose rollick. "Extraordinary."

"No matter." The viscount clicked his tongue. "Without connections, no one will marry her."

"It's good you've no intention of marrying her then."

"Strike me, if I'm entangled with such a destitute shrew."

"You're a friend of Lady Isabella's former fiancé, Lord Emsley." Nicholas's fist balled at his side. "Imagine the earl's reaction when he learns you've called his daughter a shrew."

"I doubt the man pays attention to anything outside the card rooms."

"Perhaps, but I can assure you, he'll care about assumptions of his wealth, especially if they are false," Nicholas said. "As for Lady Isabella, I doubt any father completely abandons his children. I'd tread lightly, my lord. A man of his rank could see you run through for your falsehoods."

When Nicholas faced the hall again, he lost sight of Lady Isabella and Lord Daniel. It wasn't until he turned down the corridor that led to the powder and more private sitting rooms that he saw them. Was the fire-cat up to her old tricks? Did she know of her former fiancé's attendance, and planned to make him jealous by lavishing favors on Lord Daniel? Years ago, she'd been young and naive, but even then, she'd tempted him as a way to make her lover jealous, and Nicholas wondered how far she'd go to gain Emsley's attention now that he had spurned her.

Towards the center of the long, carpeted hallway, he passed Lord Daniel's retreating form. The man did not look angry, in fact, the opposite could be said from the smile that lifted the corners of his mouth. Nicholas's fingers curled deeper into his pockets, and he continued forward. The walls lined with portraits of the duchess and her family during their happier moments a stark contrast to the sharp possessiveness curling his fist. He wasn't familiar with the bites of hot and cold current running along his skin. Nor the stabs of… He shook his head to dispel the vice tightening around his chest with no luck. He was jealous, he thought with dismay.

He stopped a few feet from the powder room, and he braced himself against the opposite wall, waiting for Lady Isabella to exit, when Lord Emsley stepped to the door. Nicholas straightened, took a step forward, then stopped when the man scanned both directions to be sure no one paid him particular heed, then turned the lock. The door opened, and Emsley slipped through.

Nicholas stared at the closed door for a long, angry moment and wondered if he should intervene, then decided against it. Lady Isabella did not need more scandal, and she was not his business. Across the passageway was an adjoining room he'd discovered earlier in the evening when he'd had enough of the upper class, a darkened office off limits to party goers, which he entered. Not bothering to light any lamps, he maneuvered to the shelf and opened the cigar box. He took his cigar from his breast pocket then clipped the head. Once again, he'd forgotten to guard his emotions around Lady Isabella. Tonight proved he hadn't truly forgotten the lady. Instead, he had merely tucked her away in some distant corner of his heart. Nicholas frowned. Yes, his heart, he admitted, for her boldness and defiance to the rules of good ton had secured her place there. Tom had given many names of ladies over the years who would have welcomed his aid and marriage to escape poverty or the like, yet he'd sought none. Not until Lady Isabella. And now he was angry...and jealous—two emotions he kept well in check. He was a fool to think his need for a wife could be anything more than a business proposal.

Yet, Lady Isabella's actions tonight served to harden his opinion of the upper-class—marriage to an aristocrat offered the connections he needed to expand his business and an improved status for his daughter, nothing more. She'd squashed any considerations that he'd look elsewhere for a wife with her public disobedience of rules, but any desires he might have harbored about their upcoming arrangement being anything more than a contract had been dashed. He no longer needed to woo her to his side, or to convince the lady that lineage was of no consequence. His protection and wealth would suffice.

French doors led to a corner of the balcony that wrapped around the side of the townhouse and eluded light from the hall. The length of a room, this end of the balcony offered a view of the neighbor's property instead of the favored gardens. He took a match from his pocket, then scratched it along the brick wall. The stick lit, and he cupped his hands around the foot of the cigar and inhaled. Back and forth, his thumb and forefinger turned the head between his lips, and he blew smoke until it clouded his vision. So, the lady had planned a secret assignation, he mused, and she'd done it under the nose of the ton.

CHAPTER 4

*T*he door to the powder room opened and Isabella rubbed her exposed arms. The faint scent of sandalwood tickled her nose. She turned to look over her shoulder and her eyes met Emsley's. Isabella inhaled deeply. She should have recognized the scent of his aftershave tonic.

"I didn't expect to see you tonight, but I'm delighted you came." Lord Emsley walked further into the room. He was dressed in a dark shade of gray and his green necktie matched his eyes. Eyes she had remembered more clearly than she cared to admit. "You look as I recall…"

She turned towards him. "Heartbroken?"

He tilted his head to the side. "Radiant."

It was difficult enough keeping her composure after seeing that rogue Nicholas, now Emsley had followed her. Her fingers tightened around the fabric of her skirt. How had she ever fancied herself in love with him? She was bone-tired and in no mood for his antics or deception. She'd made new friendships with Lord Daniel and his aunt, and had rekindled an old one in Lady Godric, but she'd accomplished little else.

It did not bode well that he'd sought her company in the ladies' quarters. If anyone had seen him enter…knew that they were alone…her appearance tonight would be for naught. There would be no hope of tutoring well-born children. "I wish to be alone," Isabella said.

"We need to talk."

"I have nothing to say to you." Sweat ran along her spine. He should be in the country, basking in matrimonial bliss, not here destroying what was left of her tattered reputation.

"You loved me once." A slight curve at the corners of his lips softened his voice. "Do you remember the day I proposed? You were knee deep in muck when I found you."

"We were to have a picnic," she said. "I couldn't decide on a spot. I was frantic with indecision when I fell off my mount. I could not help that the pool was more mud than water."

"You never do anything simply, do you?" He closed the distance between them.

She reached for her necklace before remembering it wasn't around her neck. The gift from her mother had been stolen weeks after moving into her home. She closed her eyes and rested her hand against her chest. It was another loss, another piece of her life that was snatched away while she had been too naive to see the danger. She wasn't that girl anymore.

"I remember you saying you loved me. We were going to have a life filled with children and happiness, everything you lacked in your nursery." Lowering her lashes, she turned from him. "They were all lies, and I was foolish to believe them."

"I did—do love you."

She shook her head. "You married someone else and left me in ruins." From his reflection in the glass, she saw his lips flatten into a thin line.

"I had no idea your father would—"

"You had no idea running off and marrying someone else would cause scandal, or that my father would toss me, his unmarriageable daughter, aside?" Her father had called her a spinster, and a soiled one at that.

He moved further into the powder room, close enough to see her trembling lower lip. Her fingers curled. This was to be her night—if not to be fully embraced again by the gentry, then at least to remind the ton of her good breeding. Who better to tutor their sons and daughters if not one of their own?

She'd spent hours, days dreading the sight of Emsley. She'd been bold with her rebuff in the mirror—her chin had tilted up, not with the slight quiver she now felt, nor did she stare into eyes that held regret. Emsley's did, and that almost undid her. She owed him nothing.

"If you'd waited…" Emsley said, his eyes dark. "Did you not read my message?"

Isabella froze. His message on the night things had ended had been a few lines scribbled on elegant paper. "You said your choice ensured our future. Pray tell, how could marriage to another woman benefit *us*?" When he stared at her, Isabella had a sinking feeling she would not care for his answer. "I say again, sir: we have nothing to discuss."

"I apologized."

Isabella stepped away from him. "Not for the hurt you caused me and my family…the humiliation, but for the haste of your decision."

"I had to think beyond our wedding. My father squandered our family's wealth; your dowry would not have cleared my debt. I will not live in ruin because of him. I thought you understood that."

"Because my father also gambled my fortune? I understand you chose the path that filled your coffers." Isabella realized he had not trusted in their future, and she could not tolerate his faithlessness.

"I did this for us, Isabella."

Emsley grabbed her arm. She flinched. Through the sleeve of her dress, she felt the cold sting of his rings against her warm flesh. She always thought he wore them as a show of wealth, but when she spied the ruby that once belonged to her father, she knew he boasted his winnings.

"That you would continue to wear that token of my father's is a demonstration of your character. Good evening." She yanked her arm from his grip. Isabella's gaze shifted, and she saw, to her dismay, Emsley's new wife standing in the door of the powder room. Was the girl embarrassed that her husband had sought Isabella's company?

"There must be something James and I can do for you?" Lady Emsley tugged on the tips of her glove then slipped it off her hand. Then she gave her husband a sidelong glance, willing him to silence before facing Isabella again. "His offer in his message was quite generous, I assure you."

Isabella swallowed, anger making her throat dry. "No thank you, I don't need a hand out."

"You're no ninny, Lady Isabella. My husband still fancies you."

"Catharina!"

"Well, it's true." Lady Emsley glanced towards her husband.

"You approve of…this?" Isabella shuddered as the words left her mouth. Had the woman not been cold, Isabella would have felt pity.

"Would it please you if I approved?" She smiled then. The act transforming her fine features into nothing short of a beautiful fairy. It was that beauty and money that had likely turned Emsley's head. "Emsley and I share an agreement, you see. He gets my dowry. My father gets a grandson with a title, and I'm free from Father's iron will. And after the child is born, we both agree to do as we please." The woman stepped closer. "And you, Lady Isabella, shall be taken care of."

"I don—" Isabella started to object at the absurdity of the situation. Clearly they were mad.

"I'll even aid in finding a husband if you still wish…"

Emsley grumbled from across the room. But Isabella was too stunned to take her gaze from the woman standing a few feet away to pay Emsley any mind at the moment.

The woman raised a brow, effectively silencing Emsley's growl of disapproval.

Isabella sucked in a breath of air. She looked between the two. For the first time, Emsley's ambitions and greed frightened her. The wine she drank earlier did cartwheels in her stomach, and it took a moment to sweep the cloud of disbelief from her brain. Some nerve, sashaying into the room and offering her husband as if he were some prize instead of a bee in her bonnet. She was surprised the woman did not hide her intentions… Then again, Lady Emsley was not English. "I'm no one's mistress," Isabella said. "I don't need charity from you, Lord Emsley." She turned her attention fully to Lady Emsley. "And I don't need *you* to find me a husband."

"Isabella."

She walked out the room, slammed the door, and received more than one curious glance from the guests as she walked towards the back balcony for some much needed fresh air. For the second time, Emsley had managed to humiliate her. Blinking rapidly, she willed her tears not to fall. He did not deserve them. Oh, why had she waited for him, years longer than any woman would have, to watch him marry a wretched child of eighteen? She hurried further along the balcony where shadows of light from the hall no longer played against the brick.

Secluded in darkness, the palm of her hand slapped the rail. Damn you, Emsley! At four and twenty, she should be married with children, not a social pariah being offered unsavory deals by a greedy child. She gripped the rail, surprised the low whimpers filling the air came from her. She must not cry. He didn't deserve her tears.

A hand held her shoulder, then spun her around. The chest that greeted her was broad beneath the jacket. She inhaled smoke and the sweet aroma of ripened cherries. Cigar and brandy. Her eyes searched the dark for any hint of identity. Her lips parted in silent protest when the first touch of calloused fingers brushed along her cheek, tilting her chin.

"Are you drowning, Lady Isabella?" His Scottish accent was a bath in hot springs. His thumb brushed the tip of her nose. Lingered. Her nostrils flared and the scent of him invaded her senses. His hands snaked around her waist, guiding her closer.

"You," Isabella whispered.

"Aye, me." He kissed her cheek. "Is your nose still covered in freckles, lass?"

"No!"

"Liar." He brushed the tip of her nose with his. "Did he kiss you?" His lids lowered to watch her mouth. "I'll be damned if I kiss you after him."

"No." She shivered, the sensation curling her toes in anticipation. "Emsley didn't kiss me." The man holding her in strong arms was something old, from her past, something forgotten. Isabella relaxed, molding against the captain. Oh, but she needed this, to feel like a woman again, alive and desired. His tongue brushed against her lips, not once but twice, tracing the outline of her mouth—a delightful distraction from her recent episode.

"Let me in, lass."

His warm breath fanned her face. She had dreamed of

this, years ago, when she was young and thought the world not full of danger but adventure. His gaze moved from her mouth, wet from the tantalizing brushes of his tongue, to her eyes. In the darkness of the night, his eyes were black fire. Hot. Wicked.

"What a bonnie reward for my second rescue."

"You've botched your count, sir."

"A new tally is in order then."

"Brilliant."

He smiled. His lips descended in slow torture, groaning his approval when his tongue brushed hers. All rational thoughts scattered. He explored her mouth. Heat pooled. Fanned out. The shudder that shook her was not from anger, but fear and desire.

The sea, that's what he was. Raging waves that didn't settle in the wee hours of dawn.

A strangled cry arose. But this man, breathless as he made her, was a stranger. They were too close and the scoundrel too warm and tempting. Isabella didn't have the time or luxury to sort her emotions. She shoved his chest and his hands loosened, but not enough to be decent. His head rose above hers, eyes bright with longing. Isabella moaned, a bolt of desire running up her thighs.

"Unhand me."

"Nae, I approve of where you're standing."

CHAPTER 5

*N*icholas gasped when the woman in his hold shuddered, sending a shock of awareness through him. She was a bonnie lass, with wee brown freckles dashed on the tip of her nose. He tried to convince himself that his immediate attraction and the betrayal of his body was due to the fact that he hadn't bedded a woman in months —an unease he'd yet to rectify since he docked—and even as he tried to lift the bolt of arousal from his head, he knew that was a lie.

"You've received your reward. Now, if you'll excuse me, sir."

"Aye, but I've rescued you twice."

"No decent gentleman—"

His head dipped to whisper into her ear. "I'll let go if you promise to give me what I want."

At her sharp intake of breath, he knew she was not as innocent or unmoved as she pretended.

In normal times, he would woo a lady, but these were not normal circumstances and he hadn't interest in brothels or bedding widows, not since he glimpsed the fire-cat embraced in a waltz moments ago. She had claimed both his desire and interest.

When he had docked, Tom mentioned that Lady Isabella was not under her father's protection. The man was convinced it was Nicholas's only chance to stand among the ton as an equal. With no other choice, a woman of privilege might consider marrying a Scottish bastard that made his trade at sea. Well, Lady Isabella was in more than a little trouble, and he intended to bolt the door to her exit far above her bonnie head so she couldn't escape.

Tom was correct in his assessment of her circumstances, however, that knowledge did little to ease Nicholas's annoyance that Lady Isabella so easily hardened his body.

The lady in his arms was warm and alive, not at all the cold lass he'd envisioned. Her head, covered in thick curls, leaned against his arm. He was sure he could not resist if she were to seduce him, yet he could not trust her with his heart. Not after his own father, an aristocrat, chose peerage over him, leaving Nicholas and his mother to fend for themselves. He was not so low as to blame Isabella for his scars, but he could not swear, given the choice, she would not choose the ton.

Lady Isabella was dangerous, Nicholas decided, and it would do him good to remember that before she poked her fingers at his emotional wounds.

His lips connected with soft skin just below her earlobe. Nicholas took the shudder that vibrated through her as encouragement. His tongue flicked, drawing lazy circles over the sensitive flesh. Her body responded to his simple play. He bit down. Isabella gasped, her head tilted. Her hands, hesitant at first, reached up to encircle his neck. His hips flexed and thrust towards expectant warmth. Their bodies meshed, leaving no doubt as to what he wanted, craved, desired.

Their breaths mingled as his tongue explored her mouth,

inviting dual play. She followed his lead and her tongue moved against his teeth. A shudder ran from him to her, until neither knew where it began or ended.

She broke their kiss, pressed her cheek against his chest and gasped for air.

"Nicholas," he whispered into her ear.

She looked at him.

"My name. Nicholas Ferguson. We were not properly introduced before." When she continued to stare at him, Nicholas released their embrace, and stood beside her. "You are not charmed with my name."

"Of course, Nicholas is a fine name."

He chuckled. "Tell me, what heap of trouble have you gotten yourself into?" He easily saw the spirited lass from years ago and that pleased him. Nae, he did not want her hardened by the streets of London.

"I was jilted." Her chin quivered.

Ah, that was his problem with high society. While brothels and mistresses were acceptable behavior for men, any stitch of rumor proved difficult for a lady. Looking at the stolen color from her cheeks, he suspected more to her plight and that she'd only divulged that bit of information because it was common knowledge if he cared to ferret out information from any in the ballroom. "That can't be all, lass?"

She worried her lower lip and looked into the darkness for a long time. He was afraid she would cry or refuse to answer.

"I'm not here to throw stones," he said. "You can trust me."

"I'm afraid I haven't trusted anyone for a long time."

"But can you trust me?"

She faced him, her eyes glossed with unshed tears. "It's of no great importance, is it. One more person knowing will not change my fate. This time there is no one to blame. Tonight had been a foolish idea. I had hoped..." Her lashes lowered before she turned away. "If you must know, sir, he told his friends I was a cold fish. I only heard whispers, of course." Her fingers gripped the rail. "It would explain why no other suiter showed interest. The only way to know I'm not affectionate—rigid was the word he used—is to 'sample the goods,' you might say."

He stiffened, resisting the urge to ask if there was any truth behind the words. Isabella was correct, it no longer mattered, he realized, standing behind her. He did not dare move any closer to the scent of her perfume or her pinned hair that revealed the slender curve of her neck.

"You see, Captain, not only am I soiled, I misjudged his character by miles."

Knowing someone else had touched her, tasted her, hurt her, didn't sit well. He did not intend to add threads of gossip to her life, but there was little choice. Tom had not mentioned that piece of gossip, and he had an unsettling feeling the man knew. "Do you mind that I make my trade at sea?"

She faced him, her forehead wrinkling. "I don't see what that has to do with me... But if you make an honest living and earn an honest pay?"

"I do."

"Then what does it matter?"

It mattered to him. "I hope you remember that." He covered her hand that gripped the rail with his as the balcony doors pushed open and bathed them in light. Isabella stilled. Her eyes went cold. Nicholas saw fear and embarrassment flash across her face, little shudders running the length of her. His grip on her hand tightened. Her eyes locked with his in a silent plea. For what, his protection? If she hoped to compose her emotions, he did not intend to give her any time. Tom insisted he attend the ball to seek potential clients. His cousin urged him to think of his daughter's future. What Nicholas found was a solution to both his plights.

His mouth dried. *Mine.* That was the thought that went through him when she had danced earlier.

"Lady Isabella, have you been taken advantage of?" Emsley asked.

Nicholas shifted to face the man that blocked the balcony, with the duchess's nephew hard on his heels. He was not one for spectacles, but this once, Nicholas wanted to announce his intent, see their shocked faces when they discovered he had bested them. More than that, he wanted all of London to know that Lady Isabella would no longer cower. Not with him behind her.

"Come along, Lady Isabella," Emsley said.

The man's gaze was cold when it met Nicholas's eyes. He expected jealousy, embarrassment, or even rage, but not the void of emotion he found staring back at him.

"Another one," someone whispered. "Her poor mother must be rolling in her grave."

"Hush, Margret."

"Her father, Lord Carolus, will have no choice but to completely disown her now," another said.

Nicholas squeezed Isabella's hand as she stepped beside him. She stood brave, but he felt her anger in the fist that clenched his fingers. He did not think she realized she still touched him.

"What do you want, Emsley?" Isabella asked.

"Did he force himself on you?"

"Don't worry. He shall not have to marry me. He will not save you from guilt."

The crowd tightened. Lord Daniel pushed his way to the front, putting another barrier between Isabella and Emsley.

Emsley's eyes narrowed. "Not because I turned from marriage... You've made a spectacle with this gentleman." His lips pinched when he saw their joined hands. "You don't have to… I am sure with time you'll find a suitable match."

The man all but called her a whore, then declared himself out of her reach. Before Nicholas realized, his fist snapped forward. The crowd gasped. Emsley staggered backward, his right hand reaching to cover his jaw. Nicholas saw a glimpse of disbelief shadow his eyes before it was replaced by that seething rage he had sensed earlier. "Lady Isabella is my betrothed. It would do you well to remember that the next time you are in her presence."

He turned toward Isabella, offered his hand and willed her to take hold of it. When she did, he guided them through the ballroom. For a brief moment, he wondered if she understood the implications of his statement. Her eyes widened as she read each face they passed, and his callus fingers tightened around slender ones until she met his gaze. At that moment, it did not matter if his announcement shocked her, because his every muscle said she was his.

CHAPTER 6

*B*etrothed.

That word, it whispered past her lips when she exhaled. It was a noose around her neck, choking all rational thought.

Hands clutched in her lap, she sat across from Captain Nicholas in his private carriage. The vehicle was light, smart, and built for comfort rather than mere elegance. She glanced up from under thick lashes and their eyes locked.

Except for asking directions to her home, he had said few words, and those were clipped as he relayed them to his driver. She sensed the reason for his foul mood. Served him right. Once again, he'd acted out of turn.

He looked at her as if sensing the direction of her thoughts. His lips thinned—no doubt to keep his outrage at bay—and his eyes were dark, not from their earlier lust, but anger. He'd already regretted his impulsive decision, she imagined, as well he should.

Any wicked notion Isabella had to let him stew until she reached the safety of her home quickly vanished. He had saved her further embarrassment, now it was her turn. She would release him from his commitment. It was only fair. She had nothing to offer. No dowry, not her father's backing or name, heavens, not even the dignity of an unsoiled reputation. Isabella remembered the eyes and ears that had gathered around the balcony and could not resist rubbing the gooseflesh that rose along her exposed arms.

Tipping her chin, she prepared to set him free. She had been in this position once before and would face the ton a second time. She had discovered she was stronger and far more capable than most believed. "You should not have gone to such lengths to defend me." A nervous smile curved her lips. "But I must say, seeing Emsley's shock was worth the entire fiasco."

His jaw flexed.

"Thank you," she said. When he did not respond or move, other than the clenching and unclenching of his fist, she waved towards the door. "You may stop the carriage, sir—"

"Call me Nicholas."

"Mr. Ferguson, there is no need to go any further. We are well away from the prying eyes at the party, and a brisk walk—"

"I'll take you home."

Her confidence wavered at his conviction. "But there's no need."

"I don't break my oaths." He continued as if she had not spoken. "And I've promised to marry you."

Isabella gasped. She had anticipated that he would be stubborn, but for him to insist on standing by a rash decision was beyond her. "Don't be ridiculous."

"A man is nothing without his word," he said.

"So, you'll marry me out of some silly notion of honor?" she asked. "Don't you see, I'm giving you reprieve."

His eyes drifted from her face to her neckline, then to her bodice, narrowing when her breasts rose and fell. A splash of heat tingled along her skin, pooling in the exact spot where his eyes lingered. What was he doing?

"I'm marrying you because I damn well choose to."

"Well, I won't marry you. We don't love each other, and—"

In a swift move, he pulled her to the edge of her seat, surrounding her legs between his open ones. Heat hummed, settled where their thighs touched. Her breath hitched.

"Nae. I'll have you, in every way a man can have a woman." Beneath her chin, his forefinger tilted her head until she looked into his eyes. "A husband and his wife."

It took sheer will for Nicholas not to loosen the pins to her hair and let those deep waves tumble free, to bury his hands and nose until he had his fill. Instead, he sat back until his shoulders braced the carriage wall. Isabella. The name suited her. She was all bells, from her thick wavy hair to her lush mouth. He could have done worse, and shuddered at the thought of an unresponsive woman. No, Lady Isabella would do fine.

The wheels of the carriage landed in a hole, jolting her forward. His hands shot out, taking her shoulders into his grip, steadying her.

"Are you alright?"

Isabella's eyes lifted. "Thank you," she said, and pushed back into her seat.

His fingers itched to be back on those warm shoulders, and he curled them into fists to resist the urge. He thumped his balled hand against the framing, once, twice, in quick succession. "Watch the pots, man!"

"Can't we come to an arrangement, Captain?"

His brows rose.

"I don't think you want to marry. In fact, I think your words were a surprise to both of us."

He did not answer.

"You're an outsider. Let me teach you of polite society." Her astute perception stunned him.

"You think I wish to mingle with your peers?" he asked to conceal the fact that she'd assessed him correctly. And in a mere matter of a carriage ride.

"Why else would the captain of a cargo ship attend a ball, if not for wealthy clients?"

Intrigued, he asked, "And what does the wee lass want for her lessons?" When she bit her lower lip, his eyes narrowed. "You would risk further embarrassment than marry?"

"In time, people will forget, move on."

"You don't believe that."

She flushed, turned away.

For the remainder of their journey, he did little else but think on his words. He had never reacted to any woman so strongly.

He brushed aside the small pinch of guilt knotting his chest, remembering his need for a wife before his next voyage. Their marriage would be a mutually beneficial arrangement—he needed a mother for his daughter, and Isabella needed a husband for the security of marriage.

When the carriage stopped, he swung the door open, looking at the houses hidden behind thick shadows before hopping onto the street. He offered Isabella his hand.

"Five minutes," he said to his driver.

When Chambers nodded, he led Isabella up the path to the front of her small townhome. The night blanketed the faded paint and chipped stones that threatened to career down onto him. "How long have you lived here?" Nicholas's fingers pried a loose brick from the wall before tossing it onto a patch of dried grass. "Doesn't the landlord make repairs?"

Her gaze lingered where the stone landed. "It's not so old."

"Practically rustic." He dusted his fingers on his pant leg.

When the door opened, she stood at the entrance like a shield. He almost laughed. If she had intended to change his mind about marriage a few moments ago with talk of teaching him about the ways of polite society, she had strengthened his resolve instead when he took note of the state of her home. The fact that she attended her door told him she lived alone and without the protection due her station. Every instinct warned to hire a guard at once, but he knew she would not appreciate his highhandedness, least not this night. Not until she had time to think about his proposal of marriage. Taking a step, Nicholas leaned forward, bracing his palms against the aging door frame. He never backed down from a challenge. Jesu, may he roast in hell if he started now. His head dipped until their faces were mere inches apart. "Don't you ken, lass. Nothing will keep me from you now."

"Don't call me that," she whispered, backing further into the room.

He grinned. He would give her time, as much as this night provided. Halfway down the narrow path he stopped. "Chambers will pick you up at ten."

"I have appointments."

"Ten," he repeated, then entered his carriage. The townhouse door slammed. Rattled. He looked out the quarter lights, expecting the wee house to crumble around her ears.

CHAPTER 7

*H*arold Duncan glanced up from his drink as Virginia snuck into Nicholas's library. Her heavy robe was pulled tight, hiding what he knew was the black silk nightgown he'd gifted her the last time he was on land. He admired the slender curve of her waist and rounded bottom. A long thick braid held golden hair together. He stared at the braid over the rim of his glass, making note to set it free before the night ended.

Hours after they had docked, he wandered to the library, poured himself a brandy, and thought of his future. A life he hoped would include Virginia. In fact, Harold had done little else except think of her from the time they had started home. He woke many nights from vivid dreams of her writhing beneath him, and, by the saints, he was going to see each of those dreams come true.

With Nicholas determined to find a mother for young Cassie, the question of his own future and the life he wanted for himself nipped at his heels.

The door closed. The distinctive click of a turning key reached his ears. They were sealed in. He didn't speak as she took her sweet time turning to face him. Her shoulders were rigid when she finally looked at him. It occurred to Harold that she was never truly relaxed around him, except in moments of passion. Well it was high time he asked for more, he decided. If he was going to make a decision regarding Virginia, he wanted a hell of a lot more than a warm woman in his bed. He also needed one out of it.

Not taking his eyes from Virginia, he leaned forward, rubbing his left leg, just above the knee.

"You haven't used the healing oils, I see."

"The pain is an old reminder why I can't return to the Highlands."

"It will get worse, you know."

"Not if you nurse it."

Her lashes fanned, her eyes meeting his. "The doctor—"

"That quack wants to reset the fracture, a break that happened when I was six years old at the hands of greedy uncles."

Virginia's fingers knotted together. She took small steps forward. They went through a moment's awkwardness each time he returned from long trips. Did she consider fleeing or would she brave his arms around her, wee kisses, and whispered words of endearment?

"You're a grown man now, have you thought of returning to the Highlands and taking control of the lands and clan your father ruled?"

"To what end? My father is dead, and my mother died not long after we fled."

He read wariness in the depths of her eyes and knew the reason she asked these questions. She anticipated both his rejection and departure. He also knew the reasons for her caution with men, deep-seated reasons. His finger circled the rim of his empty glass, and he wondered how long her reasons would be enough, how long would he be willing to stay at bay.

"In England, the lands could be acquired in the courts, without bloodshed, my claim to them proven with the papers of my birth. But it wasn't the same when my mother left the Highlands." He closed his eyes. "I believe my uncles had my father killed, and my mother realized it and fled." He looked at Virginia. "They will try again the moment I set foot in Scotland."

She nodded, then walked closer, a subtle shifting of her expression telling him that she accepted his reasoning. "I didn't think you'd come home this soon."

"Nor I."

"Was your trip a success?"

"For the most part." Harold relaxed further into his chair, stretching his legs. "We had already departed the coast of Africa with our cargo when Nicholas decided to return home without delay." He refilled his glass from the bottle of liquor on the small side table. "We came upon six-year-old Cassie asking two cabin lads why boys itched and decided it was time to end her voyage days." He chuckled, recalling the memory. "I don't think Nicholas paid heed to her gender or her curious nature until that moment, though I've told him, from the time she was able to walk, living aboard was nae place to raise a bairn."

"Oh…"

Harold chuckled. "You could imagine Nicholas's anger when the lads answered Cassie's wee question before we could stop their discussion. The lads told her, they didn't ken, only that 'men itched on occasion.'

"'All pirates?' Cassie had asked, her nose wrinkling.

"'Especially pirates,' the lads had said."

Virginia's eyes widened, then she threw back her head and laughed.

Something shifted in Harold, a barrier perhaps, as the sound fluttered over his skin, settling deep. Now, he wanted nothing more than to have those lips on him.

"Nicholas has come to the conclusion it's time to find the child a mother." He took another sip of his drink, eyes focused on her reaction. She sobered, and if it were not for the lack of lighting in the room, Harold would swear she paled slightly. "He is bent on the notion it is time Cassie learned to be a proper lady." He made no attempt to mask his opinion on the matter. It was much more than sea being in the blood, Harold thought. Cassie was a sailor in the making. God help them when she found her sea legs chopped and given a mother to boot.

"The party—"

"Aye."

"You didn't mention a wife, only a mother."

He wasn't convinced Nicholas accepted the notion of a wife and the duties that came along with the title of husband.

"He doesn't see it as a true marriage," she said.

It was a statement. That was what he suspected Virginia wanted: the security of marriage without the obligations of one. Harold shrugged, not trusting himself to words. Anger slowly licking along his spine.

"He has yet to ask me." Another statement. She turned those chestnut eyes on him.

"Why would Nicholas ask you, Virginia?"

"You said yourself, he only desires a mother for the child. As Cassie's aunt, I would be the most logical choice."

After all they had been through, all they'd shared, she was still bent on a marriage with no real commitment. Anyone but him. Harold swallowed the bitter taste in his mouth. Anyone who did not ask for love and children. Years later and her past still haunted any future they might have. Didn't she know the passion they shared was rare? If she thought he would let her marry another man, she did not know the first thing about him.

"And you...?" Her fingers twisted.

"What about me?" His eyes narrowed. Hope dared not take root.

Her head shook, gazed focused on some distant wall.

Well, it was time he took what *he* wanted. Before he realized his intent, Harold set his glass down and pulled Virginia to him. She fell onto his lap. Her surprised gasp was swiftly swallowed when his mouth covered hers. There was nothing gentle about his hold. His lips were firm and demanding, coaxing a response.

"You would dare share what we have with another lover?"

Virginia sighed. Her husband, God rest his soul, had never showed any interest in the physical.

Heat started in the pit of her stomach and she trembled. Desire stirred. Her breath hitched. Her nipples pressed against the restraints of her nightgown. The world fell away, leaving them in a daze of colors and sensations.

Her body went limp. Neglected yearning fulfilled under Harold's tutored hands. Her back arched. Heat. Delicious heat pooled along her core. *This* was what she wanted, but not what she needed. Hadn't she spent months learning to be an aunt to Cassie and that Nicholas was what she wanted? Even entertaining fanciful thoughts of marrying Nicholas— oh not because she loved him, but because he'd never demand anything from her—only to fall in love with Harold, feelings she had learned not to trust. Emotions that scared her more deeply than an indifferent marriage.

Virginia looked up at him. "No Harold, we mustn't."

She watched his head lift, eyes slowly opening. They were brilliant with desire.

"We mustn't," she repeated, if only to remind herself. She watched his eyes change from hunger to anger, darkening.

"Mustn't, Virginia?" His voice hoarse. A finger stroked her cheek, moved down the length of her neck, before fluttering over her robe. "We've waited long enough, don't you think? I mean to have you."

She started to rise. There was something in his voice, a promise perhaps. She was afraid he meant every word. Afraid she wanted him to. Her only refuge was to flee. Escape the wanton passion he so easily stirred.

Harold shifted her until she straddled his thighs. His grip loosened on her shoulders, skimming past her collar, her chest. Their eyes locked as he moved his hands in line with her breasts. Skilled fingers parted her robe.

Her head fell back with a small cry when he took one nipple between his teeth. Harold sucked and teased, drawing more of her into his mouth. Wild with desire, she cried his name. Desire he stirred. When her nails dug into his shoulders, there was no turning back. She had let loose an appetite that matched his.

"No!" she cried when his lips deserted her nipple.

Harold chuckled. "I'm nae done."

He moved to the other nipple, giving it equal attention as his hands moved across her back and down its slender length. He gripped the material separating them and yanked it up to bunch at her waist.

Virginia drew a sharp breath as her skin instantly chilled, then heated when his hands covered her backside. He massaged the flesh, just as he had done with her breasts. When strong hands ran along the curve of her thighs, shaping her, her hips thrust backwards, filling his seeking hands.

She groaned, trembled, before crying out. She was only aware of the wanting, needing his heat to last forever. One of his hands slipped between their bodies. Seeking. Moving urgently towards her core. His thumb pressed, massaging back and forth, mimicking the movements of his tongue. He massaged the hardened bud between her folds. She shuddered, her legs squeezing under his attention, only to be opened wider by his powerful thighs.

"You are ready for me," he mumbled from between the valley of her breasts.

She thought she would go crazy when the hand stroking her vanished, but within moments it returned, grasping her hips.

"Your eyes, lass." Virginia's eyes slowly opened. "I want to see them when I fill you."

His hips flexed, his shaft impaling her. They both trembled, enjoying the warmth and fullness of each other. Then his hands were on her backside and they were moving. Each flex of his hips taking him deeper into liquid heat, every squeeze and roll of her hips drawing them closer to a long-awaited climax. She met him thrust for thrust. His strokes becoming urgent and powerful until they were gasping for release.

"Virginia." His grunted demand was all it took.

They carried each other over the edge, riding the waves of pleasure until they were no more than panting, sweaty limbs.

Moments later, Virginia stirred to soft kisses on her neck. "It's late... I should go." Her words died when she tried to move and found her hips pinned under his large hands. Virginia's eyes widened as he stood, easily supporting her.

"Again."

"Again?"

"Aye," he groaned, bringing them to the large sofa.

CHAPTER 8

The brass knocker thumped against the door. Without glancing at her timepiece, Isabella knew her eleven o'clock student was early. Her stomach knotted. Her ten o'clock had cancelled by messenger, and this early arrival could only mean more bad news. She pressed two fingers to the bridge between her eyes in an attempt to dispel the headache throbbing there. She never received so many callers in one morning, each delivering their share of bad news.

Again, her life had twisted, tangled in a web of chaos. One impulsive act and her livelihood threatened to slip away. No, she wouldn't sit and watch her modest income vanish.

"Shall I send them away, miss?" Pashkin asked, standing at the large drawing room door.

"We both know I can't afford such luxury." Isabella sighed when Pashkin hesitated. "You may speak frankly."

"You're paid less than any teacher in London, miss."

He was correct. She earned less than a decent governess, if she counted shillings. "What would you have me do, not work?"

"No, m'lady."

"What of the vendors at the market, the rent? Who will compensate your wife for her cooking?" There lay her dilemma: entertain spoiled mothers or accept Nicholas's offer.

Isabella groaned. No matter how angry she grew, the arrogant captain was never far from her thoughts. Over and over, her mind returned to him and the expert way he had manipulated her. He wasn't gentle. No, his mouth was demanding against hers, coaxing, urging her to give more than she was willing. In spite of herself, she found her mind drifting back to the way his lips had felt against hers. The way heat had rushed through her as his tongue slipped into her mouth. She felt warmth pool in her belly—

"Lady Thompson." Pashkin snapped Isabella out of her thoughts seconds before a thin-faced woman in a plum-colored dress burst into the room.

"Leave us." Lady Thompson's hand cut the air.

Isabella's brows drew together at the woman's tone. Her gaze moved to a stone-faced Pashkin who was still rooted in place. "Thank you, Pashkin. I'll be fine. Could you ask Edyeth to prepare tea?"

He hesitated for an instant before turning on his heel. Even then, he left the drawing room door open a crack.

Isabella took a deep, calming breath. Her neck was tight with tension and her head throbbed. When she turned, deadpan eyes assessed her. Lady Thompson was never casually dismissed, Isabella mused, especially by one of lower rank.

"Edyeth?" Lady Thompson repeated. "Really, Isabella, simply call her cook."

Isabella bit her lip. Edyeth and Pashkin were more than help, they were friends.

"Your indiscretions are being gossiped about throughout town."

Isabella straightened at Lady Thompson's chastising tone.

"I'll not have my daughter's music teacher associated with wanton behavior."

Isabella's eyes narrowed as the older woman slipped her gloves off, clearly intending to prolong her visit. "I'm sorry to hear that, Baroness. We were making such progress," Isabella said. It was difficult containing herself, but the thought of mounting bills kept her from saying more.

Lady Thompson's lips pinched at the mention of her lower rank.

In truth, little Elizabeth would never possess musical talents. At ten, the child's hands rivalled a lumberjack's, and she didn't have patience for the art. She was adept at figures, however, if only her mother thought numbers a valuable quality in a lady.

"In any regard, I will not have our name sullied."

Sullied. Isabella flinched. If she could toss the older woman from her house without kindling further scandal, she would. "May I remind you, Lady Thompson, Captain Nicholas and I are betrothed." Her hands twisted in her lap. "I don't see how a show of affection between two who are to wed—"

"You can't possibly be considering marriage! He's a scoundrel and blackguard. Surely even you see that?"

Isabella sat speechless. What could she possibly say in defense? She didn't know Nicholas, and if it weren't for Emsley's cowardly betrayal, they would not have met again. She'd heard stories of the women that trailed after him the moment he docked, the brothels, the parties. Stories of women foolish enough to lose their hearts. She couldn't blame them. With Nicholas's dark hair and stormy eyes, even she found herself drawn to him.

"…may continue her lessons."

Yanked from her thoughts, Isabella eyed the woman warily.

"Once you've cut all association with the captain," Lady Thompson finished, then rose in a swirl of frills and lace. She paused at the doorway. "Without your father's protection against such vile men, society will forgive your current lapse in judgment, but no one forgives a trollop." Lady Thompson walked out the door.

Isabella reached for the small centerpiece, ready to hurl the bauble against the door Lady Thompson exited when Pashkin appeared at the doorway. "You have another caller, miss." He eyed her raised arm with trepidation. "I'll fetch the broom."

Isabella squeezed her eyes shut. She wouldn't create more work for her employees, no matter how angry hearing Lady Thompson's words made her. "Is it my last student cancelling her lesson?"

"No, miss."

Isabella sighed in relief.

"A messenger delivered a note cancelling earlier."

Her eyes snapped open, seeing a card between Pashkin's firm fingers. "Send the caller away, Pashkin." She eyed the centerpiece one last time before placing it on the table. She couldn't afford to break a single object, not if it meant she could sell the item. Oh how she wished it was Emsley's head in the palm of her hands.

Lord Daniel stepped into the room. "Tsk, tsk, is that any way to treat your friends?"

She eyed Lord Daniel with a mixture of relief and wryness, hoping he wasn't another trial here to remind her of her circumstances. "Our friendship is still to be determined."

His smile was devilish, making her lips twitch to return the gesture. "You wound me, my lady."

"After the party, I didn't expect to see you again." His family was generous in showing their acceptance of her. Daniel had not judged. In fact, he'd drawn attention when he stopped Emsley's pursuit, giving her the chance to escape to the balcony. "Wait!" Isabella said to Pashkin when the man moved to leave.

Daniel gave her a friendly smile. "You needn't be afraid of me."

"I'm neither married nor widowed, and at the moment, unchaperoned." Isabella could not afford another scrap of scandal.

"Yes, but are you afraid?"

"Not of you."

Daniel smiled. From the inner pocket of his coat, he took out a newspaper then unfolded the curled bundle. "Have you read today's edition of the Scarlet? It brims with your approaching nuptials." Daniel dropped the folded newspaper onto the coffee table before Isabella. "Almost every page has thoughts on the matter. It's as if the editor purposely sprinkled bits here and there to ensure each page flipped."

"Nuptials?" The door shut, sealing them in together as Pashkin slipped out of the room.

"Why didn't you tell me you were engaged?" Daniel sat in the chair opposite her.

"I wasn't... I'm not!" Her eyes fixed on the inked sheet of paper. There it was, in the center of the page for all to read: *Captain Nicholas Ferguson and Lady Isabella Pennington to be married on the ninth.*

"Really?" Daniel asked, staring at the same words that had stopped her blood.

"What I'm trying to say is, I wasn't engaged until last evening, and that was not my doing."

Daniel watched her, his eyes weary. "Perhaps the Gazette next time; it is certainly more tasteful."

Isabella barely heard him. "The ninth!" She looked up from the paper. "But today's the…"

"Seventh," he finished.

Once more, her eyes darted to the page, her hands trembling as she focused on the print too large for the space.

It is a tale for the romantic at heart. Captain Nicholas, rider of the sea, sailed home to capture the reluctant Lady Isabella, who promised she would not flee her obligations as she did once before...

"Flee?" Isabella gaped at the words, her hands fumbling, crinkling the smooth sheets.

With the lovers finally united, and all ties to Lord James Emsley severed, they may be wed. That is, if Lady Isabella has not yet set her eyes on another.

Isabella's eyes widened as she read the last line. "They think… They think me a tart!"

"The Scarlet has excellent writers. Don't you agree?" he said in a dry tone. "The copies are selling as fast as they are pressed."

This was all Emsley's fault. He was the one who wouldn't commit. He had jilted her. He had married someone else. *She* had waited through his excuses not to marry. And when she could wait no more, he had ended their betrothal. Her fate sealed by a few carefully placed words.

No matter what she had said, pleaded, nothing changed. Her father blamed her for not enriching their coffers and linking the two names together. For weeks he'd searched for another suitor, as if she were some prized pig. But the rumors had only grown more scandals, reaching ballrooms and clubs alike. Finding none willing to marry, and having her sister's future to consider, her loving father had tossed her out.

Isabella gave an unladylike snort at the memory. She'd

been such a fool putting her trust in a man. She was a fool yet for still believing in love. She read the last line of the Scarlet again. To think, the dangerous captain, setting sail to save her from herself, from her adventurous ways. It seemed the captain was not the only one keeping tally of her rescues. Had he intended on seeking her out at the party, seducing her? The rascal.

She did not know which bothered her more, the ton thinking she was not faithful in her engagement, or thinking of her as the adventurous sort. Did Nicholas think her so bold? Certainly not.

But he did. She remembered his caresses, the strokes of his tongue against hers, her automatic response to his touch. Isabella squeezed her eyes closed.

She didn't need saving, Isabella reminded herself, and if she did, Captain Nicholas would not be her rescuer. With her resolve set, Isabella straightened her back. She flipped the page to the next entry.

Daniel plucked the papers from her hands. "I think you've understood the gist of the tale."

"I prefer not to be mentioned in the dailies at all." Her forehead creased. "You don't believe the newspapers?"

"Not one word. Although…" He winked. "The bits on adventure might prove interesting."

Isabella flushed, her eyes darting between her knotted fingers and the folded paper. No wonder the agency refused to find her new students. She'd visited them earlier in the day, hoping to replace the students she'd lost only to be told it was impossible. All her letters of reference meant little in light of her recent scandal. Here she had thought the woman behind the plain wooden desk, with glasses perched on the tip of her nose, had meant the scandal a few months ago, when in truth she had undoubtedly been referring to the one being flaunted this very moment in the newspapers.

The additional strain on her finances changed everything.

There was Nicholas. She could accept his offer. If she married him, she'd have security. He himself had promised that much. He'd never love her. She was certain of that. Hadn't he said their marriage would be a convenient arrangement? There was the possibility of children...a family.

"We could elope, prove them right." Daniel took one of her hands into both of his.

Isabella laughed. "To the country."

He looked incredibly young, so much more than the night before. His grin was still the same, she was pleased to note.

"And what would we do?" Isabella laughed again, and Daniel's long lashes fanned his deep blue eyes.

"Anything that pleases you, my lady. We could marry."

"Why?" Oh but he was tempting! She was glad this man was her friend as she found both his company and banter comforting.

"I find your situation most unfortunate. Were you a gent, no one would bat an eye. A bit of dallying would be permitted. And I despise being told what I must do."

"I see." She tried and failed to stop her lips from curving into a smile at his outrage.

Prove them right, what an agreeable notion. If only she was so brave. "The young ladies of London would never forgive me that slight, at least until they've had the opportunity to properly come out." Isabella placed a finger on his lips to halt his protest. "Perish the thought. You don't have to marry, Daniel, not now. Not until you've broken at least a dozen hearts."

His grip tightened on her hand as he shifted to the edge of the chesterfield. Their knees touched. "You don't have to marry either. You will never have to do anything you don't want to again."

He was wrong. She did have to marry. In that, she agreed with the captain. Today proved there'd be no more students, no support from Lady Thompson—the woman's loose tongue would inflict more gossip than Emsley's betrayal ever could. This time there was far more at stake. She had nowhere to go if she were kicked to the street. Despite the circumstances, she was starting to relish her new independence, but that too had cost her the one piece of jewelry she'd kept from her mother. Marriage would save what little reputation she had and see the larder stocked.

Isabella sighed. She wasn't naive to think that marrying the captain would not have its own charges. There was no mention of affection or promises of love. After marriage to the captain, she was sure there would be many things she would have to do, whether she agreed or not. Nicholas Ferguson didn't seem the type that enjoyed a passive marriage.

Isabella looked at Daniel only to find his face, his lips, closer than they were before.

His forehead rested against hers. Her eyes closed. It wasn't the same as the carriage ride. Where Nicholas took what he wanted by force, Daniel used kindness. Where Nicholas's fingers had dug into her flesh, Daniel's were gentle. In the carriage with Nicholas, there was passion and heat, nothing she'd ever felt before. It licked at her skin even now. With Daniel, there was none. No draining of the senses, no clogging of the mind with wicked desires.

After all she'd been through today, losing what little independence she had, she should hate Nicholas. Instead, Isabella found she desired his touch, wanted his rough ways. Her mouth moistened, skin prickled.

"Say so and I'll tuck you away in my country tower."

Isabella smiled. "Rescue all the ladies, do you?"

"Only rebellious friends."

CHAPTER 9

"You're right, it's time I wed." Instead of celebrating his good fortune and safe return to London, Nicholas was perched at the edge of his desk while his cousin campaigned for all the reasons he should marry. "And fill my nursery."

"And why not expand our business while you're at it." Harold reclined further into his chair, stretching his left leg.

"We're making money; the small shops keep our business lucrative."

"Shipping cargo is expanding. I know you intend to expand with it, Nicholas, and that means your clients need to trust you." Harold held up a hand. "Not the shopkeepers. I'm speaking of the men with money."

"I'm nae a London elite."

Harold smirked. "You have their blood, that's good enough. Money graces the halls of parliament and drinks brandy. They play at politics while waving their titles."

"You believe this lass will provide me an introduction."

Nicholas avoided high society. He thought the lot of them pretentious. He had looked for a wife before, but none had held his interest for any length of time. And no woman had since matched Isabella's spirit.

Yet he sensed the change in her circumstances had robbed her of her innocence.

"We both know you desire more than politics," Harold said.

Nicholas faced Harold again. His cousin did not meet his eyes. Harold relaxed further into his chair, but his easy manner didn't fool Nicholas. "I'm not ashamed of my desires. A docile lass will never do, especially for a wife." He preferred one that was adventurous in the bed chamber. Jesu, Nicholas couldn't remember a time, even in his youth, when a woman hadn't kenned how to pleasure him. Yet, none had Isabella's vim and vigor.

"I don't know the details, but she'll need your help, Nicholas. God forbid Emsley gets his hands on her again."

"He was at the party."

"I heard they were locked away for quite a while, but I don't believe anything was amiss."

"Think you?"

Harold straightened. "By all accounts, Lord Emsley was not happy when he left the room."

A surge of possessiveness tightened Nicholas's stomach at knowing Isabella had not been with the other man. Forcing the thought aside, he said, "He's determined."

"That makes him dangerous, and you cutting him down made him more unpredictable," Harold said, then frowned. "I wouldn't put it past Emsley to harm Isabella if he's determined to have her. I tell you, the man's mad."

"Isabella..." The thought that she could vanish from his life again stirred a madness in Nicholas.

He wondered how far the man was willing to go to secure his grip in Isabella's life. If Emsley's own marriage had not deterred his advances, then there was little hope that Isabella's marriage to Nicholas would stop the man. And if Harold's judgment was correct and Emsley had lost his faculties, then the rest of his family might also be in danger.

"There is another matter: Cass," Nicholas reminded Harold. He was reluctant to take her on another voyage. On that front, it wasn't the danger to her life that scared him, it was her lack of interest in being a lady.

Harold nodded. "The child needs a mother," he said, misunderstanding Nicholas's meaning. "In truth, a bairn, mayhap two, might tie your heart strings."

"This is no love match."

"You need each other. You a wife and she, roof and coin."

"You think she'll welcome the chance to fill my nursery after she reads in the dailies that I've saved her from herself?" Nicholas's eyes rolled heavenward. Isabella was likely to drench him in cold water for meddling in her affairs. "There will be but one request to fill her duties."

Harold smirked.

"My concern is Cassie," Nicholas said, pleased he managed to wipe the smile from Harold's face. "I plan to continue captaining our cargo ship." On long voyages, his bed would be warmed in foreign lands if his wife turned cold. "Lady Isabella and I are both adults. No need for illusions." The words barely left his mouth when he felt a trickle of regret. Isabella was still liquid lava in his veins. He still tasted her on his tongue. It was the lure, he reminded himself. The spark he had seen in her eyes when she'd faced her lover before the ton. That heat washed over his skin even now.

He walked to the liquor cabinet and poured two brandies. He drank the first, refilling his glass before offering the second to Harold.

"Lady Isabella agrees to such terms of wedlock?"

"I'll broach the particulars today." He stared into his glass, thinking if he was bold enough to stake claim to things he had no right to, Isabella might make demands of her own. Throwing back his head, he drained his glass. He remembered his bold claim to have her in the carriage, make her his wife, followed by her swift rejection. His fingers tightened around the empty glass. She had been eager to escape him.

What he needed was marriage to Isabella and a mother for Cassie. Their union would provide advantages for both of them. He sighed. What he *wanted*...hoped their marriage could be was of no importance.

"And if the lady says nae?"

"She'll have me."

"How can you be so sure, Nicholas? A woman's mind is not practical. We spend half our time trying to please them, give them what we think they desire, only to find they wanted another path."

"She's already said aye before the ton."

"Under duress," Harold pointed out.

Nicholas fixed hard eyes on his cousin. "I'll marry Isabella, even if she's kicking and screaming before the priest."

Lady Isabella would be more than a tutor for Cassie. Even if he admitted it to no one else, he was a greedy man. He wanted a thriving business, home, and family—all the things that were denied his mother and him years ago. It was also time Harold and he filled their emptiness with families of their own. Mayhaps then the ghosts of their past would stop haunting them.

"What of Virginia?"

"Virginia?" Nicholas's brows drew together.

"She is the closest family Cassie has, being stepsister to the girl's mother. She loves the child. You claim to only desire a mother. Why not marry her?"

Nicholas chuckled. "She is in love with you." He chuckled

again when Harold met his gaze. "And you with her. I may be lots of things, blind is not one of them."

Harold rubbed his leg and sighed. "She asked me once to tutor her in what pleases you. I thought it odd at first," he admitted between sips of drink. "She's no innocent to the particulars of bedding. Yet, the eagerness in her request revealed a woman lacking in the receiving of pleasure."

Nicholas sobered. "Let me guess. You taught her to please *you*."

"Naturally." They both laughed.

"You devil."

"Aye." Harold grew quiet. "She doesn't cringe from the man I am, or my touch, and she doesn't care that I walk with a wee limp."

"Then why haven't you settled?"

"I gave her the impression I don't want marriage." Harold shook his head. "After that gutless husband, she deserves better. She thinks herself blackened. At first, it didn't matter." He swirled his drink.

"You've changed your mind?" Nicholas guessed.

"Her husband left her not a shilling upon his death. With no other kin, Virginia took the protection you offered because the child was all that remained of family. I don't want the memories of her husband to be all she has to hold fast to. Except for moments of passion, the lass will consent to naught else."

"It seems we are both surrounded by stubborn lasses."

"Women like flowery words, something you'll soon find out, Nicholas. In addition, promises of love and tenderness, to be told their eyes are clear blue waters any man would want to drown in."

Nicholas threw back his head and laughed. "You sound like a nursemaid."

"Or the idiot that parades the halls of the cathouse Temptress, praising the whore that wrung his cock dry."

They were both grinning when a knock came on the door.

Nicholas turned when Chambers stuck his head through the door. The man's color was pale as he took a short step into the room, fingers clutching the brim of his hat.

"Where is she, Chambers?"

"The lady sends her regards, sir. She is unable to visit and wants to reschedule for a time she chooses."

"She means never." Nicholas cursed. Snatching his hat and coat, he stalked from the room.

"Chambers." Harold stopped the man when he turned to follow Nicholas. "Were those the lassie's words?"

Chambers averted his eyes. "No sir. The lady said, 'Tell the captain I retract my acceptance of marriage, so there's no need to meet.' That was after her first message."

Harold's brows rose. "Her first message?"

"That the captain go to hell, sir."

When the door clicked shut behind Chambers, Harold laughed. "It's about time Captain Nicholas Ferguson met his match."

CHAPTER 10

*I*t was well past the noon meal by the time Daniel and Isabella sat back in their chairs. They had discussed at length the newspaper, the captain, and exhausted all decent options for employment. It wasn't that she resisted hard work. However, her gentle upbringing left her little skill in the kitchen other than making and pouring tea. She also had little knowledge of carrying out the duties of a lady's maid, though she'd had one all her life.

Daniel leaned forward and held her gaze. "All will be set to rights, you'll see."

She was about to respond when the parlor door swung open.

"Is this one of your appointments, Lady Isabella?"

Isabella gasped, her hand covering her pounding heart. Nicholas. Though Nicholas spoke quietly, there was no mistaking the ice behind the words. His eyes travelled to Daniel before resting on her.

"How long have you been standing there? And where is Pashkin?"

"Long enough to see the reason you left me waiting."

Nicholas strode into the room, hands buried in the pockets of his breeches. "As for your butler, he's happy to have a master."

Traitor. Isabella bit her lip.

She watched Nicholas cross the parlor to the liquor cabinet, the sound of clinking glass filling the silence. The scent of sherry drifted around them before he took a long swallow of his drink.

Her hands shook as he sat in the chair opposite Daniel and herself. He stretched his long legs in front of him, the old furniture giving to his bidding as if welcoming its master after an extended departure.

Daniel broke the silence, clearing his throat. "This is not the docks, sir. Your usual tactics will not work in this instance."

Nicholas gave a dismissive grunt.

"Have you any idea what you've done? Y-you had the betrothal announced in the papers." Isabella pointed to the discarded Scarlet on the coffee table. "All of them."

"The natural course of action with these sorts of things," Nicholas said.

"But I did not consent."

"Neither did you discount the claims last evening before your peers."

Isabella winced. He spoke the truth. She had faltered before Emsley, who thought to proposition her as his mistress. Grateful as she was for Nicholas's rescue from that situation, it by no means meant she would tie herself to him for the rest of their lives. With a deep breath, she loosened her laced fingers.

"Have you read the dailies, sir?"

Nicholas shrugged.

"Then you know what they say," she said, guessing his indifference was a pretense.

"I don't read gossip," he said, sipping his drink. "It's irritating when they are correct and more vexing when they are wrong."

Isabella sighed. "What I'm saying, Captain, is that we are not compatible."

"We seemed suited last night." It was whispered so softly she almost didn't hear it. His tone was as if he regretted causing her distress. Isabella looked at him, stilled by the softening in the depths of Nicholas's gaze. His eyes were a shade lighter in the daylight—deep sea blue. Then he blinked and all traces of tenderness gave way to a deeper blue that was edged with determination. Sea before the storm, she thought and shivered.

"Well, in spite of that, I'm afraid I have to reject your proposal. You see, I no longer have a reputation to protect." She pushed the Scarlet across the smooth surface of the table towards Nicholas.

"Are you now saving me from a life of misfortune, Lady Isabella?"

"Yes." The sound was a breathless whisper.

"And you shall not have to marry the captain, Lady Isabella, as my offer still stands," Daniel said.

Her cheeks flamed. Consumed by Nicholas's presence, she'd forgotten about Daniel. Nicholas had proved adept at distracting her from the world around.

"What offer?" Nicholas leveled his gaze on Daniel, giving him pause for the first time.

"I have proposed marriage." Daniel stepped closer to Isabella.

Nicholas frowned and discarded his glass on the coffee table. From the set of his mouth, she suspected he was hiding disappointment and that the marriage meant more than he let on. And he had not ranted. Or bellowed in the fashion of 'the barbarian' nobility perceived all Scots to be.

"You've decided to flee then, Isabella?" Nicholas's question was not defeat, but an acknowledgement of a challenge.

She inhaled sharply. He had read the papers. Was that what he thought of her, then? A silly aristocrat's daughter who did as she pleased without thought. Selfish. Just then, she wanted nothing more than to prove him wrong. She valued his opinion, she realized with alarm.

Isabella shook her head in an effort to gather her thoughts. Surely, she did not owe him marriage for restoring a moment's dignity. Looking at the sharp set of his jaw, she had a sinking feeling she would come to be indebted for a lot more. There was no love between them. All her life, she craved a union with affection rather than tolerance. Though her father arranged marriage, Isabella had come to care for Emsley. It was why Emsley's lack of loyalty and betrayal had hurt her so deeply. Nicholas was a different sort of creature —wild, dangerous—what part of herself would she lose if she ever found herself in love with him?

"If your intention towards the lady is to restore her good name, you can recognize the advantages, Captain, of withdrawing your hand," Daniel said. "In due time, as my wife, she will be accepted in all social circles."

"My intent," Nicholas said coolly, "is to acquire a wife of social stature, climb the ranks, and open doors my wealth alone cannot afford."

Daniel winced. "What of love?"

"Do you admit to being in love, my lord?"

Daniel shifted in his seat.

"Is that all you desire, sir?" Isabella asked, eyes wide. She understood his motives well enough. Respected his honesty. However, hearing the words spoken plainly and openly was another matter. He was dousing any hope she had of winning a true marriage, and it took all her will not to cringe.

"Like you, Lady Isabella, I've learned to be practical and not make impossible demands, especially pertaining to a man of my character." He paused for a moment and closed his eyes. "I believe there will be a time when a man's worth will have little bearing on blood, but instead on the merit of his investments and inventions."

It was the first time she'd glimpsed Nicholas's true self, his thoughts, and it fascinated her to think of such an era.

"Until then, I'm determined to marry Lady Isabella."

"You're mad," Daniel said.

Nicholas ignored Daniel's last words, his smile cold. "All other intentions regarding my wife are none of your concern. I suggest you find your own bride, my lord."

Isabella flushed.

Beside her, Daniel's eyes narrowed. "All of London knows, sir, you would sooner be at sea than mingle with the ton."

Nicholas did not rebuke Daniel's claim, nor did he release Isabella from his gaze. "Even I, a bastard, recognize the advantages of a gentry wife."

When he glanced at Daniel, his jaw hardened, making the bones along his cheek sharper. This was not the same man from the balcony who took life in stride. This man could draw blood.

"Enough," she said, rising to her feet, wishing her knees would stop shaking. Married, Nicholas had the power to hurt her more deeply than Emsley ever could. That would not do. She had no yearning to wed a man who saw her as nothing more than an elevated step stool. Nicholas was no gentleman, she reminded herself. Turning towards Daniel, she said, "I must speak with the captain alone."

Daniel hesitated, then nodded. "I'll wait in the parlor."

"It will not help matters." She shook her head. "We must come to an understanding."

Daniel ran rigid fingers through his powdered hair. Had he aged in the past hour? Daniel's eyes moved between the captain and Isabella, as though realizing defeat for the first time. Her heart squeezed. They'd become fast friends in a short time, and she hated how this situation was hurting him.

"Do not hesitate to send word if…"

She nodded her gratitude and took a step towards Daniel. Nicholas's hand reached out, cool fingers enclosing her wrist, halting Isabella at his side.

Daniel inhaled sharply.

Isabella followed her friend's gaze, her flesh prickling at the sight of Nicholas's dark fingers against her ungloved hand. Such contrast. Was he dark everywhere? Her eyes moved up the length of his arm, and when they rested on his face, she blushed. His grip tightened as if reading her thoughts.

Daniel cleared his throat. Grateful for the distraction, she turned towards her friend and murmured her thanks, promising to send word if needed.

The parlor door closed, followed a short time later by the audible opening and closing of the front door. When she faced Nicholas again, he was frowning.

"Do you love him?"

"What if I did?" She tilted her head to the side.

He blinked. "If you love him, I'll release you."

He sat rigid, awaiting her answer, his gaze holding hers. She saw through his bravado. "You're jealous?"

He stood and she took a step backwards, her head tipping up to meet his eyes. Wary, guarded eyes.

"You shall have it then, your freedom."

She smiled. "I've always had that."

"It was never my intention to snuff it out."

Her long lashes fanned her cheek. "Why the change of heart?"

"Because lass, I have no desire to play gentry games, not when others depend on me. I can give you a home, coin to spend as you wish. My kin can be yours, people that will care for you as only family can. Aye, and I can offer bits of passion if you'll have it, but I can't give you love."

She did not believe him incapable of love. Isabella frowned. Honest in his dealing, yes, but incapable? "I do not love Daniel," she said after a time.

"He wants to marry you."

"Only to save me from you."

"The uncivilized captain." He smoothed a stray lock of hair behind her ear.

"Yes." She shivered when his fingers brushed the outline of her ear. "Yet, I do nothing except think of you."

"Let me care for you, Isabella." His arms encircled her back, drawing her flush against his chest. He kissed her hair, her right temple, then the left. His lips moved over her forehead, brushing lightly over the lines of distress between her brows until they melted away to softness. To him, she was delicate and innocent to the harshness of the world, everything he was not. She was sunshine. Light that both tempted and beckoned, but always beyond his reach. He kissed the outline of her ear, drawing a gasp against his collar that inflamed his skin.

Nicholas lowered them onto the velvet sofa. He sat on the edge of the seat, hip brushing the delicate curve of her waist.

"Mr. Ferguson." His name was a husky whisper.

Slowly, he lowered his head to hers, anticipating her rejection, receiving none. Their breaths mingled for an instant before their lips touched. Her lips were softer, sweeter than he remembered.

He coaxed, and she yielded. He kissed the side of her

mouth with a gentleness foreign to him. She trembled, and his lips curved at the small movement. His lips moved to the length of her throat and she angled her head, exposing more of her creamy skin. She sighed, and her sound of pleasure made him hungry. She'd be a generous lover, not withholding her satisfaction from their passions, and the knowledge made him eager to explore all of her delights. He kissed below her ear, taking the soft lobe between his teeth, and groaned when he felt her hand against his chest. He kissed her cheek. Her freckled nose... She was looking at him with eyes the color of rich chestnut. Eyes clouded in desire.

"My brave lass, you should close your eyes."

"Then I wouldn't see you."

Nicholas shivered at the thought of her watching.

His lovers always closed their eyes, shutting him out, and he had not minded before because the act was no more than a means to slake his lust. Except for their mutual release, no words of passion were spoken. He wanted more with Isabella. He wanted to be part of her lovemaking, and her to share his.

His tongue moistened her lips. He blew gently. Her eyes widened, and she gasped at the intimacy of warm air against her cool mouth.

Nicholas chuckled.

This time when his mouth covered hers, it was hard and demanding. His tongue slid between her parted lips in an exploration of need. Warm and moist. He skimmed the ridges of her teeth, the roof of her mouth.

Her arms laced around his neck, fingers gripping the thick strands of his hair, holding him close. When he thought she would give no more, Isabella held his tongue captive and sucked. He murmured his approval, letting her have her way, relinquishing control as his mouth twisted this way and that. She nipped at his lips, then licked, mimicking his earlier play before seizing his mouth again.

His heart drummed in his ear. He wanted her hands to touch him everywhere. Needed to feel her skin against his.

Bunched above her knees, the laces on the fabric of her dress tickled his arm. His finger made lazy circles at her ankles, caressing the warm flesh under her stockings. She murmured her pleasure into his open mouth, her thighs shifting restlessly in welcome. His hand moved up her leg, caressing the sensitive flesh behind her knees. He swallowed her shallow breaths, greedy for all of her.

Her thighs squeezed around his hand. Nicholas could not remember wanting anything as badly as he did her pleasure in this moment. His chest tightened, each breath painful with desire. He kissed her ear with open-mouthed eagerness, willing her to trust him. "Jesu, Isabella, let me have this."

Silence dragged, until a single word filled the air. "Yes."

He wasn't sure who said it. It no longer mattered.

Nicholas inhaled sharply when her thighs parted, falling away with his gentle teasing. Beneath layers of material, he felt her moist heat. He murmured words of encouragement when her nails dug into his shoulders, delighted in her excitement and wanton pleading.

"That's it," he coaxed. When his hand brushed the delicate curls, they both gasped.

Sweet heavens. Nicholas wanted nothing more than to taste her. Burying his face in the curve of her throat, he breathed deep, found her core, and stroked the engorged bud. His other hand tightened around her shoulder as she moaned, writhing beneath him. He too shuddered, panting for every ounce of self-restraint he possessed. *Jesu*, if he did not end this agony soon, he would take her.

"Look at me, lass."

When she did, Nicholas kissed her. Her back arched. He swallowed her scream. Her hips arched up to meet the demand of his fingers. He held her, drawing out the last of her climax until she went slack, exhausted.

"HOW MANY SERVANTS DO YOU HAVE?" he asked after a time. He was propped up on his elbow, fingers tracing the base of her throat. His gentle touch was doing wicked things along the curves at the top of her breasts. She felt comforted by his warmth and weight pressed against her side. Even fully clothed, she felt his heat and imagined what it would be like to have his lean and naked body pressed against hers. Isabella sighed when his touch left her breasts to brush a stray lock of hair from her forehead.

"Two." Her brows drew together. "The Berths: Pashkin and his wife, Edyeth."

"No chaperone or lady's maid." He looked about the room. "You have no protection here, lass." He held up his hand to still her objections. "A lady in this part of town will soon draw attention, whether or not they possess trinkets."

"Mr. Berths—"

"Did not escort you yesterday evening," he said. "Sooner or later someone will seek you out."

Isabella sniffed. "I have little of value."

Nicholas shook his head. "A lady of wealth living alone always has something of value. No thief will believe your circumstance when you support servants."

"In exchange for smaller wages and a home, they fill the roles of cook and butler. I could not afford them otherwise."

"There are worse men than me lurking about, lass." They stared at each other. "Let me protect you."

"What are you suggesting?" Her cheeks paled, losing their flush.

"Come home with me."

"Leave...?" Isabella sat up. "You can't mean for me to leave my home?"

"Aye, leave." Nicholas's chest squeezed. He would be damned if he left her within grasping of Daniel or anyone else wanting to take advantage of her lack of protection. Even now, after he had reassured himself she was his, jealousy gnawed at his bones.

Cassie, Nicholas reminded himself as his heart tightened in his chest, he was marrying for Cassie. To give her what he could not: a mother, a home away from the constant dangers of sea, and a chance at respectability. He had made a promise. However, sweet Cassie was not the only one in need of protection. Whether she believed it or not, so was Isabella. She pretended to be wild and carefree, not caring what society thought of her and the scandals, but Nicholas saw beyond her walls. Moreover, what lay beneath tugged at his soul. She was vulnerable and in need of a place to fit in, to call her own. That suited him. He would give her a place. In his world.

He ran tense fingers through his hair. She didn't care for him, so he'd do the next best thing, he thought. He would tie her to him, make her see only he could really stir her passion. Only he could make her blood run hot, give her what she needed.

The door opened. Nicholas did not turn and was grateful that the back of the sofa hid their tousled clothing. He squared his shoulders, stormy eyes holding shocked ones, and barked an order to the unfortunate soul that crossed the threshold. "Pack Lady Isabella's trunks. Have them ready by two."

"You're mad," Isabella whispered, her eyes widening at his words.

He felt daft. No woman had ever driven him to such lengths. The first time he laid eyes on her, Nicholas had wanted more—more than a night in her arms or a quick tumble. In that moment, he had desired true affection, maybe even love. He swallowed past the growing tightness in his throat, realizing that before Isabella, he hadn't the need for such emotions.

"It's not proper." Her fingers smoothed her skirts. "For an unwed lady to be in the home of a bachelor."

"Neither is it proper for an unwed lady to be in the company of rogues unchaperoned."

Isabella squeezed her eyes shut, color creeping up her neck. "Daniel is no rogue, he's a friend."

He raised a dark brow. "You seem bent on shattering what's left of your reputation."

"At least Daniel had the good sense of a private meeting."

Nicholas chuckled. "You were responsive on the balcony, as well. I was content smoking my cigar until you came, in need of rescuing."

Isabella flushed. "Rescuing... Why you..."

"Shall I remind you?" The side of his mouth curved in triumph. She retreated further along the sofa. He let his gaze roam the entire length of her, penetrating the wall she desperately tried to build between them. He may never have her love, but he had her desire. Everywhere his eyes lingered he saw proof of that: her bosom swelled above the low-cut gown, her skin reddened into a heated flush, her lips swollen and moist. His eyes travelled lower still, to the sensuous flare of her hips. At her swift intake of air, his eyes fastened on the subtle trembling of her lower lip.

"I won't marry you," she said, a note of defiance in her voice.

"Aye, you'll have me."

She blinked at the husky rasp in his voice.

"And..." He tilted her chin, drawing her close; the fresh

smell of woman and the lemons she used in her tea tickling his nose. "There will be no one else."

"I'm fully capable of managing my own affairs."

He smiled. She would never admit to the advantage of marrying him. He was not of her peerage, and he had put her reputation further at risk. And yet, he needed her, Cassie needed her, and, whether she admitted it or not, his wealth would restore Isabella to the life she was accustomed. She could be as stubborn as she liked, but Nicholas knew she was not foolish, and she would come to see the situation the same way he did.

"And what a splendid job you've done."

Her lips thinned.

"Tell me, Isabella; are you indebted to your servants?"

She hesitated. It was the only answer he needed. He had no idea how she intended to gain an income, but he knew she was far too delicate to step outside the protection of the ton. He had witnessed men and women reduced to shameless acts for a slice of moldy bread, and he would be damned if he watched her experience the same condition.

Nicholas narrowed his eyes. There were other ways for a woman of her pedigree to turn a coin, such as paramour to some wealthy rogue or faithless husband. The thought of her lavishing her attention on another gentleman did not sit well, either.

No, he was correct in his assessment of Isabella: she was an investment, his investment.

"I've always paid them first and make no protest to Edyeth or Pashkin finding other employ."

"And the market, how do you plan to pay the vendors?"

"That's not fair—" Her hands knotted.

No, it was not. Life between women and men were not fair no matter how much he wished it so. He should feel like a cad for using the circumstances to his advantage and

causing her distress. "And the landlord, Isabella, do you plan to pay him with favors?" Anticipating her outrage, Nicholas caught her wrist easily in his large hand. "Or did you plan to take a lover? Daniel, perhaps?"

Her lips parted in wordless denial.

He held her close for as long as he dared. "Go."

Isabella jumped to her feet, her hands making quick work righting her skirts. In another circumstance, he would have laughed at her modesty, especially after what they had just shared.

She paused, her eyes dropping to the evidence of his arousal.

"Go," he repeated and smiled tightly. She backed away. "Oh, and lass—"

"Don't call me that."

"Be ready to leave."

"You still mean to…?"

"Aye," he said. "Even more now that I know the state of affairs."

CHAPTER 11

*I*sabella gathered her skirt in both hands and took the stairs two at a time, not stopping until she reached her quarters. She braced her back against the solid wooden frame of her door and took a deep breath, willing her racing heart to slow. She opened her eyes, looking around the simple room, her gaze touching furnishings she had come to appreciate for their small comfort. There was no solace in them now, only the thunder of her pulse in her ears and the knowledge that Nicholas waited downstairs, expecting her to do his bidding.

A gentle breeze blew into the room, the curtains dancing. Isabella thought of climbing out the window as she had done countless times as a child in her father's home. Her lips trembled at the idea of rebelling. The thought was shattered by the knowledge that Nicholas would be waiting in the garden beneath the window if she dared to flee.

Two thumps drummed against the wooden door at her back. The vibration, rather than the sudden burst of sound, startled her. She turned, stepped backwards. Did he come to watch her pack?

"I brought you tea, m'lady."

Isabella looked first to Edyeth before her eyes rested on the tray she held. She moved aside when the older woman brushed into the room. "I thought you were... Oh, never mind."

"M'lady?"

"We're in private, Edyeth. Call me Isabella."

"Mr. Ferguson will think me brazen for addressing you by your Christian name."

"That doesn't change the fact that we are friends." Isabella gave Edyeth's arm a gentle squeeze. "No one cares that we're close."

Edyeth wrinkled her nose. "We both know that's a tale. Now, why don't you have a seat and a sip of tea?" She set the tray on the small round table Isabella often used as a desk. "Then we can get down to the business of packing. Your Mr. Ferguson is insistent on making you his wife."

"He's not my mister anything." Isabella rubbed her temples.

The older woman's brows arched. "You met him at the ball, did you not?"

Isabella nodded.

"Agreed to marry him, no?"

Isabella sat in the chair and said, "The entire event was rather swift."

"Then he be yours, alright." Edyeth chuckled.

"Oh Edyeth, what have I done?" Isabella brought the steaming cup of tea to her lips.

"You were hurting. Pains of the heart can make a woman do things with no thought at all." Edyeth shook her head. "When you came home from that party, you had more life in you than I'd ever seen. I'm guessing Mr. Ferguson had something to do with that."

Isabella closed her eyes. "He only wants what my status can offer."

Edyeth clicked her tongue. "Then you have your work cut out for you. Show him there's more to gain than status. If that man doesn't see your compassion after your trying, I'll bring you back myself."

After a couple of minutes of the two women sharing their tea in silence, Edyeth heaved a sigh and pushed to her feet, pulling two trunks from under the bed and coughing when they came out with a layer of dust. She spread the wide base of her white apron over the boxes, wiping the top of both trunks and examining the clean surface.

"It's not like before, Edyeth. There's no walking away from marriage, a husband."

"I don't believe Mr. Ferguson is anything like that man who hurt you." Edyeth held Isabella's gaze over the trunks. "I think he's an honest toff."

"How can you be sure?"

"He told you exactly what he wanted, didn't he? Men like the captain start out the way they mean to continue. Harsh as it may be, I believe if you'd truly looked at Lord Emsley's character, you'd have seen who he really was, but you were in love. There's no seeing straight with those emotions churning in your heart." Edyeth stood.

"Wait," Isabella said, seeing her friend was about to lift the trunks. Isabella set her cup down and walked towards the bed, taking hold of the handle. Together they hoisted the first, then second trunk onto the bed and unlatched the buckles.

Edyeth nodded her thanks and wiped her palms on her apron. "You deserve better than this life you were tossed into, m'lady. I firmly believe our Lord sent Mr. Ferguson to restore your good name and maybe offer a glimpse at happiness."

Isabella's nose wrinkled. "You can't know that."

"That the good Lord wants you happy?" The older woman's hands gripped her hips when she faced Isabella. "Of course, I can. He wishes all His children to be happy," she said matter of factly, as if such things were common knowledge.

"Me and my Pashkin were strangers to you when you offered us lodgings and what wages you could piece together." Edyeth raised her palm, stopping Isabella's protest. "Granted, my Pashkin did save you from that ruffian, but you didn't have to take us in like you did." Edyeth smiled. "I'm glad you did, for my sister's home was crowded with her own children. What I'm trying to say is, you are the most kindhearted lady I know, and Mr. Ferguson is sure to see that."

That wasn't exactly what Isabella wanted to hear, but she had no intention of telling Edyeth that. Especially not now when Edyeth believed Nicholas was an opportunity at a new beginning.

Edyeth tilted her head to the side when Isabella said nothing and took several dresses from the closet, laying them across the trunk.

"And if he doesn't, I could have my Pashkin show him to the door. But that man of yours doesn't look the type to be taking orders, no matter who they be coming from."

Until now, Isabella hadn't spared the Berths' wellbeing much thought. It was selfish of her not to consider the two other people in her household, who were more than servants. "I'm afraid you're right." She had no desire to stir the captain's anger and risk their livelihoods. Placing her shoes on the floor of the trunk, they folded the dresses, stacking them until the larger trunk was full.

They were closing the empty closet when the door to her room opened and Nicholas filled the entryway. Pashkin stood behind Nicholas, and to his right, the carriage driver from the previous night.

"Chambers and Pashkin are here to help with your trunks."

"We haven't finished," Edyeth said sternly.

"It's all right," Isabella said when the men took hold of the closed box and were out the door as fast as they had entered. "Go pack your belongings," she told the other woman.

"You mean to take us with you?" Edyeth looked from Isabella to Nicholas.

Isabella's eyes met Nicholas's over Edyeth's white cap. "Of course. The captain has insisted." She waited for Nicholas to respond to the challenge and watched as the captain's only response was to brace his broad shoulders against the wall. The older woman hurried out the room, stopping only to thank the captain for his generosity.

"I don't remember a discussion about your servants."

"Don't you?" Her brows creased. "When you inquired about them earlier I assumed… It must be the excitement of moving or the suddenness of it all," she said, lowering her lashes and pressing the back of her hand against her forehead.

His lips twitched. "Are you about to swoon?"

"I've never fainted a day in my life. Pass me the silver case and bottles from the dresser, will you?" He pushed off the wall, his fingers making quick work gathering the items before handing them to her. She pointed to the dresser. "And the compartments, we haven't emptied those yet." Rolling the perfume and powder box in towels, she placed them in the bottom of the small trunk.

"Is this to be my reward for my charity?"

If he expected sympathy after sending her helper away, she did not intend to give him any. He wanted them packed quickly, so he would have to help. Isabella was about to tell him that when, from beneath her lashes, she caught a glimpse of the garment in his hands. Her face heated as she watched him examine her corset.

"Give me that."

"Nae."

Her pulse raced and she found herself wanting to box the devilish smile from his face. "It's not proper." She advanced, only to have him raise the garment higher above her head.

"A difference of opinion. A mon ought to be able-bodied in the art of handling his wife's undergarments. Now is this a corset or stays, I always get them mixed up."

"Mr. Ferguson!" She took hold of the dangling strings and tugged, only to have the material strain in protest. She quickly released the strings.

He took the garment to the bed, his long fingers untangling the knots she'd created. "I happen to be skilled at unfastening women's things."

She snatched the garment from his hold, folding it before placing the wrinkled corset into the box. Isabella wasted no time emptying the rest of the drawers herself while Nicholas chuckled from his place at the corner of the bed. Once again, he had distracted her. "Keep your experienced fingers away from my clothing," she warned, waving an undergarment at him only to groan when he grinned.

Nicholas relaxed against her bed, perched on his elbow. "I've hired a hackney to take the Berths and your things to my home."

"Would it not be better if I accompanied them?"

He stared at her for a long moment as if deliberating. "I have business in town and would appreciate your companionship."

Isabella wasn't so sure. It had been a long time since she went into town. She was always mindful not to linger or attract the attention of Emsley's friends. The top of the trunk snapped shut, and she latched the lid into place. "Edyeth will need help unpacking. I would be more help to you at your home."

"Afraid I'll embarrass you?"

"No"

"Shred the last of your repute?" He stood then.

"Of course not." Isabella backed away from the bed.

"Aye, it's settled then." He hoisted the trunk off the mattress.

"You're an intelligent sort, Mr. Ferguson." She took advantage when he paused at the formality of his name. "You must see, with no chaperone this arrangement will cause further scandal. I know you care little for the rules of society, but I'll be of no use if I'm further shunned." Isabella clutched his arm.

He searched her face, then nodded.

She sighed, "Thank you."

His voice was low when he next spoke. "The Berths will be my guests. Mrs. Berths your lady companion."

"Don't be ridiculous." She had expected to remain in her home.

"No one will object to you wanting to know the family you're marrying. Peers do it all the time when the family is travelling from out of the country or the like. And you've come with not one chaperone, but two. Your peers consider you a spinster, and in doing so, allow you a morsel of freedom."

"Yes, but…"

"Lass, I'm not leaving you here another night."

"Because you want to be sure we marry." Her lips thinned.

"No, because I can't protect you if you're here."

"Contrary to your beliefs, I'm capable of—"

"Protecting yourself," he finished. "You're coming with me."

She touched his arm when he turned. "Promise, no matter what happens, you'll care for the Berths…" If she needed to leave London, she couldn't afford to take the Berths with her. They'd been good to her. She needed Nicholas's word that they'd remain in his household.

He stared at her for a measured time.

"It's the least you can do since I'm giving up my rented townhouse."

He sighed and nodded.

Isabella followed him. They descended the stairs and walked out the front door of her home to his waiting carriage. With each step, he barked orders as if the Berths were always part of his household. The carriage door latched, the wheels starting to roll. In the bright afternoon sun, she noticed the crumbling bricks under the windowsill. She leaned against her seat, letting the thick drape fall, cutting off her past as she stared at the man who held her future.

Beside her, Edyeth squeezed her hand. "May your new home bring you much joy, m'lady."

Isabella's fingers curled around Edyeth's.

A boot swiftly dragged along the floor of the carriage. Pashkin grumbled in response to being kicked by his wife. "Thank ye, Mr. Ferguson, for keeping us on."

"You are welcome. I trust you will be the best of chaperones to Lady Isabella."

"Edyeth and me both, sir."

Soon the carriage stopped. "Where are we?" Isabella asked, moving the curtain aside.

"Broad Street." Nicholas opened the door and lifted Isabella down from the carriage, setting her feet on the sidewalk. Before she had a chance to ask his intent, they were entering a merchant's shop, the Berths following a short distance behind.

"Jenkins," Nicholas called when they entered.

The man behind the counter turned, a wide grin stretching his mouth. Isabella had never seen Nicholas smile so broadly. She'd seen him angry, playful, and once even glimpsed something close to tenderness, but not this peaceful happiness that required no thought. It gave her hope that she could survive marriage to this man.

"Captain." The men hugged. "I wondered when you'd stop by."

"I'd like you to meet someone." Nicholas took his friend by the shoulders. "This is Lady Isabella Pennington, my fiancée. Mr. Jenkins and I met the first time I stepped on a ship."

"Pleasure to meet you, sir."

Jenkins took Isabella's outstretched hand in his larger one, giving it a firm shake. She looked from one man to the other.

"And these are her chaperones, Mr. and Mrs. Berths."

Jenkins nodded and smiled. "I read about the engagement in the papers. Couldn't believe a mere woman tamed the lad." He laughed, a booming sound that filled the shop.

"Did you not read the entire article, sir?" Isabella asked. "I'm no mere woman. I'm the slayer of hearts."

Jenkins laughed again, slapping Nicholas on the back. "You came to place a new order, yes?"

Nicholas nodded. "Can you have it ready in three days?"

Jenkins rubbed his jaw. "I ought to see your list first." He faced Isabella. "Why don't you have a look around?"

She did just that, examining the wares as the men continued their discussion at the counter. Her fingers slipped over a fabric woven with gold threads, the bolt rich and detailed. She found herself imagining a golden dress, the dimming light of sunset dancing off the threadwork.

Her pause caught Nicholas's attention, and he walked

over to her, examining the fabric over her shoulder. "You like it?"

"It's beautiful."

"Then you shall have it."

She faced Nicholas. "There's no need. I don't believe we'll be invited to many parties this Season."

"You'll have to plan a ball of your own."

Her eyes widened. "You would have a bunch of snobs parade through your home?"

"Nae, our home. I think they'll be too curious not to accept your invitation."

He took the bolt of fabric from beneath her fingers, handing it to Jenkins, along with a deep blue bolt and a coral spool. "Add these to the tally, will you, Jenkins?"

The other man nodded and the two shook hands, arranging a time in three days that Nicholas would return to pick up his wares. With their business concluded, Nicholas turned his attention back to Isabella, offering her his arm.

Folding her arm under his, he guided them from the shop. "Are you hungry, Isabella?"

Nicholas thoroughly confused her. She hadn't expected kindness after Daniel's visit, and she certainly didn't expect to be strolling through town and being introduced to his friends, which was more than Emsley had ever done. When she did meet Emsley's friends, she always left the encounter feeling soiled. Isabella shivered.

"Are you alright?" Nicholas frowned.

"Yes, thank you."

The next time they stopped, he was guiding them into a dining house.

A serving girl approached them. Nicholas leaned close and whispered into Isabella's ear, "If you feel strongly about being seen with me, we don't need to stay."

Isabella shook her head. "I was only recalling how cruel people can be."

"I can't guarantee no one will be mean or cruel to you, lass. Jesu, I can't even guarantee anger will not come from me. But I swear, I will try to protect you from the brunt of it."

She nodded, believing he meant his words. Standing close, his strength was a living, breathing support, and Isabella wanted desperately to cling to it, to him. If only she wasn't afraid to let go of her independence. To be at the mercy of love. Even after giving her word to Nicholas, agreeing to his notions of marriage, the thought of living a half-filled life seemed unfair.

"Two tables, please," he said to the serving girl, disrupting Isabella's thoughts. "You may seat Mr. and Mrs. Berths within view," he ordered, making it clear he wished privacy.

"Yes, sir. Follow me, sir."

Seated close to the fire, she let the warmth drive the chill of doubt from her bones. Nicholas believed she could offer him something. She'd teach him what she knew of the ton and would accept the benefits he offered her in exchange.

"How old were you when you first boarded a ship?" She pressed the subject further when he did not reply. "When you introduced your friend, Mr. Jenkins, you mentioned knowing him when you first boarded a ship."

He stared at her for a long moment. Isabella began to think he had no intention of revealing anything from his past. Then he shrugged. "Twelve, mayhap thirteen."

Her heart broke. He was no more than a child. "Where was your mother?"

"Sick mostly."

From the way his fingers briefly tightened around his silverware, she knew talk of is mother still caused pain. Tears clouded her vision when she thought of the responsibilities he had faced at a tender age.

"I was bigger than the lads my age." He shrugged again, and this time she knew he cared far more about his past than he led on. "It was easy enough to board a ship, earn my keep."

"You could have been killed." She shivered. Her eyes touched on the Berths, but they were engrossed in their own conversation and eating their meal.

Nicholas chuckled. "From fists, yes. The sea, no. It's where I can forget. The past doesn't matter at sea, only surviving each day." He paused. "It's safe."

Isabella gasped. Surely she'd misheard. Nothing she'd ever heard about sailing was safe. "Safe, Mr. Ferguson?"

He looked at her. "From nightmares and London..."

"From remembering what happened to your mother," she said, guessing that was part of the reason he'd spent so many years sailing instead of fortifying his business connections in London.

He nodded.

"The sea does not question your birth before folding you under," he continued. "It's the one place title does not matter, except if a lad is unlucky enough to be taken captive for ransom or slavery. The skills to reason and think logically when under attack and a strong sword arm are a man's greatest assets. The first time I stepped on a ship, I knew I'd captain my own. I saw how things could be if men trusted each other. Good men wouldn't lose their lives because their mates coveted their belongings or because their captain thought them no more than a means."

Isabella frowned. That was no life for a child. Even now the streets were crowded with orphans who picked the pockets of unsuspecting men, and it was a challenge to imagine Nicholas as one of them, struggling to survive. Her chest tightened. "And your father, where was he?"

Leaning forward, he rested both elbows on the table,

distance disappearing between them. "I'm a bastard, Isabella, you know that."

Undeterred, she shook her head. Bastard or not, he still had a father. What man abandons his child? But she knew of many aristocrats who did. Had her father not done the same? Holding his gaze, she asked again, "Where was he, Nicholas, when his twelve-year-old son sought to make a living at sea?"

"In the country with his new wife, I assume."

She gasped. He knew. He had known of his father the entire time. She'd expected a defensive shrug or to be told he did not know of his sire. His honesty made her want to hold the young boy, comfort the man across the table.

"Lord Jeffery Ferguson, inheritor of Venture Estate. Marriage to my mother would not have given him property or maintained his lifestyle."

"For wealth, he abandoned you and your mother entirely?" She'd only met Lord Jeffery once, at her father's country home, and struggled to remember any details of the man that was linked to Nicholas. "Yet, she gave you his name?" There was only one reason a mother did that—hope.

"Is that not the way?" He took a sip of wine she didn't remember being served. "My mother was born and raised in the Highlands. Bairns are given the names of their clans."

Isabella sensed there was more to his mother's decision than that. Honor, perhaps.

"Or mayhap she intended to shame the man into fulfilling his duty."

Isabella frowned. "That was a brave thing to do."

"My mother would have done anything to see me fed, including taking naught for herself."

When Lord Jeffery had visited her father, it had been hunting season and he'd arrived at their country home with a boy her age. A boy with blond hair and rich blue eyes that mirrored Nicholas's. "You have a brother. Does he know of you?"

"Aye." He sliced through the beef cutlet on his plate, only rigid fingers around his knife betrayed his unease.

Isabella tore her gaze away from Nicholas. Abandoned by his father because of rank and having to support his mother at a young age, he had reason to hate the upper class. It would only be a matter of time before he came to resent her. After all, she was one of them, and he insisted on marrying into a class he despised.

"Lady Isabella."

She turned towards the voice, rasped with age and cigars, as the older gentleman moved towards their table. "Lord Eaton." She started to rise and was waved back into her seat.

"You must be Captain Nicholas Ferguson." Nicholas shook Lord Eaton's outstretched hand.

A business introduction. Isabella was pleased. Lord Eaton didn't miss an opportunity to be introduced to an entrepreneur, especially ones that sat at his tables.

"All of London is raving about the quality of your latest shipment, sir."

"I doubt all of London knows of me yet," Nicholas said.

The older man laughed. "I'd be honored to have you and your finer spirits at my tables. I think we can agree on the advantages." Neither did Lord Eaton miss an opportunity at having the finest quality alcohol, Isabella thought, as the man walked away.

"Lord Eaton is the owner of Brown's Gentleman's Club," she told Nicholas. "I believe he's just offered you membership."

"How are you acquainted with Lord Eaton?"

Isabella did not meet Nicholas's gaze. "My father patron-izes the most reputable clubs. Brown's has the highest standards."

"Am I to find Lord Emsley at Brown's?"

Lowering her lashes, she nodded. "I'm afraid he's a frequent member."

"And you would have him toss the wee detail, that you were once his, at every encounter?"

"The question, sir, is not whether *I* can set Emsley behind me, but whether you can trust that I have. Emsley is no longer part of my future, and I refuse to live the rest of my life avoiding encounters. If you want to grow your business and gain access to the homes of the well-to-do, you'd benefit from accepting Lord Eaton's offer and establishing a relationship with the gentlemen that frequent his club."

She noticed Nicholas's mouth was curved slightly before all traces were once again hidden behind his stone jaw.

"You'll consider Lord Eaton's offer?" she asked.

"I agree, Isabella, accepting the man's offer is sound reasoning. As for your companions, they will soon realize you are out of their reach."

CHAPTER 12

"*A*re the rooms ready?" Nicholas asked his butler when the man's tall slender frame exited the kitchen.

Winston paused, his eyes widening. "They will be, sir."

"Did the hired driver not alert you to Lady Isabella's arrival?"

"No, sir." Winston turned, heading back towards the kitchen.

It seemed his message alerting the household of their arrival was not delivered. He hadn't sent a note or made sure the driver understood. His only thought had been on keeping Isabella close and out of Daniel's reach.

He had tried charming her during their meal, sharing bits of his past, though each revelation had made him uneasy. Isabella had listened and, to his surprise, defended the decisions he had made in his youth. Yet, even as he did not regret their conversation, Nicholas wondered if she might use her new knowledge against him.

When they sat in the close quarters of the carriage, the space made cramped with parcels, he had glanced down several times and noticed the creamy tops of her breasts and their delicious valley. A path he was cocksure led to hell. Her tilted chin—defiance, he was sure, stemmed from regard for another man, one she would rather kiss and lavish her affections on—had stopped him from pursuing any wicked thoughts. He had cursed himself for not hiring a second carriage after their late afternoon lunch. He'd cursed her for that perfume she chose to don, which made him think of tangled limbs, silk sheets, and long deep thrusts. An hour later, his breeches were still too tight for comfort.

"Are there no rooms available to house guests?"

Winston cleared his throat. "Only the usual one, sir."

Nicholas's gaze drifted over to the woman standing beside him. Their eyes met, a slight shiver quivering her bottom lip. His eyes locked on the movement. He could only guess at what he looked like. He'd been in an aroused state for the better part of the day. It was dangerous to place her in his adjoining rooms. Her scent was still wrapped around him like a cloak. Now looking at her crimson neckline, he'd have it no other way.

"That will do." He never took his eyes off her. Reaching forward, he cupped her chin between his fingers. "Have her trunks taken up at once." And for the sake of his groin, sure it would deflate with a touch of anger, he said, "Have Miss Conley heat water for a bath; Lady Isabella has had a most adventurous morning before we went into town and no doubt wants to wash away the memories."

"Very good, sir."

Heat flaring across every delicate feature of her face, Isabella's breath hitched. She became the loveliest shade of red when angered, he observed. Nicholas sighed, immediately regretting his harsh words. "Isabella, I'm—"

Jerking her chin out of his grip, Isabella walked up the stairs until their eyes were leveled. "You are a most perplexing and irritating man, Captain." Her voice lowered.

"That you would try to manipulate...mention our romantic encounter in front of the staff..."

Nicholas closed the distance. He knew this Isabella. Defiant. Strong willed. Gone was their earlier comradery, replaced by spit and fire. "And you, lass, are stubborn."

"I was manipulated once before and will not be made a fool again, sir." She shook her head. "Marriage to you will not do."

"Despite what society thinks, I know you value your reputation and the Berths' well-being. You would not be foolish enough to throw that all away out of spite."

She gasped. "You wouldn't."

He would not turn her servants onto the streets, but he wasn't going to tell her that, not when the Berths' livelihood seemed to be her sole consideration at the moment.

"You promised them employ."

"They will have a place under my roof as long as you are my wife."

A soft groan escaped Isabella's mouth before she turned, climbing the remaining stairs. He had intended to woo her; instead he had done the opposite, destroying the little favor he'd gained. Looking down at his breeches, Nicholas cursed.

Harold walked into the room, stopping at Nicholas's side. "You have a way with the lassies."

Nicholas ignored his cousin. "The woman doesna ken she nae has a choice."

"You forced your will by announcing the nuptials in the dailies. Drove her from her home. Threatened to toss the people she considers friends out onto the street to fend for themselves... No wonder why her resolve is set."

"I tried to woo her."

Harold laughed. "With what, brute strength? Have you not heard a word I said?"

"It is difficult to remember how bonnie her eyes are when I find the lass planning to run off with another mon."

Nicholas uttered a curse when Harold laughed again. When he found himself able to move without causing damage to his groin, Nicholas headed towards the study, Harold on his heels. He frowned. "Where's Cassie?" He looked over his shoulder, expecting the familiar trot of little feet as she turned the corner. He also expected Miss Conley and Virginia to fill his ear about his daughter's unladylike manner. He received neither.

"Virginia took Cassie on a short outing. She did not think it wise to have our little imp scare the lassie off or rebel against our hard work before you have a chance to show her the right of things. If you ask me, you are doing a fine job of scaring Lady Isabella on your own." Harold grinned.

"I did not ask you." Nicholas scowled. Talking to Cassie would have to happen sooner than later if he hoped to avoid another female's fury. The child was stubborn, to say the least, and he wanted to be the first to mention Isabella to her. He decided to talk to Cassie at breakfast. In the meantime, he'd take Harold's advice on appealing to Isabella. "The men?"

"Ready to sail when you are."

CHAPTER 13

*I*sabella faced the thick wood door set in the wall opposite the large bed in her new chambers. All her instincts warned that behind it lay Nicholas's rooms. The man was insufferable. Nothing she did deterred him. What she did not understand was why he insisted on marrying *her*.

The large lavish bedchamber, green and gold threads woven into the decorative pillows, bed covers and curtains, reminded her of his wealth and thriving business. She ran her fingers along one of four polished bed posts, each reaching above her head.

Fathers would welcome him for their daughters. He was handsome and desirable, with growing wealth. Her skin was still on fire from their earlier encounter—and he could be charming.

Isabella frowned. Entrance into the nobility was not as simple as marrying above one's station. Did he seek the connections of her father? Isabella hoped not. Her father did not intend to forgive her slight, and he no doubt thought her engagement another attempt to snub him. The father she knew would not warm to the idea of a husband who made his livelihood by trade.

She could offer Nicholas nothing. That thought chilled her. Emsley had wanted her dowry. Power and money, she understood. What would Nicholas do when he grew tired of their arrangement? What would *she* do? With no family or money, she would be dependent on his support.

That would not do.

It was late evening when she and Edyeth finished unpacking the trunks. Sleep evaded her. Walking to the adjoining door, she touched the tips of her fingers to the wood, then flattened her palm. Her forehead rested against the polished surface. No sound came from the other room. She had hoped to hear his footsteps, exchange a few words while she had the courage and the household was asleep. Though his proposal of marriage was more than reasonable, she wanted to make demands of her own. Turning from the door, Isabella gasped and stared into the greenest pair of eyes.

"I did not intend to frighten you."

Isabella looked for a spark of resemblance to Nicholas and found none. What she did find was a woman no more than three years her senior with knowing hazel eyes.

"He's not there, you know."

Isabella flushed.

"I'm Virginia." A smile curved the woman's lips.

"I'm pleased to meet you," Isabella said, returning the smile. "Are you Nicholas's sister?"

"In a way, I suppose you're correct, only we're not related by blood." At Isabella's confused frown, Virginia continued, "Nicholas has a way of saving people from themselves, as you'll soon find."

"You mean capturing and taking hostage?"

Virginia's eyes sparkled. "I've been waiting to meet the woman who's sent Nicholas into a wild frenzy."

Isabella felt a tightening in her chest. Surely this woman was wrong. "You're mistaken. He doesn't act like a man who wants me here. One moment he's kind and charming and the next he's..."

"Unbearable?"

"And stubborn."

"Let's not forget ill tempered," Virginia said. They laughed. "I'll help you unpack. I would have welcomed you sooner but ..."

"I've already emptied the trunks, thank you." Isabella walked to the door, opened it. "I don't mean to be rude, but I must speak with Mr. Ferguson."

"Off to do battle? May I offer a suggestion?" Virginia's green eyes danced.

Isabella paused.

"Nicholas is used to getting his way. He's been this way since childhood," Virginia said. "And it's not all empty bravado." Virginia's head tilted to the side. "A battle of wits will only serve to entice him... Use your charm, and you might catch him unaware."

Isabella's brows drew together. "Why are you helping me?" They were strangers by all accounts. Nicholas had brought her into his home only hours ago, and the two women had exchanged only a handful of words. She had expected hostility, not kindness.

Virginia laughed. "If we're to be sisters, Isabella, what better way to foster our relationship?"

"He may well toss me aside after tonight."

"Then I'll help you gather your things... But I doubt he'll do anything of the sort." Virginia smiled. "I believe you can make him listen to reason."

CHAPTER 14

*N*icholas heard the library door open, then close. He looked up from the desk, his hands hovering over the note he had started to pen. It was hours since her arrival at his home and he had expected her protest sooner. Instead, she had kept to herself, refusing the refreshments he'd sent to her room. Not knowing her thoughts irritated him. He preferred spit and fire any day.

He watched her graceful movement as she walked across the room. She was a beautiful woman. Warm and soft with the right touch of delicateness, her hips purposely swaying to provoke him.

He detected no anger, but Isabella was a woman of education and he had felt the bite of her words. He straightened in his chair. They might as well resolve their differences before dawn, or at least he hoped they could. This business of finding a wife proved vexing, a greater task than he had anticipated.

"Mr. Ferguson."

His skin tightened at the use of his proper name. "Isabella."

She settled in a nearby chair with the same grace she had used to walk into the library.

"Where is your chaperone?"

"It's late. I've sent her to bed."

If he did not know better, he'd think she was warming to the idea of marriage. He relaxed. "Are your rooms suitable?"

The slow lifting of her eyes from beneath her lashes was enough to heat his blood. Folding his arms across his chest, Nicholas ignored the feeling. This was a marriage of convenience, he reminded himself. A union Isabella had protested from the start.

She nodded. "They are comfortable, thank you."

"Since you are without a chaperone to protect you from indelicate advances, I presume you did not seek me out to show your gratitude."

She looked down briefly before holding his gaze. "You've made it impossible for us to marry without furthering gossip, dashing any chance of me earning suitable income. I have terms."

"In case I go back on my word?"

"Yes."

There was a pause. He was being generous, he thought, offering her a better life than she could possibly have without his aid. Yet, she had terms—she had come here hoping to bargain. Intrigued, he said, "Alright."

"But first, a question. What is it you expect of me, and why must we marry at all?"

Ah, she had realized their rooms joined.

He rarely expected people to do anything without the promise of coin. However, he hoped Isabella was different.

"I have a daughter," he said. "She needs a mother, or, at the very least, a woman's guidance."

Isabella stared at him, and he suspected his admission surprised her.

"You can pave her way into society."

"You do not need a wife for that when you can hire a governess."

"A wife can open far more doors than a governess."

"You would marry for my title alone?" Her eyes widened.

He raised a brow. "Was Emsley not besotted with your dowry?"

Her cheeks warmed. "What of love?" She looked away, focusing on some distant nonsense over his shoulder.

"Is that what you wish for, Isabella? Love?"

Her eyes met his again, and what shone in their depths made him pause. Dare he hope that she would accept more from him, that she could love a man like him, so different from her peers?

"What I wish is for us to come to an agreement." Her chin angled up.

He almost laughed at his lapse in judgment. He ran his hand over his face, letting the bristle from a day's beard prickle his palm. Isabella heated his blood from their first encounter, but it was time he set aside notions of passion or love. He was a good father and a good captain with loyal men. It was more than most men had.

"Is she your illegitimate child?"

"No."

Her brows pinched. "You were never married."

"Cassie is my ward," he clarified. He had made a serious error if Isabella could not accept Cassie.

"The ton will never accept your orphan, sir..."

He walked around the desk and placed his hands on her shoulders. He ignored her wide eyes and shocked gasp. "And you, could you accept her? She was born in wedlock by parents who loved her enough to trust her upbringing to me, and I aim for her to grow in wedlock. She's nae a bastard and will nae be treated with any affection other than kindness, even if ye cannot see fit to love her."

Isabella wiggled out of his grip. "I only meant that my current reputation will not aid you in this." Her eyes flashed.

He had frightened her. Nicholas took a seat on the other end of the chesterfield, the fight draining from his bones. "In time, high society will forget your scandal, move on to the next. I don't want Cassie to have the life I had. I want her to have choices."

"What if she doesn't choose a life of nobility?"

"Knowing she can choose is enough."

Isabella tilted her head to the side, and her voice was soft when she next spoke. "You love her very much."

He didn't answer. There was no need.

"Is this all you need from me, then?" she asked. "A mother for your ward?" Her hands tightened around her waist. "What will happen when you tire of me? I will be no better off than I am now."

"I'm not Emsley. I honor my word."

Her eyes cast downwards.

He sighed. "Isabella, this is as much your home as it is mine. You will have all the rights of a wife."

"Will I, sir?"

"Aye, lass."

What kind of a man did she think he was? He would give her the respect due her station. Rising from the sofa, he picked up his quill. "Tom," he said, scribbling a reminder across a sheet of parchment from his desk. "He's my solicitor. I'll have him open an account at the bank under your name. You wouldn't ever have to ask for pin money, Isabella." He scribbled with more vigor. "Virginia is usually given the monies for the household, Miss Conley, food and such. I'll turn over next month's pouch to you."

"I'm not your housekeeper, sir."

Nicholas's hand stilled over the note. He had erred, thinking that turning over the pouch would give her more freedom as mistress of the house. He took pride in pulling his purse-strings. Isabella, he noted, thought differently.

Isabella sat up. "I think Miss Conley is capable of running the kitchen. I would, however, like to know what the expenses are."

Nicholas nodded, glad his future wife wasn't naive.

"What of the two employees from my household?" she asked. "I confess, I pay them a ridiculously small sum, but they depend on me for room and board. We've grown to look out for each other." Her eyes softened as she spoke of her employees, fingers knotting together. The confidence he had grown to admire slipped away.

"Isabella," he began.

"I'm sure we could make a place for them," she said. "Any position at all…"

"Stop!" Nicholas pinched the bridge of his nose. "Isabella, they are your employees, and if you want them with you, we'll find duties for them here."

"Thank you."

"My God, what type of malicious gossip have you heard, to think I'd turn away two people you care about?" He held up his hand, sensing her denials. He already knew her reaction to him was no one else's fault but his own. If he'd been gentler and more refined, then perhaps she wouldn't find him so distasteful.

"If we're to have a marriage where we are not at constant odds, it's best we lay our demands before the ceremony."

"Is that all we're to have then?"

Nae. The word weighed heavy on his tongue. She made him dream of possibilities. Ones he couldn't have.

Holding her gaze, he reminded himself not to look too deeply into her question. It was more than likely her delicate way of reassurance that he'd keep his distance. He looked away. Did she also want reassurances he wouldn't burden her with wifely duties?

"I've taken the liberty of acquiring special licenses." Nicholas kept his expression neutral when she flinched. She must detest him. To set herself free from one cad only to marry another. If nothing else became of their marriage, he planned to give her time to settle her feelings for her paramour.

"What of my desires?" she asked. "Have you thought of them?"

Nicholas sighed. He had, more times than he could count. He moved beside her on the seat. "Surely you see the advantages of marriage."

"What of my friends?"

"You mean Daniel?"

She nodded, eyes holding his.

"You will be free to...conduct your life as you wish."

Her eyes watered before she hugged him.

She was going to be the death of him. The women he'd slept with had all had lovers, he'd not been their first. However, none had had lovers while they'd been involved. That was the only rule he'd ever extended to them, and for the life of him, he didn't understand why he was making an exception for Isabella.

"I have two requests." He shifted back, creating distance between them. "Care for my daughter."

She nodded.

"I promise not to press you with husbandly demands." He closed his eyes. "I have a home in the country, it is yours."

"And you will live here?"

"I'll be at sea often."

She looked at him, then dropped her gaze. "Who will greet you on your return?"

Was that disappointment? Nicholas inhaled, stilling his pulse. His family traveled with him. This would be his first journey without Cassie. Except for the servants, no one welcomed *him* home, at least not the way Isabella suggested. The merchants wanted their goods, bankers their money. The servants fussed over Cassie while she relayed excited tales of bandits and pirates. Virginia awaited Harold.

"*Everyone* leaves, Isabella," he finally said.

Nicholas looked away from the softening in her eyes. He had no use for pity, especially from Isabella.

"If I refuse?" she asked.

He leaned forward, their knees brushing. Heat burned beneath layers of clothing. "Do you have more terms, lass?"

"Don't call me that." Her whispered words held no conviction.

"In exchange for the care of one child, I am offering freedom and financial support." His finger tilted her chin until there was little choice but to look at him. "Think on it. A wife has far more freedom than that of an unmarried woman."

She trembled against his touch, her lips parting. "You ask for nothing more?" Clouded eyes searched his.

His hand dropped to his thighs. Even now, as she negotiated the terms of their marriage, he thought he felt her flinch from his touch. "Our marriage will be as you wish it. I only ask that we consummate the marriage. Endure my touch for one night, and you shall never have to endure another."

"What of children?"

Hope surged again and he swallowed. "If you get with child, I'll visit the bairn often, of course. On that we must agree." His eyes held hers. He planned to be a different type of father, devoted and loving. By the Gods, nothing would make him abandon his child. "The country home would be yours. You'll be free of me there to live a life at your discretion."

"What if I don't want to be tucked away in the country?"

"Separate dwelling will keep us from each other's throats."

"I can live here," she suggested.

He searched her face before nodding. "If that would make you happy." It would not be the first time he was driven from his home. This time, at least, it was on his terms. "Will you accept our bargain, then?" His breath held.

"*Yes*," she whispered.

A slow smile tilted the corners of his mouth. "My brave lass." Then, his lips brushed hers.

CHAPTER 15

"I've sold my soul to the devil."

"Surely you've saved a bit for yourself?"

"I've negotiated a portion for myself. But he intends to have it all."

"A man like Nicholas is never satisfied with a mere soul, especially when he is challenged on every front," Virginia teased.

Isabella groaned. The cup touched her lips and she took another sip of tea. Her discussion with Nicholas had not turned out as she intended. He still wanted to marry. Cassie —she had not expected his plea for Cassie. He was capable of love. He just couldn't muster any of that for her. Nicholas was right about her need for protection, and he'd used those weaknesses to his advantage.

In a day, they'd be man and wife. She would be his. The thought both frightened and intrigued her. Her face grew warm and a slight rose tinted her cheeks. "I'm an expensive governess."

"I very much doubt that."

"He desires more children, though he didn't say as much."

She frowned. "I expected... Oh, I don't know what I expected." Isabella closed her eyes.

"It has to do with his childhood." Virginia took a sip of her own tea.

Isabella opened her eyes. Nicholas spoke of his past rarely and readily accepted disappointments as though he expected them, except when it came to Harold and Cassie. He trusted them.

"He was made a man at the age of a boy. His father..." Virginia's mouth pinched with sympathy. "...was...is an aristocrat who had no need for a son he considered below his station. I believe Nicholas means to give any children he sires what he never had."

Isabella's eyes lowered. Many wives did not love their husbands. In fact, many did not love their children. Children were unavoidable when one needed an heir.

Isabella's fingers tightened around the hot cup. Her punishment for loving Emsley should not be a loveless arrangement to Nicholas. Could she marry him, knowing he did not love her? Could she watch day after day as she cared for their children, see the love in his eyes and know none of it belonged to her. That would be torture. How could she bear his children, lie in his bed, give herself over to his lovemaking without falling in love with him? "Oh, Virginia..."

Virginia patted her knees in sympathy. "Have you said yes to your arrangement?"

She nodded. "I fear the vessel connecting my brain to my lips was severed at the time."

Virginia chuckled. "Nicholas has that effect."

Her heart skipped as a new thought occurred. Did Virginia also harbor feelings for Nicholas? She stared at her new friend, then shook away her unease.

"I do believe he cares for you, Isabella."

"I doubt that. I have what he wants, and in my current dilemma...I'm afraid he's correct."

"He also wants to restore your good name."

"Only so his children may have the rights denied to him."

Virginia sipped her tea. "Do you care for him? Could you love him, Isabella?"

"Don't you understand? I've made the mistake once in being with a man who only desired what I could give, and I've grown to hate the bitter taste of it."

Isabella brought the hot cup to her lips, welcoming the soothing flavor against her tongue. The warmth calmed her and she clung to the familiar taste. "When I'm not thinking of wringing his neck, I see how thoughtful and considerate he is. He's made a family in his home. He is...overbearing, yet he's offered freedom."

"Yes, but could you love him?"

Isabella swirled the liquid in her cup. "I don't know."

"Oh dear." Virginia set both their teacups on the side table. "I've known Nicholas for four years and he is smitten with you. Love doesn't always come first in a marriage, especially among your class."

Isabella's heart leapt against her chest. "He's made no promises."

Virginia clasped both of Isabella's hands in hers. "Neither have you."

$\mathcal{N}$icholas sat at the table, his daughter at his right, an empty chair to his left. Harold had abandoned his seat for one beside Virginia. Isabella had not joined them for supper, and Nicholas wondered if she intended to avoid him.

Virginia asked, "Do you suppose Isabella would object to Cassie at the table?"

"In my house, we don't have before the mast. Our family dines together, at the table."

Looking at Cassie, he decided there was no good way to tell the child she would not join him on his next voyage. Jesu, he hoped the child took to Isabella, or at least saw Isabella as a new adventure. "Stop playing with your eggs," he said to Cassie for the third time.

Elbow on the table, Cassie's head rested against her small knuckles. The child was not excited to hear of her new mother. This, coupled with the fact that Isabella did not seek out Cassie after supper, deepened his worry. Even now, he saw the spark behind his daughter's eyes each time she glanced at him. Cassie was an intelligent lass. It would not take her long to decide Isabella was not interested in gaining a new daughter.

"Jesu, Cassie, with such a long frown a mon would think I planned to toss you overboard."

"She don't like me!"

"Does not," Virginia murmured.

"She doesn't know you," Nicholas said.

Cassie looked around the table. "She don't like any of us."

"It's me she doesn't like," Nicholas said before Virginia corrected the child.

Cassie's eyes widened. "If she don't like my pa then I don't like her. Send her away!"

"Cassie," Virginia gasped.

"She'll take you away."

Nicholas's chest tightened. Cassie was afraid of losing him and their time together.

"You don't want me anymore." Cassie didn't look at him, her eyes focused on the pieces of food tossed about on her plate. "And I don't want you."

Pushing his chair back, Nicholas lifted Cassie from her seat, settling her on his knees. He hugged her. Her shoulders slumped, nose pressing deep against his chest, and she began to cry. Nicholas tightened his arms around her.

"Now lass, you know that's not true." He closed his eyes against the hurt he heard in her voice. "A wee lass needs a mama as much as she does her papa. A life at sea is nae good for you. You should have never set foot aboard a ship."

"But…"

"A mother can teach you things I can't. Isabella knows of society, and politeness, and will have you accepted in circles that are closed to me."

"I have Aunt Virginia." Cassie turned in his lap.

When he looked at the aunt in question for help, he

received a smirk in return. Both Virginia and Harold were enjoying the exchange at his expense. "And you always will."

"And me, Cass, ye will always have me."

"I know, Uncle Harold. You get me out of trouble."

Harold twisted in his seat, he, too, not meeting Nicholas's glare. Kissing the top of his daughter's head, Nicholas eased her away from him. The smile Cassie sent his way would have melted his heart if he didn't know better.

"Hire another governess, Papa."

He folded his arms. "Nae."

"I'll be good, Papa."

His eyes narrowed. "The first one called you possessed." This was how Cassie came to travel with him. She'd cry for days if he spent long amounts of time away. Even as a babe, it was as if she knew she'd lost those closest to her and he could not refuse the little comfort she'd sought from him.

"And the second," he said sternly, "couldn't listen to any more of your tales of pirates and walking the plank." What he didn't tell her was that the woman had insisted on a heavy hand. He'd had no choice but to fire her. Possessed or not, no child deserved the punishment that governess had in mind. He'd even refused the letters of reference she'd insisted upon. "Jesu, Cassie, you told the woman tales of missing limbs."

Cassie frowned. "Uncle Harold says not to forget the important bits. It wouldn't be a good story without one-eyed pirates on ghost legs."

"You weren't supposed to frighten the woman, lass." With his thumb, Nicholas smoothed her creased brow. "Do you trust me, Cassie?" He knew the truth of it, but needed to hear her answer. Sometimes they needed no words. He knew his daughter's mind as well as he knew his own. A bond, he suspected, would only grow.

She nodded.

"And what of your Uncle Harold, do you trust him?" He

intended to pay his cousin double for his role in the details of Cassie's story telling.

Once again, she nodded without hesitation.

"As do I. It was your Uncle Harold who suggested I find a wife and you a mother." Nicholas smiled when he heard Harold's swift intake of air.

Holding his own breath, he waited as a range of emotions crossed his daughter's delicate features. Confusion, betrayal, anger—he recognized those quick flashes of fire like that of an explosion. Again, she buried her nose against his shirt. She was always a strong lass, ready for adventures, but now she seemed vulnerable huddled in his arms.

"Good morning."

The room grew still. Isabella had chosen this moment to enter. Not sure how much she'd heard, Nicholas murmured a greeting in return.

"And you must be Cassie?" Isabella stood a mere foot from them.

"It's not polite to ignore a greeting, lass."

"My papa said you don't like him."

Aye, his daughter had found the source of her emotions, it only made sense she would direct them towards their cause. Isabella's eyes held his for a moment, and, when she spoke, Nicholas held his breath.

"I admit, I didn't like the way he asked me to marry him."

He'd never lied to his daughter, and was grateful Isabella hadn't sought to do so too.

"Did Papa steal you away?" Cassie pushed from his chest, glimpsing Isabella for the first time. Her eyes widened, though the reason was unclear.

"Cassie," Nicholas warned.

"It's alright." Isabella pulled out the chair beside them and took a seat.

Nicholas's shoulders stiffened. Was this some new game?

Did she intend to use Cassie to free herself from him? He was about to tell her she needn't bother. That she was free if only to protect Cassie.

"In a way, I suppose he did." Isabella nodded.

Holding his breath, Nicholas's eyes fixed on Harold. Damn his cousin for encouraging Cassie with wild tales.

Those brown eyes widened. "That's what pirates do. My papa has the fiercest ship. Maybe we'll take you on it one day, right Papa?" She turned to look at Nicholas, who nodded. He hadn't expected the meeting to go so well, and he was willing to agree to almost anything to keep the peace between the two spitfires in his life. Cassie nodded and turned back to Isabella. "Tell me how Papa captured you."

Harold coughed.

"Tell you what, I saw a beautiful pond from my window..."

"Our fishing hole."

Isabella's lips twitched. "Show me your fishing hole and I'll share my tale."

Cassie sprang to her feet. Isabella's smile barely shielded her shock at seeing Cassie in breeches. She tugged at her father's hand.

"I think this is a trip for you and Isabella." Nicholas tapped her nose with a finger.

Her small face turned to meet Isabella's. "Can't Papa come?"

"Of course, your papa can come." Isabella's lips pursed.

Standing, he decided to stay a step or two behind the lassies.

A short time later, Nicholas sat on the cool blades of grass, reclining against his elbows as the ladies skirted the pond hand in hand. He listened to their rapid chatter. Occasionally Cassie pointed to waves in the water where fish swam just below the surface. He was mindful not to interrupt, giving Cassie the time she needed to bond with Isabella before he was again at sea. The late morning sun pierced the treetops, bathing them in ribbons of warmth. He closed his eyes.

Their laughter reached his ears, the sound unguarded and pure. He waited for their voices to soothe him again, and when that small delight was denied, he opened his eyes to find Isabella's gaze on him.

Cassie tugged Isabella's hand. "You don't mind my stories?" She tossed a small pebble into the water, delighted when it skipped the surface.

"Lady Cassie, I don't mind your stories in the least."

"I'm not a lady, I'm a second mate."

"Of course you're a lady. You want to be captain one day, don't you?"

Cassie nodded.

"Then your father needs your help." Isabella silenced his protest with a glare. "You see, it takes an intelligent and courageous lady to command both land and sea."

"I'm smart!"

Isabella's brows drew together in thought. "I'll make you a bargain. You teach me all you know of the sea, and I'll teach you all I know of being a lady and proper schooling. That way we're both prepared for anything your father decides to throw at us."

Cassie looked to her father. He nodded, not believing his ears. Isabella had reached his daughter where threats and harsh words had not. She'd used the child's love for the sea to reach an agreement. Though he knew Cassie would never truly give up the notion of sailing, she would now gain respectability and a choice at a future that had eluded him and Harold.

For the first time, he saw what Harold had seen, and was now more convinced he'd made the right choice in a mother for his daughter. Though, he was not so sure Isabella had softened in regards to becoming his wife.

"It's a deal," Cassie said, voice serious.

Nicholas sat up, realizing what his daughter was about to do. He cringed as Cassie spat in her little hand before slapping small fingers to the palm of Isabella's outstretched one.

Though Isabella folded larger fingers over Cassie's without reproach, Nicholas knew she was appalled by the stiffening of her shoulders, but had the good sense to know this was one of Cassie's first lessons in life at sea.

CHAPTER 17

The horse's hooves clopped on the brick road to Isabella's father, Lord Carolus Pennington's home, Nicholas's carriage slowing as it turned the corner.

It was a nice enough neighborhood. The houses were grand and gave the appearance of money. The trees were tall, trunks sturdy with age. The lawns were so manicured even dogs avoided them. Nicholas, too, might have been impressed if he hadn't looked into Lord Carolus's financial holdings. The man had gambled away everything, including his daughter's dowry. He might have done the same with the house and small estate if it hadn't been in his late wife's name and passed down from mother to daughters. The property would now go to Isabella's younger sister, Catherine, since Lord Carolus no longer considered Isabella family.

He imagined Isabella and her sister running in the front lawn, being chased by their parents. Would her father have allowed such liberties? The nobility were sticklers for their rules. He had tolerated far worse than chasing Cassie for a chance to hear her laugh. He wondered again what sort of man Lord Carolus was.

Nicholas steeled himself against the sense of sorrow twisting in his gut as he thought of Isabella and her father being at odds. His father had shown little interest in his upbringing, and his mother, the bravest person he'd ever known, had almost turned to brothels to put food on the table. Those were the longest days of his life. The nights had been even longer. Stepping onto the docks of his first ship at the age of thirteen, he became a man when he should have been a boy. He still felt his mother's arms tight around his shoulders, telling him to be safe, to write, that she loved him. Even then, he'd been strong willed. He'd sent home every spare penny for five years, until his mother passed. Nicholas closed his eyes against the haunting memory. The next time he had boarded a ship after laying her to rest, it was his own, with Harold old enough to be at his side.

As he arrived in the circular drive, his stomach clenched. Was this the life Isabella wanted? Was he denying her a life of luxury, with people she loved and cared for? His life was a tangled mess. He only knew the importance of a mother, his mother, and wanted one for Cassie. His father had been long absent from his life, but he was a good father to Cassie. He loved his daughter as if she was of his blood.

Above his head, leaves the color of butterscotch flickered on the branches. The bark peeled in thick flakes from the trees' trunks. Along the drive, neglected flowers struggled to bloom, stifled by vines of weeds that suffocated the garden's simple beauty.

The carriage stopped. Pushing open the door, he planted both feet on the ground before Chambers left his perch.

There was no warm welcoming feeling of home here, not the kind that Isabella had brought to his house since she'd arrived. Then again, this was not his home, and the only person that ever truly loved him was his mother, and she was dead.

Nicholas shrugged aside his current dark mood, steeling his features before the butler opened the door. Without waiting for an invitation, he stepped into the hall, startling the butler with the intrusion. He didn't care, he was inside and not even the devil himself could toss him out before his business was concluded.

"Captain Ferguson to see Lord Carolus," he announced before the servant fully recovered.

"Look here, you can't barge in at such an ungodly hour."

Nicholas was mildly irritated that the man had not gone to do his bidding. But he did notice the butler had created a sizeable distance between them. Ungodly hour? What was it with the wealthy? For as long as he could remember, he'd risen with the sun. "I can and did. I'll wake the entire household if I must."

The butler paled. "Are you expected?"

Nicholas smiled coldly. They both knew he wasn't from the *ungodly* hour he'd arrived at. He followed the nervous man to a modest parlor dressed with two uncomfortable looking chairs and a coffee table. Lowering his bulk into one of the seats, he was dismayed to find himself correct about the seat. Stretching his long legs, he groaned when his knee bumped the side of the doll-sized table. He was a caged beast in the small room, and he had a sinking feeling this was exactly how the house's master made all unwanted guests feel.

Giving up on comfort, Nicholas walked to the window overlooking the southern lawn. The land stretched far, wrapping around a duck pond. Lush gardens wove around a stone trail, and he found himself wondering if Isabella's bedroom faced such a stunning view. Did she wake to the sight of lilies and sunshine? How many times had she stared out this very window and dreamed of her future? Had she imagined how it would be, married to an earl or perhaps a duke? As a daughter of the Earl of Pennington the opportunities were endless. Instead, she'd found herself stuck with him, an illegitimate captain.

He'd worked hard for his fortune, holding onto it with sweat and blood. More often the latter. He was proud of himself, his finances were secure. He owned two properties, lived in one and collected income on the other, and his shipping business and investments were thriving.

Nicholas only regretted not being able to give Isabella the title she deserved. He'd always prided himself in knowing he'd treated his paramours with kindness, making their time together special. He had never been less than honest about his intentions. Each woman had welcomed him with fire and eagerness, fully aware they shared no more than affection. It had always been that way, and he'd moved on to the next woman knowing he'd left the last with a new taste for passion.

For as long as he could remember, women had always wanted the same from him. None had shown any real ardor beyond desire. And he'd done the same. From a young age, he'd steeled himself against love, locking such feelings away as to not be used against him.

This was different.

Isabella was to be his wife. He saw in her more fire than any lover he'd known. He'd admired her courage when she'd faced Emsley and the ton with her head held high. The farce had cost her dearly. When he comforted her during her time of vulnerability, Nicholas had never felt more needed. She was strong willed, and bonnie. And she needed him as much as he needed her. Isabella was everything he'd spent his entire life avoiding.

The thought of treating Isabella with the same amount of affection he showed his lovers felt cold, detached. Yet, he wanted no illusions between them. It was better this way, he reminded himself. Of noble blood, she desired one of her own rank, perhaps Lord Daniel. And he would forever be the husband she cared naught for.

Cassie was not the only reason to marry Isabella. She'd intrigued him from their first meeting in the lake. Then again on the night of the party when he had encountered her on the balcony. She had also aroused him beyond measure, and his only thought was to bury himself to the hilt between the sleekness of her thighs.

Usually the attention of another gentleman was his way of escape, allowing him another adventure. One that was equally grand and filled with promise. But for the first time, knowing the woman that captivated him desired another man made his blood cold.

Until their last voyage, Nicholas had had no intention of marrying. He'd sworn to a life of bachelorhood until he realized what his crew had always known. Cassie was no lad to be raised at sea, but a lady, whether born of noble blood or not. And so by God, he would see her raised as such.

He only hoped Isabella would grow to love Cassie as much as he did, even if that affection did not include him. Strange, such burdensome emotions had never affected him before. Nicholas had always taken what he wanted, and what couldn't be taken he achieved by purchase or persuasion. Having forced Isabella into marriage did not prove rewarding. Instead, guilt nipped at his heels at having to use her slight by society to his benefit. It was why he'd come here today, to return some of what was taken, and in turn, Nicholas hoped it gave her the freedom to pursue what made her happy. Feeling the bite of regret, he shoved his hands into the pockets of his pants.

"My lord will see you now, Captain."

He had promised Isabella security, and one of the ways to

ensure her comfort was to provide the means in which she could again walk among the ton.

The door opened to the library. The butler announced Nicholas's arrival as they entered.

"If you came to collect a dowry, there's none." The older gentleman had yet to lift his head from the ledger his quill scribbled across or offer Nicholas a proper greeting.

Nicholas studied the man. Hair peppered with gray, there was still an air of youth about him, though his broad shoulders sagged as if they held the world's burdens atop them. The lines creasing his features could be blamed on age rather than wisdom.

"I did not come for money. Not that you have any to give." Pennington's head snapped to attention then. This pleased Nicholas.

"If not for her dowry, then what? To ask her hand?"

Nicholas snorted at the accusing tone. He'd given no thought to Isabella's father when he'd announced their engagement to the dailies. In fact, his only thought had been honoring his word. "I had hoped to be enlightened as to why Lord Emsley did not honor his vows to your daughter."

It was Pennington's time to snort. The sound, one of derision, grated Nicholas's ear, as if the topic was of little consequence.

"I've yet to see how this involves me."

"Jesu, you are her father."

"She gave up that privilege when she defied me."

Was the man dull witted? Had he even looked in on Isabella's health since she'd left his home? What kind of man was he that he could so easily set aside his own daughter? For that matter, what type of man was Lord Emsley? Sure, he himself had no intent towards marriage—Nicholas had never imagined that course for his life. But he'd also never gone back on a promise. What was a man without the honor of his word?

He did not want to believe the ton, that Isabella had developed a taste for lovers, cuckolding Lord Emsley before they were married. Somehow knowing she'd once been faithful made a difference. Damn it, he knew why her past nagged at him. Hadn't she escaped to the balcony that night, fleeing from Lord Emsley? Hadn't Lord Daniel Steel been close? Only it had been he who'd rescued her.

Walking to the large windows, Nicholas took in the view of another part of the property. "I don't believe for a moment you tossed your daughter to her own fate simply because of defiance." The man could not be that cold.

"That's none of your affair."

"You are wrong." With his back still turned, he stuck his hands into his pockets. "I'm to be her husband. Whatever causes her pain concerns me." Nicholas had never believed anything more. He faced the older man then, really looking at him. He seemed to have aged a great deal from the time Nicholas had entered the room. The lines etching his forehead were deepened by worry far beyond Nicholas's expectation. Eyes sunken with fear, Lord Carolus Pennington resembled young sailors as they fended off pirates for the first time. This was different, though, not the type of fear that followed the knowledge of quick death, but one expected to be slow and merciless.

They studied each other with prolonged silence. No doubt Lord Carolus weighed what he thought of Nicholas's character. The moments stretched on until he wondered if he'd wasted his time in thinking a renewed relationship with her father would serve Isabella well among her peers. He would soon be her protector after all. But with his constant voyages to secure new cargo for the merchants, Nicholas needed to know Isabella had support beyond his household.

Finally, Pennington nodded as if satisfied with what he'd found.

"I gather you know of my gambling?" Pennington asked warily.

With a nod, Nicholas allowed the older man to continue. His voice was no longer curt, lightened by the chance to unburden his troubles.

"I'd developed a taste for card, you see." His brows knitted, remembering the precise moment it started. "My father dealt me my first hand." Pennington nodded towards a small round table in the far corner of the library. "He taught me a gentleman's game... Gin. Until last year I'd never lost more than what I carried in my purse.

"It was only natural that, when Lord Emsley showed interest in the game, I shared my skills."

Nicholas's fingers curled into fists at the thought of Isabella being used as stakes in a game between gentlemen.

"Nothing like that, sir," Pennington said after looking into Nicholas's eyes. "This was well after he'd showed interest in Isabella and asked for her hand." Pennington lowered his head. "I've done many things, but gambling away one of my daughters is by any means...low."

The muscles on Nicholas's shoulder relaxed. The man had not been so foolish as to gamble Isabella's hand in marriage. Though it would explain Emsley's reluctance to a marriage he'd won, or worse, lost in a bet.

"We frequented the game rooms at the back of Baker's. It was there in a game of Ace that I lost." With a hopeless thunder of a sound, Pennington threw back his head and laughed. Though it echoed around them, filling each dark corner of the room, it did not lighten the space.

"I was such a dunce not to have seen it earlier. He was an expert cards man, and of course by then he'd also learned my habits. My pockets were dry and I was ready to call it quits when he convinced me to play another hand. You see, we were all having a jolly good time and we were deep in our cups. I stayed, and played, and lost most of Isabella's dowry before I knew it had happened.

"You could imagine my shock when Emsley arrived the next day with my signature on a Baker's note to collect. I was furious at first. I hadn't that kind of money on hand, and the small estate that supports both households could not be touched."

It all made sense now that Nicholas had the gist of the tale. He would think of a way to make Emsley pay. His fists tightened. What would have befallen Isabella had she married the man?

"I thought myself clever," Pennington groaned. "That after they married and he found he'd been paid with Isabella's dowry, the jest would fall on him."

"But that's not what happened, is it Pennington? He called off the engagement soon after." As if he had knowledge of Pennington's finances.

Nodding, Pennington said, "Isabella was beside herself. Emotions were high. The gossip. Emsley's new marriage. She blamed me." The man was rambling now. "You see, I'd sided with Emsley in the delay of their nuptials for another Season, thinking the man needed time to adjust to the idea of marriage and its responsibility. We both said things we regretted. With scandal about, no one would marry her. I had her sister to consider." Lord Pennington's fist slammed against the desk. "Isabella rented an apartment, resigning to spinsterhood."

"Does Catherine know?"

"For a few days now. I've sent her sister to the country." He pointed to the sheets of paper, letters, Nicholas had not noticed on the desk.

"Who else knew the means by which you obtained the money?"

"My man of affairs, John Hamilton."

Nicholas nodded.

"My God, man, you think it all a ruse?"

"I don't know, but I'm damn well going to find out."

Taking a folded bank draft out of his pocket, he placed it on the table before Pennington. "I have made arrangements for Isabella to have her own account. Tom Jenkins, my solicitor, will see to it. If you truly intend to make amends with your daughter, give her this as a gift after we are wed. I believe it's the sum of her dowry?"

Pennington studied the bank draft suspiciously before turning his gaze back to Nicholas. "What are your intentions towards my daughter?"

"She's in need of a protector, and I'm in need of a wife. Anyone who sets out to harm her will pay dearly."

Ignoring the older man's slight curving of the mouth, Nicholas gathered his coat. "Consider this your invitation to the nuptials." With that, he left the study.

Nicholas showed himself out of Pennington's home, not waiting for the butler—not that the man would show him any more courtesy than slamming the door at his back. Taking the stairs two at a time, he halted mid-step as he spotted a familiar figure bracing against the wall from the corner of his eye. With an annoyed grunt, Nicholas continued his descent knowing Harold would follow close behind.

"Ye followed me."

"I was bored."

Nicholas shook his head.

"And in need of adventure," Harold confessed. "From the looks of your scowl, I might have already missed the lot of it."

Shrugging, Nicholas climbed into their carriage. With a

flick of Chambers' wrist, the reins snapped, sending the horses into a steady gallop.

"What would make a man with coin abandon his kin?" Harold asked.

"He no longer holds substantial wealth."

Harold frowned.

"He gambled most of it away," Nicholas said.

"That wasnae vera smart."

"I donna think it was intentional. Pennington thought Emsley loved his daughter."

"But Emsley was only interested in money?"

Nicholas nodded. "And when he found Isabella had no more coin, it was easy to step aside."

"Do you think he started the rumors of Isabella having lovers?" Harold asked.

"I'm almost certain. At the party, I got the impression he intended to make her his mistress."

"A greedy cad, isn't he?" Harold lips twisted in disgust. "Do you think he bedded her?"

Nicholas shifted. "It doesna matter, does it?"

"How can you be sure she doesn't still hold affection for this Emsley fellow?"

Nicholas looked out the carriage. He did not answer.

Leaning against his seat, Harold did not press him further. "Mind telling me where we are going?"

Clenching his jaw, Nicholas continued to gaze out the window. Curse ye, Harold. He didn't need an audience while stumbling through Isabella's life. She'd been embarrassed enough.

"Baker's," Nicholas finally answered.

"For a man about to set sail, ye seem bent on a journey to recover Lady Isabella's good name." With a smirk, Harold again leaned against the carriage wall.

Nicholas wanted to shout the words, "I don't give two

pence," but once said they would be a lie. He felt the over-whelming urge to protect Isabella.

He was always able to hide his true feelings from the world, but never from Harold.

Instead, he turned his gaze back to the window, the mundane filling his sight, yet he saw nothing, heard nothing, except Isabella's swift intake of breath before their lips touched and the sweetest scent he'd ever known shook the walls of his world. "Ye know as well as I do, recovering Isabella's good name will serve to increase Cassie's chances into society."

"Cassie is not of noble blood, Nicholas. While they may accept her, they will also know she doesn't belong."

"All the reason to be sure she doesn't end up a spinster on my ship," he snapped.

"If she has any of her father's determination and spirit, you'll be battling more gentlemen than ye think."

"I'm not her father." Those words hadn't filled his head in ages. Cassie had been three months when she was given to him. He'd never balked at the responsibility. It was an honor to know one of his men would think him worthy enough to raise their child. But Cassie's true father was more than one of his men. They had started out together, sailed from coast to coast. And they had survived battle after battle.

"You didn't sire her, but ye are her father, and a damned good one."

Jesu, the man had an uncanny way to knowing his thoughts.

"It's not terribly difficult to surmise your thoughts when it concerns Cassie. You scowl and clamp your jaw. It's a wonder ye havenae bit your paramours on their arse. I'm surprised you still have teeth."

"You are being a mother hen." Nicholas's lips twitched and he knew that was Harold's intent.

When they arrived at the gentlemen's establishment, it didn't take long for them to spot Lord Emsley sitting at a small corner table away from most of the other gentlemen. With a newspaper cracked and opened, he gave the illusion of reading. Nicholas had a sense the man's ears were pinned for any information of consequence. That suited him fine.

"I gather ye have a plan."

He hadn't an inkling on the proper course of action. Driven by the need to make Emsley pay for hurting Isabella had been his only motivation. He'd definitely fumbled coming to Baker's without a plan. It didn't matter at the moment. They were here. Taking a seat two tables away from Emsley, they were far enough to escape the notice of other gentlemen, yet close enough to be overheard.

He looked around the room. It was late afternoon and soon the tables would be filled with gentlemen looking to drown in their cups. The smoky room and ready banter reminded him of nights aboard his ship when the voyages were long. It was precisely those times Harold and him had used to ferret out traitors from their mix. Looking back at Emsley, Nicholas remembered how Isabella's father had lost a large amount of his fortune and decided Emsley would only be lured into a game he thought he could win.

"Is all prepared as planned for our voyage?" Nicholas asked.

When Harold's eyes widened slightly, Nicholas jerked his head in the direction behind him. They had played this game before, using it to trap disloyal crew. He only hoped the man they were about to bait was no wiser than the ones they'd played this particular game on in the past. Greed sometimes clouded a man's vision—at least he hoped it true now.

"Finalized the last order this morning." Rolling a cigar between his fingers, Harold relaxed into his seat.

"Good. Any trouble securing buyers?"

"All are willing to pay top coin upon delivery."

They were shipping their normal cargo with the exception of new fabrics, teas and coffee, but no one needed to know that.

"We'll return wealthy men." Nicholas grinned.

"And Lady Isabella?"

"We're setting sail as scheduled, two days after the nuptials. That will secure me Pennington's estates, which Isabella's mother entitled to her, now to me through marriage."

When he heard the paper crumple behind him, Nicholas smirked. The trap was set. If Emsley didn't know Pennington's property would go to Catherine, Isabella's younger sister, he did not do a thorough job investigating. That also meant John Hamilton, Pennington's solicitor, had not betrayed Isabella. Nicholas only guessed Emsley now felt cheated.

"Have ye plans for your share?" Nicholas stood, not wanting to linger. When Harold said nothing, Nicholas continued, his grin broader than before. "Baker's has the best card room in town."

If Emsley believed they had money to lose, he'd lure them into a game. Nicholas had no illusions about his ability at smaller games but, among more experienced gamblers, Harold was the best card player he knew. He was well aware that the man might even try to once again secure a hold on Isabella's life when he left. Little could be done about that. He would, however, have his man keep a close eye on her finances. He trusted Virginia to be her companion.

"Shouldn't you have warned me *I* was your plan?" Harold asked when they stepped into the busy street.

Nicholas grinned. Harold was an excellent card hand, and at the moment it was the only sport Lord Emsley took interest in. "And spoil your chance at adventure? Never." He slapped Harold's shoulder, causing him to wince. "Besides, you volunteered."

"Funny, I don't recall that." Harold's brows pinched.

"Huh, I could have sworn ye agreed."

Harold cursed. "Ye bloody well know I didn't." He might have well have been speaking to himself when Nicholas grinned, then tapped the roof of the carriage.

CHAPTER 18

*W*alking into Cassie's room, Nicholas tapped on the side of his daughter's playhouse and waited for her to emerge. He was not surprised when her head of tousled curls slipped through the makeshift curtain, a patch covering one eye.

"What do you think of a proper welcome for Isabella? A picnic perhaps."

"Pirates don't have picnics." Her head slipped back behind the curtain.

"Oh." He turned on his heels. "I'll tell Mrs. Berths you declined a slice of her chocolate cake."

Hearing her hurried movements, he smiled. His hands shot out as she rushed past him. "Don't you think you should wear one of your pretty dresses?"

"No, Papa."

Nicholas held her still. "Crumb-covered pants are no way to welcome guests, Cassie." They had turned the house on its head and still they could not find the source of her trousers. He didn't remember commissioning that many pants and thought perhaps the previous owner had sons and they had left a trunk behind.

She looked down, dusted off the knee-patches and smiled.

He raised a brow. "Didn't you make a promise?"

She nodded.

"It's settled then." He watched her open the closet. Her eyes widened, and he was sure the task of picking a dress was new to her. "And Cassie," he said. "Rid yourself of the eye patch."

CASSIE IN HAND, Nicholas went in search of Virginia and found her exiting the dining room.

"What a marvelous idea, Nicholas." She squeezed his arm. "A gathering of Isabella's closest friends is exactly what she needs. I only hope they have no plans for this afternoon."

He had not thought beyond inviting the members of his household to a picnic by the pond, but Virginia made it seem as though they were to have a party. "Closest friends?"

"Not to worry, I've taken a tally from Isabella and dispatched your driver with invitations." She paused, her fingers tapping her skirts. "It's scandalous, I know, sending invites anything short of a week's notice."

"They may not show." He didn't bother to mention that Isabella would be disappointed if that were to happen.

"They will show," she sniffed. "If for no other reason than to be sure she has settled comfortably."

"Virginia," he groaned, not pleased to have his business under scrutiny of others. "Who has she invited?"

"The Godrics, and Lord Daniel."

Nicholas scowled.

"Now, Nicholas, this is to be her welcome. I must see to

the food and sweets. Did you know the Godrics have a son Cassie's age?"

"See to Cassie, she may require your assistance," he called after Virginia. Shaking his head, he watched her turn the corner.

He'd hoped the small gathering would lighten the tension between he and Isabella before they were wed and increase Isabella's comfort in his home, their home. He smiled. All the years of his youth, he'd never imagined a family. Now with a wife and daughter, Harold and Virginia, he had more than he ever asked for.

The tunes coming softly from the music room drew his attention. Following the sound, he stood inside the door and listened for a time. Isabella's fingers were light and graceful across the keyboard. The blinds were thrown back. Light flooded the room. The brass-and-gold trimmings sparkled, dancing around the piano and its player. It was a sight he hoped to see often.

He barely noticed Mrs. Berths sitting in the chesterfield. Nicholas smiled and nodded a greeting. As chaperone, the woman looked as out of place as he felt.

"I didn't know you played," Nicholas said.

Isabella looked up. "There are a great many things you don't know about me."

"All of which you plan to teach me?"

She smiled coyly. "Perhaps."

Glad she hadn't stopped playing, he sat beside her on the bench.

"I've invited Daniel." She did not look at him.

"I've heard."

"You're not annoyed?"

"Only that you've managed the task first."

Isabella laughed. "Liar."

Smiling, he nodded towards the keyboard. "You play

beautifully."

"I remember my first lesson." She looked at him then. "I was five, perhaps six, and my instructor complained I had not yet learned to sit still. He was only appeased by my ability to play." She chuckled at the memory.

"He complained to your father," Nicholas guessed.

"No. My mother." Her smile broadened. "Poor man. Mother tried to discipline me, but I still made my instructor perspire with frustration."

Nicholas laughed. "Was she disappointed?"

"No, she wasn't disappointed. Besides, we were too busy recalling the poor man's twisted wig." She smiled fondly at the memory, and Nicholas saw great love for her mother written across her face.

"She loved you very much."

Isabella nodded. "My sister and I were terribly spoiled."

"Did your father not share the same affection?"

Her fingers touched the keys again, and soft notes surrounded them. "Once, perhaps, before mother passed and the burden of raising two girls was left to him. Mayhap, if we were not so much like our mother…"

"Spirited?"

"Yes." Isabella laughed as Cassie ran into the room, looking uncomfortable in her new day dress.

A knock came to the music room door and they turned. The first of their guests had arrived. Their conversation left him feeling hopeful that they might have more than an agreeable marriage.

Nicholas had met Lord Richard at the duchess's ball and had liked the man. When the family approached, he shook the other man's hand. He glanced towards an excited Isabella, who was awkwardly embraced by the very round Lady April.

Lord Richard introduced his son. "This is Emmitt."

"A pleasure to meet you." Isabella smiled then took the boy's hand in hers. "This is Cassie."

Isabella had barely finished her introduction when Cassie fumbled a curtsy, took the boy's hand, and headed outside with her new friend.

"So impatient." Isabella shook her head, smiling.

"Emmitt barely finishes one task before he's on to the next," April laughed.

"I'm glad you could visit," Isabella said as the group moved to the back lawn.

"An afternoon brunch before the summer heat is fully upon us is a brilliant idea," April said.

"And an excellent reason to leave the house." Richard chuckled.

April rolled her eyes, looking at her husband fondly. "Richard believes, in my condition, I should have a permanent seat on the chesterfield until the midwife delivers our child."

"Refreshments are in order. I'll have iced tea sent down for the ladies. How about sherry, Lord Richard?" Nicholas asked.

When Richard nodded, Nicholas headed towards the library. From the window, he watched the children chase each other and heard their happy laughter. Taking a deep breath, he let that joy surround him.

Drinks in hand, he risked one last glance outside and noticed Daniel's arrival in the garden and Isabella's greeting. He considered going to welcome him, then decided against it, not wanting to meet Daniel just yet and giving Isabella the time she needed.

Standing beside Lord Richard, Nicholas smiled as the children cupped water into their palms, then threw the droplets at Virginia and Lady April. The women squealed.

"If April's not careful, she'll give birth in the middle of your pond," Richard teased, taking his drink.

"I believe that is the children's intent from the way they are constantly chasing your wife."

Richard chuckled. "They have become fast friends."

"As is the way with children."

"I was surprised to receive your invitation," Richard confessed. "It is no secret, your thoughts of high society."

"It was Isabella's doing; she considers Lady April a friend, and friends are always welcome, especially if they make Isabella happy."

"Is she happy?"

Nicholas looked over the pond again. "It is difficult to judge happiness. I can only hope. Since I planned another trip, it is important for Isabella to see this as home."

"Sail? So soon?"

"That, my dear fellow, will depend on my wife."

Richard sipped his drink.

"Tell me, are you friends with Lord Emsley?" Before he went any further, Nicholas wanted to know where the man stood.

Richard cleared his throat. "I don't believe the man has many friends, at least not in my circle."

The hairs along Nicholas's arms rose. "Why is that?"

"I've seen his paramours after separation, and more than once it looked as if they'd had an encounter with his temper."

"No one reported him?"

"His father is a member of parliament and gives the boy free rein." Richard shrugged. "Besides, no mistress would report her lover at the risk of new companionship."

Nicholas grimaced, happy Isabella had not experienced Emsley's wrath. "Is he as good at cards as I'm led to believe?"

There was a brief pause. "He's a clever sort. He is bested when he becomes overconfident in his hand, but even I confess, that is seldom." Richard looked at Nicholas. "Are you entertaining a match?"

"Can I count on your support?"

"You'll need an invitation to the game."

"For my cousin," Nicholas clarified.

"Clever." Richard smiled. "Is *he* as good as I've heard?"

"Better than that."

With his newly formed comradeship, Nicholas went in search of Isabella. It was time he considered not sailing. If Lord Richard was correct in his assessment, Lord Emsley was a violent man, and leaving Isabella only in the protection of servants would not do, least not until her place in society was again secure.

When he rounded the wide trunk of the oak tree, he saw the back of Isabella's pinned curls as she sat on the garden bench. He was about to interrupt when Lord Daniel's figure came into view on the opposite side of the seat.

Then he heard his name, and Nicholas paused. Isabella still insisted on referring to him by his formal title, Captain Ferguson, and he realized it was her way of putting distance between them.

"I'm afraid arranging my own marriage has taken away the spontaneous joy that accompanies the occasion," Isabella was saying.

"A leaping shame," Daniel said.

"I have no appetite for the business end of nuptials, and for a brief moment, I wished my father was in the room with Mr. Ferguson."

"Ah, the price of independence. I wish you were spared the grim details of it."

"Mr. Ferguson is a fair man. I believe he will fulfill his commitments."

Daniel flinched. "Is there no affection, then?"

Nicholas stilled. Isabella did not immediately answer,

then she said, "Some, perhaps, though I'm not certain. In truth, his trip will allow me the time to find my place."

Nicholas turned towards the house. Any hope of remaining in London was dashed by Isabella's words. Looking around the garden towards the small group and Lord Daniel, he realized he would not be leaving Isabella without protection. She did not need him.

CHAPTER 19

"*J*enkins delivered the last of the supplies yesterday." Harold straightened his neck cloth.

Nicholas nodded.

"Have you changed your mind?"

"Nae."

Ignoring his cousin's grumbled curse, Nicholas scribbled the last of his instructions to Tom. It was best for the household that he left. Isabella had yet to show any true affection towards him.

"Jesu, mon." Harold swiped stiff fingers through his shoulder-length hair. "No mon would leave his wee bonnie bride days after marrying. Do ye forget, Emsley seeks an opportunity to lurk at her skirts, looking for ways to regain her trust."

Nicholas shook his head, reminding himself of the pact between Isabella and himself, the reasons for their marriage. "It's a marriage of convenience, nothing more. On that Isabella and I agree. She has said so repeatedly. I don't blame her. I'm harsh at times."

Harold snorted. "Try barbaric."

"Isabella…" Nicholas waved his hand, encompassing his surroundings. "Wants her good name back, and a bit of comfort, nae more."

"Ye spent the last few days hunting those that harmed her only to watch her slip through your fingers?" Harold's eyes narrowed.

Setting his note aside, Nicholas looked at Harold.

"Don't be an idiot."

"She's made it clear; she means to continue life as she pleases."

"She's to be your wife, Nicholas."

"Don't ye think I know that?"

"Ye cannot keep her at arm's length forever." Harold locked gazes with him. "You'll have to trust her."

Nicholas sighed. "Trust me, the lass doesn't want me, Harold."

There was a silence as they stared at each other. "You don't believe this Daniel fellow is her lover, do you?" Harold questioned.

"No." Nicholas sighed, then rubbed his eyes. "But she insists on resuming her life, whatever that means, and she fancies Lord Daniel."

"And Lord Emsley? Do you believe the rumors?"

"That they were romantically involved?" Nicholas thought of the few intimate moments he had shared with Isabella. "The lass disnae act virginal."

"Would it matter if the gossip holds truth?"

"No." Nicholas said with conviction. "Yet, she hasnae confided in me."

Harold paused, then swallowed the remains of his drink. "Even if Isabella acted out of wedlock, your mother would not approve of your treatment of the lass. To set sail—"

Nicholas laughed. "In the end, Mother did not believe in love. Ye know that as well as I."

Harold shook his head. "That's not all true and you know it. She loved us, though I was naught but an extra mouth. It was love that made her take me in when Ma died, and love that kept her from the streets."

Nicholas's fingers balled into a fist before he spread them wide. "Curse ye, Harold, for dredging old memories. And look what trusting in love got her. A son and nephew with nae more than names as stamps of our breeding. Highlands that don't want us, the sea that waves her bonnie arms as she is ready to fold us under, and London... London means to mark us as upstarts."

Thumps on the door halted their argument. "Pardon, sir, the priest has arrived." Winston stood at the library's entrance.

"Thank you." Harold cleared his throat.

"What else has Isabella said regarding our nuptials?" Nicholas asked, certain this new campaign to keep him on land was Virginia's doing.

"Said?" Harold startled. "Any fool could see the lady wants more than she bargained for. Now..." Harold got to his feet. They walked out of the library and towards the other guest. "The priest waits to join what no man may sunder."

Nicholas tugged at the neck cloth, each woven thread reminding him of a noose.

"Ye can still change your mind." Harold stood beside him at the foot of the stairs.

"Nae," Nicholas whispered when Cassie skipped to his side. His breath caught when he saw that her dress was not ripped or soiled at the knees. "Cassie, you are a vision."

"Thanks, Papa." She smiled, making a show of straightening her shoulders.

"Mr. Ferguson," The priest said as he approached them. "Congratulations."

Nicholas shook the man's hand. The priest was lean and

tall. His flesh pulled over the sharp angles of his face. "Thank you for blessing our union on short notice."

"I presume you acquired a special license?"

Nicholas patted his breast pocket.

"Now that you're a man of family, and responsible for their spiritual well being, I hope to see you in church."

Harold coughed.

"What of you, Mr. Duncan?" The priest faced Harold. "The church welcomes everyone."

Nicholas smiled, liking the man's bluntness.

The priest extended that bony hand to Cassie. "And you little lady, can I count on your support?"

Cassie's brows wrinkled as she looked up at her father. Nicholas nodded. "May I bring my ship?" she asked the priest.

The man's brows drew together. "Depends. Can it withstand a good sermon?"

Cassie giggled, then gripped the priest's fingers, steering him towards the library. "It's not a real ship, I'll show you."

Family. The priest's words rang true as Nicholas looked around the small group. Isabella deserved her father's presence, the white dress, a church filled with family and friends —he didn't have too many of those. She deserved roses and flowers, courting, balls and dancing, all things he didn't have time to lavish on her.

Running a wary hand through tussled hair, Nicholas vowed to give her everything she desired, whatever comforts she sought, to make up for what had been lacking in their courting. No one would ever desert her again. He swallowed. Wasn't that precisely what he was doing by setting sail? No, he shook his head. She wanted him gone. Leaving would make her happy. And…maybe in time, with enough distance, Isabella would grow to tolerate, even care for him. The thought of merely tolerating one's wife, his wife, left a bitter taste.

He risked a glance towards the top of the steps. Unease weighed. One booted leg landed on the first stair, and he felt Harold's grip on his arm.

"It's not good fortune to see the bride, cousin."

A relieved sigh flooded his chest when Virginia rounded the top of the stairs.

"Nicholas!" Dress clutched in both fists, Virginia hurried down towards them. Harold took her elbow as she drew near, steadying her. "She's... Isabella, she's not in her rooms."

When Nicholas pushed past her, heading for the second floor, Virginia touched his arm. "Maybe she went for a walk, Nicholas, to accept her new situation. She wouldn't abandon you."

The last was a plea for understanding. He hoped Virginia was correct. Nicholas took the stairs two at a time. He checked each room, closets, under every bed until he found himself searching the gardens.

Isabella was gone. Cold fingers of dread touched his nape. Fled. Her word meant nothing. His breath came in labored pants, pushing against his rib cage. His father, an aristocrat, had done the same, and he had vowed he would never be that vulnerable again.

Had she any intention of fulfilling their arrangement? "Ready the coach," he said between clenched teeth when Chambers caught up to his hurried pace. Nicholas looked at his property, land he had no time to enjoy.

"Sir." Nicholas turned to see the man hadn't moved, not a coach in sight. "Your... M'lady took da coach."

"Pashkin?" he asked about her man servant. The man nodded, taking a step back. At least the fool woman hadn't driven the coach herself. "Saddle my horse!"

CHAPTER 20

*L*ady Isabella's fingers twisted in her lap. Under long lashes, she glanced at her companion. They had been riding for hours in his open-top carriage, and she was grateful for the coolness of the day as they travelled along the countryside. So far, Daniel had left her to her thoughts. She was grateful for the silence. Biting her lip, she shook her head as another thought of Nicholas sent a whisper of awareness along her back. He'd be furious when he discovered her absence. And little Cassie, she imagined the child's hurt, and the loss of the trust they'd carefully built. Cassie would understand, Isabella thought as she wiped a tear. She'd see it as another adventure. "Do you presume—"

"He'll come," Daniel said.

Isabella nodded. She had suspected as much. Nicholas was not the type of man to be easily set aside.

"Has he treated you unkindly, Isabella?" Daniel asked, his ruthless smile replaced with a look of caution.

"No," she answered quickly. The opposite was true. "He has shown me more tolerance than my own father."

"Then why have Pashkin deliver you to my care, if not to

run away with me?" Daniel winked, and she was once again enveloped in light-hearted friendship.

"I'm fleeing. You're being a gentleman and helping me, but we are not running together," she said. "Besides, I trust you."

"I can protect you."

"Pray tell, were you also knighted?" she said, ignoring the true meaning of his words.

"No, but I'm a magnificent fencer."

Twisting in her seat, she looked around the carriage floor. Finding naught but her bag, she raised a brow. "Will you defend my honor with the swords you've forgotten on your mantel?"

He chuckled. "Why the cat and mouse?"

Only he would think she played a game to be chased. Isabella joined in his good humor. "I thought you'd enjoy a distraction."

In truth, she was terrified of committing her heart to a man who had no need for love. Their bargain was for Cassie —no word of tenderness or commitment promised. Not that she expected love from Nicholas. She, however, cared, and it frightened her.

He was not the man the world believed him to be. Nicholas was kind and considerate. He was raising Cassie as his own. That was the man she had come to care for, but the two could not be separated, because he was also a man deeply scarred by a difficult past.

"Distraction is it." Daniel entwined their fingers and squeezed lightly before kissing the back of her gloved hand. "For my sake, let's hope he's not as good a shot as he is a horseman." And before she had the chance to decipher his meaning, Daniel kissed the side of her mouth. His lips against her skin were feather light and lasting long enough to be unmistakable by the approaching rider. It wasn't the kiss that sent her heart racing, but the thought of Nicholas's reaction to Daniel's little stunt.

Isabella heard the steady gallop of a horse and peered over her shoulder. "Do you think—"

"I believe your hopes of running away with me are dashed, my lady."

Isabella gasped. "You knew." She squinted, but the rider was unrecognizable from such a distance.

"I might have given my butler our general way of travel." Daniel twisted in his seat. "You have every right to toss me under the wheel. But we both know you love the cad and you admitted he has not harmed you."

"And if he had?"

"We would have taken an alternate route."

She raised a skeptical brow at his confident answer.

"Besides, I had him looked into."

"Dear heavens."

"You don't think I would abandon you, do you?" His tone was alert, as if everything depended on her answer. His eyes held hers and Isabella realized he, too, showed the world a cover of himself.

Isabella cradled his cheek. "No Daniel. You are the dearest friend one could hope for." And she silently promised to be one in turn.

When his devilish grin returned, she matched it with a genuine smile of her own. "Well?"

Daniel chuckled. "He has sound investment and no bastards, except little Cassie," he said thoughtfully. "And, by all accounts, he cares deeply for the child."

Isabella had no intention of correcting Daniel in his assumption of Cassie; it was not her secret to share.

"Most fascinating is his numerous connections. I do believe he can return you to the *grand monde*. And with the duchess, Lady Kenningsly's fondness and my support—

though I am mere Viscount of Plainfield—you shall be back in *monde de la mode* in no time."

Squeezing his shoulder playfully, Isabella said, "I'm sure you'll inherit the dukedom and all its boring aristocratic duties soon enough."

Daniel flinched. "Good heavens, I hope not! So far, Father has given me the reins, and I'm happy in my current role. Besides, I'm fond of the old goat."

She believed him, and by the sounds of it, he truly shared a connection with his father. "Thank you, Daniel, for... indulging my foolishness."

Daniel loosened his grip on the reins. The sound of hooves pounding against the dry dirt road grew closer. Gently, he brought the carriage to a slow trot.

Isabella's chest tightened, her heart hammering. Suddenly, running away seemed silly. Though tangled in conflicting emotions, she needed to know Nicholas cared— wanted and desired her.

"Promise you'll confide in me if the match is not a happy one."

The rider was upon them now, and she dared not look at Daniel or acknowledge his words. Her breath hitched. A large, gloved hand grabbed the reins of their horses from Daniel's fist, slowing them to a halt at the side of the road. He'd found them and he was not happy.

Nicholas's jaw was hard ridges. Eyes cold, gray, stormy.

Her chin tilted upwards even as she fidgeted against the seat when the horses snorted, nostrils flaring.

"Isabella?" Daniel asked when he climbed down from the carriage. His earlier playfulness was replaced with concern as he looked from Nicholas to Isabella, and she knew he wished to say more. Block her from Nicholas's view or issue a warning, perhaps. She dreaded such a confrontation, and seeing Nicholas's dark scowl, there was no telling what he'd do if angered further.

She could only nod in response to Daniel and, after holding her gaze for a moment, as if coming to a conclusion of his own, he walked around the back of the carriage to Nicholas's large black horse.

She watched Nicholas leap to the ground. What a fool to think she'd escape Captain Ferguson's notice.

The two men stared at each other. It was maddening waiting for Nicholas's accusations. There was no mistaking the pain he tried to hide. Isabella shuddered. A flicker of fear and uncertainty battled behind Nicholas's eyes before they were swept away by the storm raging there.

What right had he to be hurt? Nicholas had barely paid her much attention in the last two days, summoning her when needed, conversing only in necessity. His lack of interest drove her escape. What had he expected? Her fingers weaved tighter at the horror of a loveless marriage, glued by cordial convenience. Or worse, distrust and anger now that she had tried to flee. She sat tense, waiting for Nicholas to explode.

The accusations never came.

His speechless gaze was more chastising than any words. How did he manage to make her feel wrong for doing what she believed right: wanting love and…passion?

It was Daniel who broke the spell. "What took you so long?"

The exchange was swift. In moments, Nicholas's bulk filled the carriage and Daniel was leaping onto Nicholas's big black stallion, securing the reins in his fist.

The small confines became charged with a current that lit her nerves. The tension was as intense as it was arousing. Small gasps whispered past her lips. Her stomach curled when their thighs brushed. Their eyes locked as he unwrapped the secrets of her traitorous body and that wicked sensation moved lower.

"Are you unharmed, Isabella?"

Her tongue ran along her dry lips. "Daniel would never…" She looked at Daniel and saw him stiffen at the mere suggestion.

"I'm well aware of what Lord Daniel is capable of," Nicholas said tightly.

"Then you know I would never harm Lady Isabella."

"Viscount," Nicholas said, sailing Daniel's abandoned hat through the air. "If I find your intentions less than honorable…"

"You'll have my head." Daniel caught the hat as it cut the air above his head. "Don't forget your promise, my lady." He shouted above the roll of wheels.

They rode at a steady gallop for a few minutes when she realized Nicholas wasn't turning their carriage around. "Where are you taking me?" she asked when he made no move to turn them around.

"Gretna Green," he said and looked at her, a brow gently arched. "Why else would an unmarried lass and a Viscount be on the North Road?"

Isabella shook her head in denial. "I only meant to leave London. I had no idea we were traveling along the Great North Road."

Nicholas let the reins fall over his thighs. Eyes closed, he took a deep calming breath. Whether to gather control of his anger or because he was now stuck with her, Isabella didn't know.

If her presence infuriated him, he shouldn't have come. She had no doubt he'd easily find another more suited to his temperament.

"Why… Why did you come after me?" She sniffed.

Still braced against the carriage, his head turned

towards her, brows raised slightly. "Because, darling Isabella." One long finger traced a line from her brow to her chin. Isabella shuddered at the unexpected contact. "Ye are mine."

"But you don't…"

"Care?" he asked warily "Love ye?"

Within moments, Isabella found herself in his lap, his eyes hooded, growing darker. She flushed. It was a compromising position for a lady, indecent, more so in plain view. And it made her blood run hot. Cigar and soap and man filled her nose. Isabella breathed deep. Too late. Her tongue flicked along dry lips, moistening them. His gaze followed the gesture. Taut muscles flexed beneath layers of fabric and she gasped.

He rested his forehead against hers, breathing deeply. Isabella's hands tentatively reached up between them, palms lying against his chest. She heard his sharp intake of air and felt his heart speed in time with her own.

"I would release you from this bargain if I could, Isabella. But I cannot."

She squeezed her eyes tightly against what his words implied. That he'd so easily let her go meant he didn't care, not truly. A bargain of necessity was all that could ever be between them. Nothing more. Eyes moist with unshed tears, Isabella blinked them back, not wanting to show any weakness. He was winning her heart, she realized.

No, he'd already won it.

As easily as he'd gathered her close, Nicholas righted her on the seat, taking the reins into both hands. The hard set of his jaw replaced their moment of tenderness. "Some of the most respected marriages among your class were not founded on love, Isabella."

It was true, she agreed.

"One does not always have such luxury. I have promised a

home, agreed to all your terms, and of course financial support. Is there something else you desire?"

"No," she quickly answered. How could she tell him what she most desired? He was a practical sort. Not swayed by emotions. Trembling hands brushed the seams of her skirt, any distractions to keep from burying her face in them.

THEY HAD BEEN TRAVELING for almost four days, stopping only to change horses, rest, and eat. The overnights had been spent at various inns along the route. It didn't matter that Nicholas had gotten them separate rooms. With no chaperone or male relative to accompany them, her reputation was lost. No one would believe she was still virginal. Isabella sighed. She did not have close male relatives in abundance and, although the thought warmed her, she certainly did not expect her father to chase after her.

She was tired. Her bottom ached from prolonged sitting and she longed for a proper bed. Although she was enjoying the sprawling landscapes and hills, she wished to stop moving and sink beneath the waters of a steaming bath.

Isabella stretched.

"Look," Nicholas said, pointing. They were nearing a hut. Nicholas slowed the horses to a halt. "Wait for me here, Isabella." Feet on the ground, he tied the reins to a post before knocking on the door. They didn't have to wait long. The door swung open. A man as built as Nicholas, but with shoulders slightly broader, stood at the entrance. From his bulk, charcoaled apron, and high boots, Isabella guessed he was the town's blacksmith.

Their hushed, rapid exchange increased her nervousness. Her fingers knotted in her lap. From the deep burr of his voice, she knew Nicholas was home among this Scottish country man. By now, all of London knew she hadn't married Nicholas as announced, as well as of his chase across the country side. Escaping the ton here was possible, on land that stretched beyond hills. She giggled nervously at the thought of high society guessing as to her whereabouts.

Both men turned. The blacksmith's gaze held, searched, before full lips curved into a broad smile. But it was Nicholas's raised brows and amused smirk that sent her heart racing.

"Come." Nicholas helped her from the carriage. "Your amusement confirmed our happiness to Ian, and he's agreed to perform a hand-fasting."

Her brows wrinkled.

"He carries out the local weddings until someone from the clergy passes through the village and can perform the ceremony."

Isabella quickly glanced at the man that now held the door open wider in welcome and received a nod in return. "I thought him the blacksmith."

Nicholas chuckled. "Aye, he is both."

"Ma name is Ian," the man introduced himself once they entered his home. "This is ma wife, Gillian, and sister Fenella."

"A pleasure to meet ye," Nicholas said. "This is Lady Isabella Pennington, and I'm Nicholas Ferguson. Thank ye for agreeing to do this on such short notice." Nicholas nodded to both women.

"Nae much is planned beyond a month in these parts." Gillian smiled. "The wee lads and lassies are more anxious to get started. The tartan cloth is nae loose when they run in search of privacy."

"Gillian!" Ian groaned.

"Well it's true! I seldom think they hear your words, husband, before they're racing to the nearest lodgings." She shook her head. "The poor priest is kept busy."

Isabella blushed.

"Fenella, why don't ye start a pot o' tea? That'll give Lady Isabella time for a wet cloth before the pipes."

Sure she was the color of a ripe apple, Isabella followed Gillian to a small room at the back of the house. It was smaller than her own powder room, with white-washed walls and a large window that flooded the room with light. Simple, but with all the essentials and a feeling of comfort.

"What a beautiful vanity." Solid oak with silver carving embedded into its legs and surface.

"Thank ye. My husband carved it and gifted it to me on our wedding day. He finished it only hours before our ceremony."

"What does it say?" Isabella ran her fingers along the inscription.

"Yer beauty shines from beyond what ye see." It was Gillian's turn to blush.

After all these years, Isabella saw a woman still in love with her husband. Envy and longing nipped at her heart.

As if sensing her insecurities, Gillian said, "Yer Nicholas seems like a fine mon. Do ye love him?"

Despite all attempts not to, she did care for him. Isabella nodded.

"Then, I pray you have the happiest of marriages. Now come, before that mon of yours thinks ye have fled."

Isabella flinched. It would do no good to incite Nicholas's anger further. Following Gillian into the front parlor, Isabella was again startled by the size of both men. They filled the room. She watched the two of them, both confident in their stature. Nicholas's mouth curved in good humor at Ian's jest.

He was six feet tall, the top of her head meeting the center of his chest. They couldn't possibly fit together, could they? Looking at the man who was soon to be her husband, she wondered if he was huge everywhere. At the direction of her wanton thoughts, a shiver started at the base of her spine as she realized tonight would be their wedding night.

Nicholas's eyes met hers, pinning her to the floor, his gaze as effective as iron chains. He took her elbow, guiding her to his side.

Ian smiled and took his place before them. Isabella swallowed. It was not how she imagined her wedding day. She glanced at Nicholas, but he stood rigid. The blacksmith spoke, his words washing over them. Herbs and spices from the tea and cakes drifted to her nose.

Eyes moist, Isabella was unable to stop a lone tear from leaking. It may not be the wedding of her dreams, but the ceremony was warm and personal. She immediately felt guilty for depriving Nicholas's family of the nuptials.

Ian's wife and sister stood as witnesses. The joining words were clear as Nicholas repeated them. She was next. Two words would seal her fate. She would be married, bound forever to a man who had made it clear he had no intention of loving her. She swallowed, studying Nicholas. Black suited him. It wrapped around him like a cloak rather than clothing. Pinned to his chest was his family's tartan brooch.

The sharp ridges of his jaw and eyes willed fear and offered protection. Hadn't he protected her that first night, made her feel whole, wanted? And wasn't that a husband's role, Isabella wondered.

Isabella glanced up and realized both Nicholas and Ian waited on her response.

"I do," she said solemnly. She did care for him, would cherish him and hold fast to the sanctuary of their marriage. Would he? Could he ever love her? Pushing the thought aside, she scolded herself.

Reaching into his pockets, Nicholas revealed a heart-shaped brooch, the plaid similar to the one he wore. She gasped when the cool pin weaved between the materials above her breast, the antique brooch delicate in his large hand.

"If ye will have it so, it's both a Luckenbooth and tartan. The weaving from my mother's clan," he explained. His head lowered, fingers brushing the pin. "It says, 'My love and wife. Friend and clansmen.'"

Strong hands circled her waist, drawing her against the solid wall of his body. Eyes alight with mischief, his lips were mere inches from hers. His breath brushing against her cheek, Nicholas uttered a single word before claiming her mouth. "Mine."

This was different from all his other kisses. Hungrier. A taste of their future. The thought of their nights being the fire to their days sent a new thrill through Isabella. This power he held frightened her.

Isabella swayed.

He nipped her lower lip, then licked away the sting. Isabella gasped, the heat that started on her lips moving downward.

He, too, moaned as his tongue swept past her lips.

Too dazed to react when Ian cleared his throat, she allowed her new husband to hold her close.

"A thousand welcomes to ye in marriage. May ye be healthy all your days. May ye be blessed with long life and peace. May ye grow old with goodness and riches." As Ian blessed them, Nicholas stared into her eyes.

Mine. His last words played over and over. She was his.

CHAPTER 21

*W*ithin the hour, he'd found the inn Ian and his wife had suggested. They were warned it was comfortable, but probably not filled with the splendors they were accustomed to. But polished silverware was not her first thought—spending the night with Nicholas was. There was no one to tutor her on what was expected. What if he found her lacking?

"Afternoon m'lady, m'lord." The innkeeper beamed. "Just married, are ye? Ian sent word ye'd be wanting a room."

"Good afternoon, sir." Isabella blushed when the man's eyes darted between them. Though she'd brushed most of the dust from her traveling drapery, it still clung to her shoes.

"I'd like a room," Nicholas said. "Tea and a bath drawn for my wife."

"I've just the room—"

Nicholas cut him off with a wave of his hand. "The best corner room you have facing the east." He tossed a few extra coins on the counter, which disappeared before having chance to settle. It surprised Isabella that he so easily sought to comfort her.

Either the word "wife" or the extra coins spurred the innkeeper into action. "Of course, sir." The innkeeper snapped his fingers and two girls stood at attention as he barked orders in rapid succession.

"You, laddie." The innkeeper addressed a young boy covered in grime. "Take care of the gentleman's horse and take his bags to his rooms straight away."

As the boy passed, Nicholas dropped a coin into his dirty hands.

"Thanks!" The lad beamed.

"Nae need for that, sir," the innkeeper shouted.

The boy grinned, showing off his white teeth. Isabella's hand reached to stroke the boy's cheek, but she instead found her arm linked with Nicholas's.

Nicholas shrugged, then plucked the coin from the boy's hand. She watched in horror as the boy ran from the lobby. The innkeeper looked pleased. She was about to chastise Nicholas when he entwined his fingers through hers. He squeezed lightly. No coin! He hadn't taken the coin from the child. It only appeared that way. She looked at him with wide eyes.

What a smart lad, Isabella thought. And cunning.

"Will ye take tea in the lunchroom, m'lady? Supper will be served shortly."

"Yes," Isabella answered. She was only postponing the inevitable, she knew, but she couldn't stop her heart from leaping against her chest.

The innkeeper moved from behind the counter, leading them into a spacious dining parlor, sitting them close to the large window.

Orange glow moved across the surface of the tablecloth. Little balls of white light danced over the cutlery and napkins. She tapped her finger on one small reflection, amused when it moved out of reach.

"Is it too bright, Isabella?" His voice was cheered by her silliness.

Isabella shook her head. "I enjoy this time of day," she told him. "The sunset, it is not bright or hot. Evenings are the right time for entertainment, yet too late for callers if one does not wish company. It is peaceful." She risked a wary glance in his direction. His eyes were soft, thoughtful.

"Aye, the wee hours before dawn as well."

He *would* appreciate the hours leading to dawn, she thought. They were gloomy. She giggled, unable to suppress the strangled noise from escaping her lips.

Nicholas frowned. His hand reached across the distance, his fingers stroking her cheek. "Your disposition on my favored time of day leaves much to be desired."

"I... I did not mean to..."

"As your husband, it is now my duty to show you why I prefer early mornings."

Their eyes held for a long moment without words. What she saw in their depths was an unspoken challenge. Looking away, Isabella felt heat gather where his fingers caressed her skin. He was deliberately needling her.

The servant came then, placing cups of tea and sweets on the table. Isabella welcomed the distraction. Nicholas was being a perfect gentleman, attentive. Was it his intent not to shadow their wedding night with hostility?

Isabella had to admit she was as curious as she was scared. She remembered the wicked things those hands had done the day he'd found Daniel in her townhouse. His hands had burned her, and no number of layers of clothing had stopped him. His touch hounded her even now. What would happen when he truly had his way? Her heart would be lost to him forever. Isabella bit her lip, pulling it between her teeth. She could ask for more time, least until they were home on familiar grounds.

"Isabella," he groaned, "stop that."

Her brows drew together as she met his stare. Slowly, she released her lower lip from the clutches of her teeth. "I... I think I'll have that bath now." Retreat, she thought. She was almost always at an advantage when she had time to think.

"Would ye like help?"

She really needed to avoid those stormy eyes.

"Let me wash ye." He leaned closer.

Isabella staggered, unable to block the image his words created. "No!" She hurried from the room. Again, he'd unraveled her wit.

Leaning against the back of his chair, Nicholas folded his arms across his chest and studied Isabella's fleeing form. She had acted virginal—very different from the day he had taken her from her home. She had writhed beneath him that day. Blossomed to his touch. That Isabella had left him aroused for the better part of the afternoon. Having her in his home didn't help. Knowing she was within reach heated his blood. So he had avoided her and held fast to the bargain they'd struck, a bloody shame. An agreement Isabella had mucked up when she chose to run away. He didn't know what game she played, but he aimed to find out.

He shrugged away any thought of Isabella as an innocent. Had she not bargained for continued involvement with the viscount, Daniel? And after a three-year engagement to Lord Emsley—knowing the man frequented hidden brothels—Nicholas was now convinced they had shared more than chaste kisses.

Was it fear, then, that made her rebuke him? Nicholas frowned. Or was she still in love with Emsley? Neither notion appealed to him as he pushed away from the table and stood.

More than an hour had passed since she'd abandoned their meal. He headed towards the stairs that led to their room, aware complete darkness did not engulf them yet. Isabella had given him a glimpse of the lightning passion she possessed and he wanted more. Of all the women he'd bedded, none drove him stir-mad like Isabella. That first night at the ball, when her reddened lips had parted for him, Nicholas knew she was his. She belonged in his bed, though she wasn't aware of it yet. The ton would laugh if they knew he desired his own wife.

Entering the room, he closed and locked the door. Nicholas shrugged out of his coat, draping it over the nearest chair in the small parlor that connected to their sleeping quarters. He half expected her to greet him at the door, protest her readiness, but no sound came from either room. Rosewood peppered the air. Nicholas breathed deep, trusting his instincts.

He moved to the entryway of their bed chamber and braced his broad shoulders against the frame. His body stiffened immediately at the sight of Isabella soaking in the hip bath. Back to him, her thick hair taunted the ground. Nicholas did not know how long he stood watching her bathe—seconds, minutes—until she sat forward, reached for the robe on the floor, and stood.

It took every ounce of restraint to remain where he was. Her skin looked soft and as creamy as fresh milk. Nicholas imagined the feel of his hands against the back of her knees, kneading the flesh there as he moved higher still, until he cupped the fullness of her bottom. Would she let him have his way? His erection throbbed painfully against his breeches.

When she stepped out of the bathwater and wrapped herself in the robe, only then did he allow himself to breathe.

The air was charged with current. Was she as aware as he? Did she feel the untapped energy between them?

She faced him suddenly, eyes wide. Her hands clutched

the front of the damp robe. "How long have you stood there?"

"Long enough. You smell very nice."

"Nicholas…"

If she meant the name as protest, with her whispered groan, it only served to fan the flames of his desire. He felt her roused alertness as keenly as he felt his own.

Nicholas did not want her hidden from his gaze. He wanted her free. She was so damn bonnie. Never had he longed to make love to a woman as he did Isabella. Cherish every shared touch. He had never made love to another woman. He'd bedded them, but he'd never savored. He'd touched without feeling.

He stepped closer. His eyes narrowed as she took a step back, then another. Still he followed.

With each step, he painted the image of tussled damp hair, wet dressing robe and flushed skin to memory. They would be his refuge during the many nights at sea.

Isabella shivered, the bed firmly at her back.

"No more running."

She was fighting her attraction to him, he realized, had been fighting for a long time. The knowledge was a dull ache in the pit of his stomach. He wanted one night of freedom. One night of trust in her arms. But he knew, even before closing the distance, one night would never be enough.

Her pink lips pursed. "You don't mean to consummate our marriage here? The walls are thin… The entire establishment would know." Isabella flushed.

Nicholas grinned, once again struck by her cocktail of naiveté and recklessness.

Fingers gentle, his hand brushed the back of her nape, working its way into her hair until it spilled from his fist. He tugged gently, causing her to gasp until her head tilted, eyes holding his. "Aye, lass."

Against the palm of his hand, her hair was soft silk. The short strands wrapped around his fingers as if to keep him there. He had no intention of leaving.

Isabella's head fell back as he slowly started freeing the robe from her grasp. "Don't call me that—lass."

"The first night we met, do ye remember that?"

She didn't answer as he unwrapped a delicate shoulder. Her neck stretched and he saw what her words denied: the quickening of her pulse. The creamy top of her breasts taunted him. So smooth. So soft.

"I told you I would have you in every way a mon can have a woman, a wife her husband. My bonnie fire-cat." He lowered his lips to the treasure he'd unwrapped.

"Don't call me that either."

Nicholas smiled against her shoulder. Fire. She was heat and he wanted to be engulfed by it, until there was no way out but to go deeper.

"Only the bargain," she whispered, as if to reassure herself.

She wanted to steel herself against him. Before he answered, his lips moved to the base of her neck. Finding her life's pulse, he licked the spot and groaned when the drumming quickened under his tongue.

"Forget the arrangement, lass. Let me love you."

He slipped the garment completely off, letting it pool at their feet. He needed this; she had possessed him for so long, Nicholas thought he'd go mad. Tonight he wanted to love her, possess her and claim her as his, even if for a short while. He wanted her to love him, not because he was her husband or because of their bargain or because she pitied his past, but for the man he was by his own right.

Her small hands clutched his shoulders.

Again he kissed the curve of her neck, the base of her ear,

until he took her earlobe between his teeth. She arched into him, burying her face into the curve of his neck.

Nicholas squeezed his eyes shut and prayed for mercy when her warm breath fanned his neck. But the Gods were otherwise occupied. She pressed against him. Nicholas cursed. He felt the swollen tips of her breasts against his chest. Jesu, what sweet torture. When he thought he could not possibly burn any hotter, she mimicked his actions and licked the flesh at the base of his neck. He sucked in a sharp breath.

"Let me love ye."

She nodded, her arms closing around his neck. It was the permission he sought. As much as he desired her, had she refused, he would have walked away.

A thrill of excitement ran along his spine. Nicholas took her into his arms, molding her against him. His lips descended, covering hers. He was a starved man. Her lips parted under the pressure of his, and this time when he claimed her mouth, his kisses were hard and demanding. Her hands moved to the back of his neck, holding his head closer. It was all the motivation he needed. Lifting her off the floor, he placed Isabella on the bed, breaking their kiss long enough to pull his shirt over his head and kick off his boots using the toe-to-heel method.

Blushing, she averted her eyes.

"Look at me, lass."

She did, with heat that matched his.

Nicholas moved onto the bed, taking her to the center with him. She was soft and lush. "Jesu, Isabella." He kissed her again. Slow this time. Savoring her flavor. He licked along the seam of her mouth, pulling her trembling lower lip between his teeth. "Ye are bonnie." Their tongues met and he shivered, the sensation taking root in his soul. Torn between prolonging their fevered loving and fulfillment, he wanted to give her as much pleasure as he could, but he could not last much longer.

He silently promised to taste her everywhere before the night was through. His mouth moved across her chest, taking one hardened peak into his mouth. His hand cupped the weight of her breasts as his tongue flicked and teased the sensitive bud. Isabella arched, driving more of herself into him and he welcomed her, giving more of himself over to her hunger.

Frantically he untied the front of his breeches, lowering them enough to free his shaft. He brought himself more fully between her thighs, spreading her with his knees until they were hip to hip. His hand moved between their bodies to test her readiness.

Slick. Warm. His fingers parted her folds until he found the source of her desire. He circled the engorged bud and her hips tilted off the bed. Her head fell back with a strangled cry.

"Nicholas, I'm on fire." Her back arched again and she rubbed wantonly against his fingers.

"Aye, love, so am I."

He adjusted his position and, with one determined thrust, he buried himself.

Isabella cried out, pushing frantically at his chest.

Nicholas froze. If the fearful woman beneath him were anything to go by, Isabella was a virgin, or had been until a moment ago. He was convinced she'd been intimate with Emsley. Her palm lifted as if to strike him. He took her wrists and pinned them above her head.

"I'm truly sorry, Isabella." He kissed away the tears from her eyes. Goddamn, he was sorry for not being gentler, for taking her so recklessly, but those feelings warred with the joy of knowing no other man had had her. He remembered the moment her maidenhead gave way to his intrusion, and he could not help the small thrill that crumbled another wall around his heart.

He shuddered, every muscle aching to move.

"Is it over?"

Nicholas did not answer with words. Instead, he took her breasts between his lips, loving them until both dark nipples hardened.

"Please…" Her eyes closed.

He kissed her cheek. "There's nae more pain, lass."

Her head shook.

"Look at me." His hand reached between their bodies, determined to give her as much pleasure as he had received. He smiled when her eyes flew open. She was liquid fire. White hot in his arms. Her hips shifted upwards and Nicholas groaned from the weight of his restraint. Still he did not move. His mouth descended in a long kiss that would leave her mouth swollen for hours. His tongue breached the walls of her mouth. She was as eager as he, and Nicholas found delight in her dual play. Her hands clutched at his shoulders, this time pulling him closer.

"Wrap your legs around me."

Slowly, her legs cradled his hips, then his waist. Her eyes widened with uncertainty. "I… I can't take anymore."

He groaned. "My wee lass, ye were made for me." She was. She was made for lovemaking and long kisses in the moonlight.

As their eyes locked, he thrust forward, burying himself to the hilt. They both gasped. She fit him perfectly. Sweet agony. Jesu, but he had to move. His jaw clenched, a slow rhythm starting.

She answered his call thrust for thrust, her back bowing. She took everything he gave, growing brazen. Her hips tilted and her inner walls fluttered, holding his cock hostage. She cried out her pleasure. Small hands clutched his buttocks.

Her heated touch was his undoing. He thrust once, twice, with powerful strokes, savoring his own release.

They were both panting. Nicholas braced himself on his elbows and gave her a slow kiss before rolling onto his back. He wanted to stay inside of her warmth forever, until he was once again taking them over the edge.

This day was not going as expected. Isabella had surprised him at every turn. When he thought they played on even ground, he was deprived of even that. She was a virgin. Nicholas pushed off the bed and headed for the washbasin. Dipping the cloth into warm water, he dampened it then wiped himself, cursing as the proof of her innocence covered the towel. Rinsing the cloth again, he took it to Isabella, surprised she had not hidden her nudity. He shook his head. Nicholas had mistaken her boldness for experience. Though she had rejected the idea of marriage, each time he had taken liberties, she had welcomed him. No, he remembered, she had participated.

Using his free hand, he spread her thighs, and then gently cleaned her. He flipped the towel over, repeating the act. She was silent as he attended her, unusually quiet. His eyes sought hers, and what stared back was a mixture of heat and reprimand.

"You apologized during… You apologized."

"For hurting you…"

Her head shook in denial. "It was more than that."

"Isabella."

"You were surprised I was not… That I was a virgin."

Nicholas raked a hand through his tussled hair. "Aye."

"You didn't think you were bedding a virgin?" She sprang to her knees. Watery eyes gave way to her true feelings.

"Nae." He tossed the towel on the side table.

She moved back further onto the bed, distancing herself. "A whore then?"

Cursing, Nicholas's hand gripped her ankle just as she moved to leap off the bed and tugged her back to him.

She squeaked. "Let go, you…you…"

"Now listen. I never said ye were a whore—"

"No. You only thought I was free with my affections."

"You're wrong."

She jerked her foot.

Nicholas held fast to her leg, fingers tightening around her ankle. "Aye, I thought you were intimate with Emsley, mayhap with Daniel," he admitted. "To that extent."

"Two lovers?" Isabella stiffened.

He did not answer.

Isabella hugged herself. It scared her to think that Emsley's gossip had reached into her marriage. That he still held power over her. It may not have mattered to Nicholas whether Emsley had bedded her, but it mattered to her. "The gossip." She looked at him, feeling hurt that he thought so little of her. "You believed them and did not care if you married a loose wife, as long as I shared my favors with you."

"Nae, Isabella, don't say such things." Nicholas's heart squeezed. He was losing her and there wasn't a damn thing he could do.

"I hate you."

He breathed deep. She was out to draw blood and he was sure she would get her fill before the night was through.

"I'll fulfill my end of the agreement and care for Cassie if you'll honor yours and provide financial support."

They were back to that damnable bargain. "Is my touch so repulsive?"

"Yes," she hissed.

Nicholas thought for the first time tonight that she had lied.

Something deep inside of him shifted, a part long forgotten. A part of him, Nicholas now realized, he had saved for his wife. A woman as brave and bold as Isabella. He masked his hurt at her rejection. After all, he knew what he was and had accepted it long ago.

He studied his wife. Isabella, so full of pride, her tilted chin reminding him she was out of his reach. No longer did he wish to fight or spend his days hoping she would see reason.

They shared unmatched passion, yet she denied it.

He had to set her free, though every fiber of his being screamed against what he was about to do.

His jaw hardened as he stripped off the remainder of his clothing, then tossed the breeches aside. "If that's what ye wish, Isabella. But I've bargained for an entire night, and the evening is far from over, lass." He climbed into bed. "I'll leave you alone to do your bidding and hope in time you'll grow up."

She gasped, but he ignored the sound.

"Heed me in this," he whispered in her ear. "I won't meddle in your affairs, whatever they be. But harm your reputation any more, or that of Cassie's, and ye will truly not like the man ye've married." He tugged her under his chest.

"Wh-What are you doing?" Her breath quickened.

"Feasting in our bargain." He claimed her mouth in a long ravishing kiss for the second time that evening and shuddered when her fingers tangled into the strands of his hair.

CHAPTER 22

"On ye signal, Captain," Harold said.

"Raise the flag!" Nicholas said.

Nicholas stood on the docks of London. He loved and hated this part of the voyage. The waiting, the anticipation. Overlooking any small detail risked lives.

The crates used for storing the goods they would purchase were secure below deck, and all the men were accounted for. The last of their supplies were loaded. Soon they'd be on their way with London to their backs. The salt air and wide-open sea was a seductive lure. There, he'd be free from his past and the weight of society. In the middle of the ocean, he could breathe.

Every time he had set sail in the past, it had felt like freedom. A chance to claim things for himself that he could not find on land. Even when he had left his mother behind, he had always felt a rush as he looked out at the large expanse of unconquerable sea in front of him.

But not this time. This time, sailing felt like running. Running from Isabella and the feelings she stirred. In his haste to find a mother for Cassie, he had married a woman he could never truly possess. The muscles along his back clenched. He would not think of his wife now. His men needed him. He *needed* to sail.

Harold stood beside him. "The men are restless."

They were caged birds with no room to fly. "They feel it, the call of the sea."

He'd promised his wife distance. Her parting words were a stinging reminder of her contempt. He'd been correct in his assumption about her anger. She'd bled him dry that night.

He had asked forgiveness, no, begged for it, to no avail.

Repeatedly they'd made love, finding pleasure together, yet still she did not relent. In the end, he'd gained no more than their agreement.

Isabella hadn't known of his past, yet her words were true, curling themselves around a part of his heart he had thought long dead. It was time to stop wanting what Isabella so easily denied. He had no one to blame except himself for trusting his wife with a piece of him.

Swallowing the last of his pride, he shook the forbidding thoughts aside as Harold released a string of curses under his breath.

To their right, another ship prepared to sail. Amrason's vessel. It was no secret the other captain planned to return to London first. Nicholas clenched his jaw. "I've counted two men that are in their cups," Nicholas said angrily.

"Amrason should be warned."

"The fool is determined." Nicholas grunted. It was only luck that the man and crew hadn't died at sea with some of their riskier stunts. Gripping the rail, Nicholas peered over the edge.

Harold's gaze moved from the departing ship to Nicholas. "You're not going to alert him, are ye?"

"A captain has no business at sea if he disnae know his

men." Nicholas turned away, leaving the task of warning Amrason to Harold.

His eyes locked on his own men, men he trusted. He had to if they were to survive each journey. They watched each other's backs, and more times than not, they returned home with no less men than they sailed with.

He stepped on deck, felt the ship sway in tune with the waves, and for the first time it did not feel like home. The thought made his breath catch. He had anticipated more than a mere rush, had expected genuine excitement. He wanted to forget, feel the wholeness he had come to appreciate with each journey.

The rightness of it was still there, along with the anticipation of adventure, but there was something missing...

His fingers clenched around the wheel. Harold nodded to the crew. Shouts echoed around him. Men bustled, adding to the noise. He closed his eyes and savored it all. He did not need to see. The wind, the water, and the planks beneath his feet were all part of his soul. He knew the calls of each man before they were voiced. The drums of his heart beat with the crew.

His soul shifted. They were free. The anchor rose. The ropes freed.

The winds were in their favor. The morning was warm despite the light mist covering the shoreline. The fog would take them away, down the Thames to the sea. And for a short time, he'd forget London.

AFTER THE SHIP'S bells rang, signaling the beginning of dog watch, Nicholas went below deck. He entered his quarters, hanging his jacket on the hook secured to the cabin wall. Small hands folded around his shoulders. Nicholas turned into the arms of Judith, an old amour.

Hair pinned into a nest of curls and bows atop her head, her long lashes fanned him. Glancing about the space, he searched for additional surprises before his gaze touched her again. "Why are ye here, Judith?"

"I thought to give you my company."

"I'm a married mon."

Her smile was a slow, inviting curving of full lips. "You brought me aboard your ship before."

"Three years gone. Not since Cassie was old enough to understand."

"Your wife's not here, is she?" Her fingers spun the short hairs at the base of his neck. "Neither is Cassie." Standing on the tips of her slippers, her arms encircled his neck before ruby lips pressed against his.

His hands moved along the length of her arm, easing out of her hold and stepping away. "I'm not interested." He crossed the room to the small map table bolted to the ship's floor. "What do ye want, Judith?"

"Your wife doesn't make you happy. I can."

His head shook. She was never one to tangle words. "Years ago, you sought more than the coin I had offered. Ye wanted a lord. Though you couldn't boast of a relationship with a peer, knowing he was above your station was enough. Have you forgotten? I still can't give you that."

She moved closer. Nicholas recognized the easy sway of full hips. "You don't believe that. Your circumstance has changed."

The palms of his hands slammed against the surface of the table. "Nae!"

Judith gasped.

"Ye made your choice."

"Nicholas?" Harold stumbled into the room. His eyes moved between them.

Nicholas straightened, folding his arms across his chest. "Ye'll stay in Harold's quarters."

"I'll stay here, with you." She pouted.

In a swift move, he took her shoulders. "Ye'll do as I say and be glad I don't bunk ye with the men."

Her lips pinched. "Turn the ship around!"

"No. It is too late to drop a rowboat. You wanted aboard, and here you will stay."

Shrugging out of his hold, she pushed past them and out the door.

"Why didn't the men stop her?" he asked Harold.

His cousin shrugged. "They assumed you knew."

Nicholas jabbed his finger in Harold's direction. "Keep her away from the men. She bats her lashes, and I'll toss her off the deck myself."

"We'll have to return sooner than planned."

"Over a bloody whore?"

"Try explaining to your wife why ye voyaged for months with your whore."

"Jesu." He ran sprawled fingers through his hair. "Aye. We'll stop to load, no more."

"The men will not be happy." Harold said.

"The men will be content to return home with full purses."

Alone in the room, Nicholas turned to the map. His finger traced the route he'd carefully planned. Fewer nights docked, the right winds and currents ensured them an early return. His finger tapped the spot indicating the Far East, and he knew that part of the trip was lost.

SLEEP DID NOT COME easy that night, nor any of the nights in the weeks they'd departed. With most of the goods loaded and the crew having little time for entertainment on exotic shores, they were anxious and randy. Two lads had been rationed to bread and water for groping Judith. The rest he'd threatened with forfeiture of their share of the wages. While that stopped the men from making advances, it did nothing about the woman sashaying on his deck. His jaw clenched, suspecting the tension on board was her intent.

Tomorrow he would have words with Judith.

Tonight he needed sleep.

It had taken hours, but he had finally been lulled to sleep by the rocking of waves slapping the side of the ship. And it was the first night that dreams of his wife had not awoken him in the middle of the night, sweating and wanting. The longer he stayed at sea, the more vivid the memory of her touch had been. Even the sea breeze, once sure and true, had turned on him, until every brush of wind against his loose strands of hair reminded him of her hands at his nape.

Tonight he slept.

He had not dreamed of Isabella, yet he was restless. The shouting above his head was not moans of pleasure. The thumping of heals and the trace of sulfur peppering the air were not from the rose water she used in her bath. And surely his wife did not possess a gun...

Nicholas jolted up, his legs swinging off the bed. Slipping his feet into his boots, he was out the door before the second shot pierced the air. At the top of the stairs, he grabbed a lad by the shoulders, halting his descent.

"We're taking fire, sir!" The lad's eyes were wild.

Dammit, he knew that. He looked from the lad to his scrambling crew. "Where are you going?"

"First mate ordered powder, Captain."

"Keep the barrels filled," he commanded. "And Jesu, keep low before you get us all killed!" He released the young man, watching him stumble below deck to the supply hold.

Another shot echoed through the air, and he prayed his third, Grey, kept their distance from the enemy ship.

He pushed past the men. Above his head, a man scaled the mainmast to the fighting top. Hurrying across the deck, he found Harold taking cover behind the quarterdeck. "Who are they?"

"Still too dark to see their flag."

"Pirates?"

"Aye, from what we can tell. The men are at their posts. They know not to waste a shot." Harold nodded towards a second ship. "We heard gunfire in the distance... It was then that I realized it was Amrason's vessel under charge."

Nicholas cursed. "Let us come to Amrason's aid, then."

Harold nodded.

Picking up one of the guns laying between them, Nicholas loaded the musket. The pirates had likely used early dawn's cover to attack. They had not anticipated clear, cloudless skies, however, or the glow that slowly broke over the sea.

"Nicholas? Nicholas?"

He stilled. Reaching over Harold, he peered around the wall. "Does the woman use common sense?"

Harold chuckled when Nicholas darted from their cover.

When he reached Judith, she clung to him. Her tucked curls now fell about her shoulders. "Oh Nicholas, thank God!"

"Get below, Judith."

She shook her head, grip tightening.

"Unless you want those men to find you—hide!"

Her eyes widened.

"Hide in the crew's quarters, among their bedding. If the pirates board they'll be more interested in merchandise than the crew's worthless belongings." He pulled her towards the stairs and gave her a nudge.

Cursing, he turned on his heels, stopping only to give the men operating the cannon their orders and watch them load the first shot.

"Fire!"

That was their only warning as the ship's cannon fired. Holding his breath, he waited for a sign that their shot hit its mark. When screams rent the air from the pirate ship, he slumped against the wall. He breathed deep and felt the subtle shift of the ship beneath him. "Grey found us a current."

The ship moved closer.

"Aye, so did they." Harold pointed as the pirates' ship moved broadside.

"Ready your guns," Nicholas yelled. He filled both hands with his pistols. Aimed. Fired. Gunshots echoed around them. Both ships answered the other's call to surrender. Closing his eyes, he heard the screams of men and prayed they were not his. Countless times they reloaded, called for gunpowder, and told his mates to stand strong. "Hold your ground!"

Saltpeter and gunpowder thickened the air, the fresh scent of sea air gone. A deck once mopped clean was mucked with blood and powder.

A few feet away, gunshots hit the end of the quarterdeck where his new crewmate huddled. The man's fingers fumbled with his weapon. Another shot hit the wall, just above Calloway's shoulder.

"Light the slow match, mon!" he said. Calloway took aim. Nicholas watched wide eyed as the spark moved up the fuse. It smoldered but did not ignite. The slow match did not touch the gunpowder.

"Jammed!" Calloway fought with his gun again.

Cursing, Nicholas grabbed the musket at his feet, aimed, and fired at the pirate slumped before the other vessel's bowsprit. When the man fell into the water, he said, "Don't just sit there, Calloway, repack that musket!"

"Aye, Captain!"

One by one he watched the pirates fall, yet still they came. As the first morning breeze drifted across the sea, he looked at the tattered sails. Leaving Harold, he moved towards the wheel. Jesu, he had no appetite for dying today.

When a round of cheers sounded, Nicholas looked towards the pirates' ship. They were leaving, turning their wheel away from Amrason's ship. He took stock of his men, his ship, and when Amrason's vessel maneuvered alongside theirs, his men stretched a plank to the deck of the other ship.

"Your men?"

"Alive because of you, Captain Nicholas."

Nicholas shook the man's outstretched hand.

"That was brave, to risk your lives and come to our aid," Amrason said.

"I'd like to think the favor will be returned one day." Nicholas looked over the ocean. "I suggest we leave these waters."

Amrason nodded before again stepping onto the plank that joined their ships. He paused. "These pirates are becoming bolder. Blackening their sails, attacking under dark skies. We would fare better together."

Nicholas shifted. "What are you suggesting?"

"We sail and return together. Pirates are less likely to attack two ships, and our lives will not be solely dependent on incompetent men."

"The first convoy." Nicholas nodded, sure this new partnership would benefit them both.

At the helm, Nicholas spun the wheel. They were still in the currents. With luck, their sails would catch the winds that would lead them home.

CHAPTER 23

"*I*sabella?"

Isabella looked up from the unfinished letter on the desk to the little girl, knowing that her undivided attention was required. Cassie sat in the corner of the library with blocks, strips of wood—peeled from the bark of a tree by one of the stable hands—and a bowl of paste prepared by Edyeth.

Isabella's lips twitched in amusement.

"When is Papa coming home?"

"Soon, darling." Isabella's voice caught. Cassie must have heard the uncertainty in her voice. She looked up from her play, a frown creasing her brow.

That answer, as well as the others she'd used in the month since Nicholas had left, was no longer sufficient. Cassie's persistence showed no sign of easing. In fact, the child grew restless with time, and no amount of reassurance placated her questions. Isabella was immensely grateful to the staff for distracting Cassie. The house now had two cooks, thanks to Nicholas for continuing to employ her two servants. He'd found a place for them here, insisting they stay for as long as they wanted it.

It had all worked remarkably well. While Miss Conley, the head cook, prepared delicious lunches and suppers, she was lacking in the art of perfecting pastry. Mrs. Berths filled that void quite well. Her scones and sweets went a long way in soothing Cassie. On many occasions, Mrs. Berths also prepared their picnic luncheons. Miss Conley often commented on the increased time she now had for the market and the creation of new dishes.

Mr. Berths, on the other hand, once Isabella's head butler, now found the extra time as second butler highly vexing, except for the moments he snuck off with his wife.

Taking the paper between her fingers, Isabella crumpled the letter she'd started, balling it in her fist before tossing it into the bin with the others. The message was meant for the madam in charge of Sound of Voices. She had hoped to gain a few more students now that she was married and the wagging tongues had quieted, finding some new gossip more entertaining. However, Isabella knew the elite society could be high handed with their forgiveness, especially if they felt snubbed.

She didn't need to seek employ now that she was married. Nicholas had entrusted her with enough coin and pin money —but the bit of freedom she'd tasted from her brief independence was alluring.

Isabella snatched another paper from her writing desk, then dipped her quill.

A month had passed since her marriage to Nicholas. In that time, she had never felt lonelier. She had gotten exactly what she had bargained for, yet the knowledge brought her no enjoyment.

"Will you go away when Papa comes home?" Cassie asked, startling Isabella from her thoughts.

"Of course not," she answered readily, wondering why Cassie would ask such a question. "This is my home now."

Cassie smiled with all the mischievousness of an imp.

"Cassie—"

"I know Papa married you because he wanted me to have a mother, and you didn't really want to marry my papa, so you ran away." Cassie smeared another clump of paste on the blocks, then spread the paste with the brush. She paused. "Next time take his ship. He can't catch you if you take his ship."

Isabella snorted back a laugh. The child was far too clever, Isabella thought. Pushing back from the desk, Isabella came to sit on the settee close to Cassie. "One of the reasons we married was because of you," she said, confident Nicholas had always been open and honest with the child, and immediately grateful with her decision when Cassie responded with a nod. "He wanted you to have a life with all the joys he could provide."

"But you don't love my papa."

At the time of their marriage, she did not, Isabella confessed. In time she'd come to know the man who was both the relentless captain and the father. He was not at all who she'd expected. The servants respected and adored him, and he was a fair master. He had not neglected Cassie to servants or shunned his responsibility because she was not of his seed. Quite the opposite.

Her heart tugged. Despite all the affection he received, he held himself separate from everyone. Looking at the world from outside instead of participating, as though he waited for its rejection and disappointment, expected it. Poor Nicholas. Isabella hugged her waist, wondering when he had lost his trust in love.

.   .   .

ISABELLA AWOKE and groaned the next morning. Tossing her arm over her eyes, she blocked the sunlight from rendering her blind. Last evening she'd opened the curtains and unlatched the windows, wanting the cool night air to dull her senses. Forgetting him was not that simple. She wanted to escape, anything to forget the memory of Nicholas's angry footsteps outside the doors of her room. Their last night together tumbled back with vivid certainty. Her husband! How had the entire event turned rotten?

"Is that what you truly desire, Isabella, to be alone? Is my touch so repulsive?"

"Yes."

Isabella squeezed her eyes shut. The emotions he had stirred scared her. She had lied. Recklessly answered out of fear.

What a ninny she was.

Something changed in him then. A quiet calm took over. She expected rage, anger perhaps, but received none. Late into the night he'd left their room. The following morning he'd packed their trunks with swift silence.

How sure she'd been of what she desired. Now she was not so convinced. She silently wept, feeling a profound sense of loss.

Their ride home from Gretna Green the following day had been filled with tension. There might as well have been a mountain between them, Isabella thought.

Later that afternoon, when the air had cooled, he'd wrapped his coat around her shoulders with cold carefulness. She'd felt his anger, frustration, and even jealousy before, but never such chill. He had avoided her touch, Isabella remembered with deep longing, a connection her body now craved. And when he'd helped her from the carriage, Nicholas hadn't held her by the waist as he typically did, but by her gloved fingers, as though they had not shared an intimate night together.

But Isabella felt his warmth from the small contact, and was sure, when their eyes met, he'd felt it too.

Frustrated, Isabella rolled onto her stomach, wishing the night had swallowed her. From the time she met Nicholas, she was torn between desire and pride. There was nothing proper about the man. He infuriated her. But by the devil, he set all her nerves on end. Her heart leapt and responded even when her head was tormented and confused by her feelings. He proved an elixir against all things wicked.

Even now, she wanted him. Her muscles stretched, taut at the reminder of his vow.

It was her own cowardice that had kept her from Nicholas that night, and pride that had kept her from asking he not sail. Instead, she sought solace in the cool night air. But the stars did not dull her hope for love, and the moon, with all its beauty, did not cease the knowledge of her disposition.

"Leave," Isabella warned when the door to her room opened.

"I'll do nothing of the sort," Virginia said. "He'll be back. He always comes home."

Isabella buried herself deeper beneath the sheets, pulling the covers over her head. Instead of retreating, the footsteps grew nearer. She sulked, any hope at solitude dashed when the bed dipped.

"Locking yourself away in your rooms won't gain Nicholas's favor. No good can come of it." Virginia's voice softened.

Her head shook. Pity would send her into another fit of tears. "I wish to be left alone." There was a brief pause. Isabella held her breath. Surely someone in this house must obey.

"Did he hurt you? He could be—but I can't imagine him uncaring with your first time."

Isabella groaned, mortified. "He was most..." She thought of the right words. "Attentive." She felt a blush color her cheeks, and immediately clutched the covers to shield her embarrassment.

Not deterred by Isabella's tight grip, Virginia eased the covers past Isabella's shoulders, rousting her from hiding before helping her to sit. "Nicholas is a complicated man," Virginia said when Isabella sat, tucking the coverlet firmly around her torso. "He's not at all the unkind beast the world knows him to be."

Isabella frowned. The first few days he'd done little else but growl and nip in her direction. "Yes, but is he capable of love?"

"That depends," Virginia said. "What's your idea of love?"

Isabella's forehead wrinkled. She never thought love needed words. She opened her mouth, then shut it. Her impressions on the subject were born from fairy tales and a sheltered life. Silly, she'd fancied herself in love once. Doubt swept over her. She hugged herself, unsure. "I do not know."

Virginia grinned. "With no expectations of how one must love, anything is possible. Don't you agree?"

Before Isabella voiced her objection, a knock on the door silenced her. It opened. A servant peeked around the frame. "Good morning, my lady. I'll return later."

"No need." Virginia instructed the girl to bring bread, cheese and tea. "And the hip bath, as well."

When the girl's hurried steps could no longer be heard, Isabella asked, "Do you love him?" They were both surprised by the question. Time slowed as they searched the other's face. A shallow knot twisted in Isabella's stomach. This was a home of secrets and hurt, banded together by a force she desperately needed to understand.

It was Virginia who broke the silence. Moving to the window, shoulder propped against the frame, she was lost in another time. Her voice faltered. "Of course I do."

Jealousy seized Isabella's chest. Her breath held. She wanted to scream, but anger eluded her. Virginia had answered with simple honesty. She stared at the other woman, clutching the sheets and trying to understand. Virginia loved him. Why hadn't they married? Then it dawned on her—*Nicholas*. "Nicholas does not love you...?"

"I think he does."

Isabella swallowed, confused.

"I think he loves all of us in his own way." She paused. "No sister could wish for a better brother. Any thought of marriage on my part was only to save us both heartache."

"Oh, Virginia..."

"You have to understand, he gave me family, a home, and darling Cassie. All the things I had thought lost. The first time I laid eyes on Nicholas..." Virginia smiled over her shoulder. "He stood outside my door with a squirming baby."

"Cassie."

Virginia nodded. "I don't think she was more than nine months. Even then she had him wrapped around her finger." Virginia sniffed. "He said my sister and husband died from fever. They named him guardian of the baby, but he thought it should be me. But I couldn't. My sister was impulsive and strong headed, kind and loving, but I think it was her wit her husband loved most. If she entrusted Cassie to Nicholas, she must have known the type of man my husband was." Virginia tapped a small spider crawling along the wall. "Pff, I had no one," she murmured. "Countless times I wanted to be selfish. Take the child. His affection for Cassie did not let me."

"Was? Your husband died?" Isabella whispered, knowing the strength it took to abandon the last shred of love.

"Not then, though I wish he had." Virginia trembled. "The

debt collectors came often. They wasted no time collecting. The chairs went first. The dining room next. It wasn't long before we slept where we walked. That was no place for a babe. Nicholas realized it, too, when he finally took stock of the house. I'd sold everything of value or given it as payment for one or more of my husband's excesses."

"I am sorry…" Isabella left the bed and held Virginia's hand.

"Pellian, my husband, came home and saw us with the babe. He was foxed and vicious." Virginia closed her eyes. "'My sister is dead. The babe has come to live with us,' I told him.

"'We can't afford another mouth,' Pellian had said.

"I had taken his hand. 'We always wanted children. Maybe now, if you stop drinking, it will be better for us.'"

Virginia swallowed. "He slapped me. The blow knocked me back a few steps. 'Keep the bloody thing,' he said. 'It might fetch us coin yet.'"

Virginia touched her cheek at the memory. "No one ever witnessed Pellian's abuse. He was careful. And never the face. When Nicholas handed me the baby, I fled. I couldn't stand the disgust or anger in Pellian's eyes. It was as if I'd betrayed him." She closed her eyes. "I was so tired. Can you understand, Isabella? So tired of living but not truly doing so.

"I don't know how much time passed, or what happened when the door closed behind me. But I remember Nicholas saying I was to live in London with him."

"That sounds very much like Nicholas," Isabella mused.

"No law would deny Pellian his wife. Most think of a wife as her husband's property. I lived in fear of him coming for me, but not once did he come looking, and when I received a letter of his death, I was happier for it." She spun, facing Isabella. "Do you find me distasteful, knowing I wanted my husband dead?"

"No!"

Nodding, Virginia again stared out the window. "Those are not the actions of a man incapable of affection. Instead of disposing of a child, Nicholas gained me."

"Poor Nicholas," Isabella said with a faint smile. She squeezed Virginia's hand in understanding. Virginia was loyal to the man who had shown her compassion and offered his home. He loved, Isabella thought with hope. It was in everything he did for the people he called family. Family went beyond blood.

Nicholas gained the trust of those in his service, loyalty and love from his family. Void of a title, he had built a world that surpassed those of his peers. Yet he did not take full pleasure in his success. He only gave the impression of being heartless. Isabella's brows creased. There was a tension between Nicholas and her, she'd felt it, strong and wild in him.

"There could be happiness in what you have..." Virginia's grip tightened on her hand.

Uncertainty replaced her smile. "I have nothing." Isabella lowered herself to the velvet-upholstered chair and hugged her knees. Resting her hot cheek on her knees, she squeezed her eyes tight. "My family abandoned me. My marriage is a bargain struck to care for an innocent child. I can't imagine happiness without love. My husband," she whispered, tears forming on her lashes, "has no need for a wife. How could I possibly be happy?"

Virginia glanced at her. "By letting go of the past," she said simply. "You have family here. Though I must warn you, some are more temperamental than others. As for your husband..." Virginia tucked a lock of hair behind Isabella's ear. "You shall have to win him."

CHAPTER 24

*I*sabella only knew one person capable of guiding her in winning her husband: the Duchess of Kenningsly. The carriage stopped. "Thank you, Chambers," she said as he helped her to the sidewalk. Glancing at the large wooden door, she climbed the stairs.

In the past weeks, she'd made great progress gaining Cassie's trust.

The child had spent the first few days wondering when she'd leave. She'd awaken many mornings to find Cassie in her bed watching her sleep, as if to disturb her meant Isabella might vanish. It wasn't until they'd shared a bed, the child tucked under the curve of her neck, that Cassie began to believe she wouldn't leave again. Isabella hated that she'd put such doubt in the child's mind. It was that determination to love Cassie as Nicholas did, and to demand more than a bargain, that drove her to the duchess's home.

She knocked, and when the door opened she stepped inside, startling the butler. It was the same butler from the party.

"Lady Isabella Pennington?" His shoulders straightened.

"Where is Lady Jane?"

"In the garden, my lady. I'll let her know she has a caller."

"That's quite alright. I know the way." She paused, staring at his arched brow of disapproval. "It's Lady Isabella Ferguson now. You ought to know I've married since my last visit." She took pleasure when the man paled, then headed in the direction of the garden.

When she exited the double doors, Isabella's steps faltered. The older lady was not alone. Daniel sat with her, sharing what looked to be the remains of a late luncheon.

He saw her first. "Lady Isabella, what a delightful surprise."

She curtsied when the duchess faced her. "I did not intend to disturb your meal."

"Nonsense." Daniel grinned and eased his chair back, reaching her side in a few long strides. Linking their arms together, he guided them to the table, seating her beside him.

"I agree; a delightful surprise," the duchess said from her place across the table. She tugged the bell pull. Moments later, fresh tea, cakes, and fruit lined the table. The servants were swift in replacing the soiled dishes.

Isabella took a sip of tea, not sure where to begin. She'd expected to find the duchess alone. Lifting a lemon cake to her lips, she found the treat even more soft and flavorful than she had expected. Each bite released a new burst of lemon zest.

Beside her, Daniel sampled his own pastry. They would not speak until she did, Isabella realized, or at least not until she'd gathered her thoughts. "It was most generous of you to entertain me at your party. And you, Daniel, for being a gentleman, honoring me with a dance," she said, careful not to implicate him in her foiled plan on her wedding day.

Daniel's brows rose. His wicked smirk widened.

The duchess huffed. "You did not come to thank me."

"Let me apologize, then, for leaving abruptly and spoiling your evening."

This time Daniel chuckled. "Hardly."

Leveling her eyes on Isabella, the older lady said, "Neither did you visit to apologize. I may not have seen you often, but you are your mother's child. She did not apologize. I expect a ramble of regret from your father, or that sister of yours, but not from you." She paused, brows drawn together. "And if I recall, you were swept away that evening." Intelligent almond eyes moved to include Daniel. "More than once."

Isabella blushed.

"Very unladylike," Daniel teased, and then grunted when the side of Isabella's slipper connected with his shin.

"Romantic on the captain's part." The duchess sipped her tea.

Daniel choked.

"Romantic?" Isabella stared at the woman. "He was nothing short of barbaric."

"Tsk." The older woman clicked her tongue. "He's more gentleman than most." Setting her cup down, she faced Isabella, her eyes sparkled with mischief. "Yet you've come to tame your barbarian."

"No!" Her face heated, she'd answered too quickly to be believed. "Only to win him," she finally admitted.

"He has not harmed you, then?" Daniel asked.

"No, Daniel," Isabella answered. He'd done nothing more than fulfilled their arrangement, giving her freedom, weeks of it. A freedom she no longer enjoyed.

"Tell me of your captain," the duchess said.

"He's not my..." she started, and then stopped when the older woman's eyes met hers.

"Do you mean to go on as you've started? Many married women live separate from their husbands. Neither dallies in the other's affairs. If so, one must learn not to look too closely at his misdeeds, and a strong stomach is necessary for gossip."

Closing her eyes, Isabella whispered, "No more gossip."

The older woman nodded. "Do you truly want him, then, and your marriage?"

"Yes."

"Claim him as yours or another will. Those are not mere words, child, they require actions."

Picking up her napkin from the table, Isabella passed the material from finger to finger. "He's a stubborn man, but not so much so that he can't see reason. He's honest and fair. And though the world sees him as ruthless and common, and he acts in kind, Nicholas has never been anything but generous to me. He's also had a sordid upbringing and embraces family as a result." Her eyes kept fixed on the napkin.

"Ah, Lady Isabella, I do believe your captain will do." The duchess smiled. "A man strong enough to face storms at sea wants to know he's captured his lady. At the very least, we can let him think so."

Isabella flushed.

"When I first saw my Henry, I knew. While the other wallflowers waited to get their dance cards filled, I decided to help mine along. In spite of my chaperone's protest, I wrote Henry's name twice, filling the spots for the first and last dance." The duchess chuckled. "I wanted him to remember me. I marched to his side and showed him my card."

Isabella easily pictured a younger lady being bold. If her no-fuss approach to aging were anything to go by, her younger self would have been lovely, easily catching the eye of every man in the room. "Did he point out your error?"

"He was too much of a gentleman. He quickly realized that other men were smitten with me. As we danced to that final song, I allowed his hand to wander down my back."

Daniel coughed. "Aunt!"

"Rest his soul. To the day he died, your uncle thought himself clever." The duchess winked. "Daniel, be a dear and fetch my wooden box from the cabinet."

"You never remarried," Isabella said when they were alone.

"No one could replace my Henry. Our son Jack and nephew Daniel fill my days. Not to mention the charities and numerous social gatherings."

Daniel returned, setting a box no larger than a cigar case on the table. The older woman opened it, sorting through the contents until she found the item she sought. "Even as a little girl you were loyal to a fault once your heart became involved, Isabella." The older woman slipped a card between them.

"Your mother was much the same. Unlike your father, frills alone will not sway Captain Ferguson. He's married you to get ahead of men who have no intent on opening the doors of society." The duchess's lips curved, teasing the laugh lines around her mouth. "I do believe you have the wit to out-fox him."

Sipping her tea, Isabella hoped the older woman was correct.

"Do you know," the duchess said, her eyes dancing. "The warehouse beside your husband's has gone on the market?"

Her fingers stilled around the cup.

"Don't you think being captain and landlord would appeal to your husband's business senses?"

"Yes, but...how would I go about acquiring it?"

The duchess smiled coyly. "What a lovely coincidence that I'm friends with the owner's wife."

Isabella returned the duchess's smile. "Marvelous indeed."

CHAPTER 25

*N*icholas stood on the main deck of his ship and overlooked the crew as they steadily approached London's docks. His fingers tightened around the rail. Would Isabella be waiting for him?

The months had not gone quickly. Nor did he forget his wife. Each day the memory of her slender frame writhing beneath him was maddening, and his current state did not lighten his mood as he felt the ache of his traitorous manhood.

He shifted, resting one boot against the rail, and cursed when his breeches tightened around him. Eyes closed, he felt the wind against his face and allowed it to ruffle his hair. Nicholas hoped it would cool his blood, but only the warmth of a woman could do that.

Isabella. He needed Isabella, his wife, to quench his needs. He gasped, easily remembering her innocent seductiveness as she had unrobed on their wedding night. Her long hair was a welcomed caress as it cascaded down her back. At that moment, he had envied those strands. Wished they were wrapped around his fingers as she submitted to her most secret desires. For weeks he'd imagined his hands in her hair as he guided her to her knees. What would her mouth feel like around him?

Uttering another curse, Nicholas jerked away from the rail. He'd been in such a foul mood the last few days that even Harold stayed clear. He regretted his treatment of the crew and vowed to make it up to them.

Filling his lungs, he shouted, "Lower the sails!"

The shore line came into view. On his command, the men moved into action. They were almost home. More shouts echoed in his ear as the first sail lowered.

"Captain!"

Nicholas spun. "Damn it, man, lower the sail." They were moving too fast, the winds guiding them firmly into the bloody docks.

"The ropes are stuck, sir. We're fetching a lad to climb."

"The sandbags. Drop the bags." Even as he uttered the words, Nicholas knew it would not be enough.

Heart hammering, he scanned the distance to the docks. There was no time. They would crash. God help him, but he had too much pride to crash upon his own dock. "My rifle," he ordered, catching the gun easily as Harold tossed it from behind the wheel.

Taking aim, he took a deep breath. One shot. The weapon relaxed in his grip. The wind calculated for, his finger flexed, squeezed.

They watched as the wheel holding the rope spun and set it free. The sail dropped and a roar of cheers went up as the ship slid like a slain beast into dock.

MERCHANTS GATHERED. There was laughter. Men, women, and children stood close. Wives awaited their husbands' return. The dock was crowded. Shop keepers tallied and noted the goods as the crew unloaded.

"We'll sort it at the warehouse, fellows," he said, slapping Harold on the back.

Wheat, grain, and silks. It was a good haul.

Harold lit a cigar and inhaled deeply before blowing a whirl of smoke. He handed the cigar to Nicholas. "See you at home."

Nicholas followed Harold's gaze and found Virginia standing among the crowd. "I'll keep your share," Nicholas called after his cousin in amusement.

"You wouldn't live long enough to spend it," Harold warned, not slowing his long strides as he pushed his way through the crowd. He had no doubt being cooped up with Judith had something to do with Harold's hurried pace.

Smiling, Nicholas rolled the cigar between his fingers. He took a long drag then released it into the air. They always shared a smoke when they returned home. This was the first time the act lasted minutes. "Here." Without shifting his gaze, he passed the cigarette to whoever stood to his right.

Reaching down, Nicholas picked his bag from where he'd dropped it at his feet and slung it over his shoulder. His day was far from over. Men needed their pay. Tom would be waiting in his office for an account of the events at sea, but that would have to wait until he dealt with the merchants.

"Congratulations, Captain, you made it." An eager lad ran beside him.

"Did you lose any men? How many injured?" a reporter added to the frenzy, pen in hand.

"The captain eats his wounded!" another laughed.

"How many did you kill?" another shouted.

"Only those who tried to kill me," he answered, trying to push through the bodies. For all his reputation was worth, the crowd closed in on him instead of moving away. Nicholas sighed; he couldn't possibly draw his pistol and threaten the lot.

A chill ran across his shoulders, coaxing every nerve along his back to life. His head snapped up as he scanned the docks for the cause of his unease. Nicholas's eyes stopped at the familiar figure standing beside his parked carriage. It was as if his subconscious had conjured Isabella purely for his distraction.

Her hair was pulled into a loose bun, with thick curls caressing the side of her face and slender neck. He groaned at the thought of setting her hair free.

He let his eyes linger, roaming over every inch of her: the top of her head, the slope of her shoulders, the softness of her breasts barely being contained by the dress's low neck-line. He saw the small shift in her posture and wondered if she was as uncomfortable as he. His eyes blazed a path back along her curves, causing his own body to stiffen in sweet agony. Their gazes met and held.

Time slipped away, and something between them shifted. They were no longer separated by the sea or time, but bonded by their own needs. By the slight lifting of her shoulders and the tilting of her chin, he sensed Isabella felt the tension too. Something significant had changed between them, though he was reluctant to name it, and the lure she ignited tightened in the pit of his stomach.

Heat. Delicious heat warmed his skin as if she had touched him. Touched him with her eyes as he had done her. He drew a ragged breath at the thought of the power of such a connection.

As quickly as it happened, the link was broken. He remembered where he stood. The voices around him breaking through the invisible barrier. And like a bucket of cold water, Daniel stepped out of the carriage to stand at her side.

His chest hurt, the wound deeper than any he'd suffered in battle. And even as his fist tightened, Nicholas threw back his head and laughed. The sun and sea salt must have addled his brain if he thought anything between them had changed.

"Nicholas, darling, give me your hand." Judith's voice brought him back to the present.

He'd forgotten all about the woman on board. He looked at her questioningly.

"The puddle." She pointed at her feet. "I don't want to get my dress wet."

Stretching his free hand back, he opened his palm and waited for her to take hold. When she did, he closed his fingers around hers, guiding her around the muddy hole.

She stood before him in a twirl of skirts, her up-turned face holding a suggestive pose. Nicholas shook his head. She had painted her face and changed clothing. But his feelings towards her had not changed.

Without warning, Judith threw herself at him, wrapping arms around his waist. "Thank you, Nicholas, for…" she blushed. "Keeping me safe aboard your ship."

He raised a dark brow. They both knew *he* had not been her protector.

"Shall we?" This time it was her hand being offered.

Nicholas scowled. He had no time for Judith's games. He had a mind to leave her where she stood. Instead, he took her arm, not trusting her to keep her mouth shut about the events at sea or adding bits of her own imagination.

Turning away from his wife and her lover, Nicholas moved them through the crowd, his dark mood etched across his face.

At the end of the dock, he crossed the narrow alley

between buildings until they stood at the stairs to the office space he rented.

"Go on up," he instructed Judith. "I'll arrange your transport home."

If she was irritated, it didn't show. Judith gathered her skirt and ascended the stairs with all the grace she possessed.

Over his shoulders, Nicholas sought one more glance at his wife, but she no longer stood at the edge of the crowd. Isabella was gone.

Nicholas climbed the steps two at a time. He was hot, tired, and disgusted with himself for allowing Isabella to rob him of all reason, but the crew did not deserve his ill treatment or his scowl. They deserved a celebration. They had risked their very lives and survived.

A round of cheers went up when he entered the room.

"Dispense the wine, will you, Tom?" The crew, Tom, Judith, and some of the gentlemen financially invested in his cargo all filled the small space outside his office. It was a successful run.

Holding his glass, he toasted, "To the bravest, most loyal crew a captain could ever have."

"The most loyal and ill-tempered captain a crew could have," one of the men countered.

"Don't forget honest," another shouted.

"He saved my life when those pirates attacked!" Calloway's voice rose above the others.

"Here, here to the captain."

"See this lot paid, Tom, and don't let them leave until their jugs are empty." That earned him another round of cheers.

In the far corner of the room, Judith looked in need of saving. A gentleman Nicholas had only seen a time or two at Brown's engaged her in what he could only guess was his attempt of wooing. Judith's gestures were polite enough, but every few minutes her eyes roamed the room. Twice she had looked pointedly at him, but he'd only nodded and raised his glass. He wouldn't give her the chance to repeat the stunt she'd pulled at the docks.

"I seem to be the only one without cause for celebration," Lord Jacob's voice interrupted Nicholas's musing.

Nicholas turned to find the straight-faced man at his side. Jacob was a constant investor in trade; one Nicholas could not afford to lose.

"In my office." Nicholas didn't wait for a reply. He led the way, closing the door the second the other man stepped past the threshold of the private office. It was quieter, and he welcomed the moment's reprieve.

"You promised a full shipment," Jacob accused without hesitation.

"Look, we both know the shipping business is risky. Shipment is not guaranteed until I dock, and it's the reason I don't charge an installment on orders." He also didn't take advances because he did as he very well pleased, he almost snapped. Nicholas's eyes narrowed. He understood power and the value of it. While men held title over him, he held the means to cripple their livelihood. No, he wasn't a lord or marquess, but that did not mean he would bend to their will.

Lord Jacob fell back into the chair with a sigh.

"The gains were no good. Drought," he said as way of explanation.

Jacob nodded.

Lifting his bag off the floor, Nicholas opened it, taking a handful of its contents out. "How stands your greenhouse?"

Jacob shrugged. "I don't see what my plants have to do with my loss in coin."

Opening his hand, Nicholas showed him the seeds. Frowning, the other man leaned forward and plucked a seed from the palm of his hands. Jacob examined the item, knowledge slowly lightening his features.

"Tea," Nicholas said, pouring the contents back into the small sack. Retying the string and sealing the bag, he wondered if the man could see opportunity, or better yet, seize it. Pulling on the string with a final tug and finding it secure, he tossed the sack to Jacob. The idea struck him at sea: why buy on behalf of merchants when he could also participate in sale. He certainly had the means to ship. A large greenhouse like Jacob's was necessary, since he was unfamiliar with how the crop would fair in the winter months.

Jacob's brows creased. "You want me to grow tea?"

"Not just any tea. The leaves are the main ingredient in an herbal blend. It's popular in the East, and by all accounts has both calming and healing properties. There is no reason the exotic blend cannot be replicated here."

"You're giving me the seeds?"

"Only if you'll consider partnering with me."

"What do you want in return?"

"You have the means to grow and I have the means to ship. If we pass the first stage and the crop survives, it could be a lucrative stream of coin."

"Why me?"

"Our dealings have always been fair. I trust you, and from my experience, it is not always so in business. This is more than tea, Jacob. Tea is drunk all hours of the day, more than alcohol in some households. Done right, we will be in every kitchen in London and across the pond. As to why I chose you? You're honest."

"And if I decline?"

Nicholas shrugged. "I'll find another partner." Truth, he didn't know anyone else with a greenhouse as large, or that possessed the necessary skills.

Whether it was Jacob's business sense or the thought of growing something new, his curiosity had been piqued. "Partners, huh," he said, eyeing the seed.

"Fifty-fifty."

Jacob rose from the chair, bag clutched in one hand as he extended the other. "Partners."

Nicholas took the outstretched hand, sealing their new bargain. "There is one more thing, partner," he said. "What do you know of Lord Emsley?"

Jacob's lips twitched.

WHEN JACOB LEFT HIS OFFICE, Nicholas knew he'd not misstepped in his choice of a business partner. More than that, now he knew more about Lord Emsley's gambling habits. The man would risk all for card. Nicholas shook his head. He'd known such men, witnessed their downfall countless times. Even now, he knew of two in debtor's jail because they could not pay off the money they owed. They'd lost their families, homes, and still they risked all over and over again.

"Come in," Nicholas said, leaning against his desk. He frowned when Tom entered his office, wiping sweat from his brow. He'd never seen the man out of sorts. Come to think of it, he'd never seen the man with so much as a hair out of place.

"I fear some of your men may have trouble finding their way home." Tom dropped heavily into Jacob's abandoned chair. "I've taken the liberty of relinquishing them of the means to add to their current state," he said, handing over the pays he'd withheld to Nicholas.

Nicholas laughed.

. . .

"Stop!"

"Isabella?"

"I must go back." Isabella's fingers trembled as she fingered the pins in her hair. "Your aunt is correct, Daniel. If I'm to win my husband, he must know I mean to try."

Daniel squeezed her gloved hand before leaning against his seat as she reached for the door. "I wondered when you'd come around."

She paused, brows raised. "You're not going to stop me, or think I'm a blundering fool?" she said, taking Chambers' out-stretched hand and stepping onto the street.

Daniel chuckled. He caught her free hand. "Your captain doesn't stand a chance against such forces."

She blushed. "See Lord Daniel is taken wherever he wishes, will you Chambers?"

"Yes m'lady."

Turning away from the carriage, she took a steadying breath, lifted her skirts above her slippers, and crossed the street that lead to the busy docks and Nicholas's office.

The celebration was still in high spirits as more ships docked. Her steps faltered. Nicholas had survived the journey. His men were all accounted for. She did not want to sour the mood with thoughts of their disagreement. Maybe she'd been rash in her decision to not prolong their meeting.

The duchess's words rang in her ears. "Nicholas requires a bold wife, an equal."

Looking around the docks as men shouted their orders for merchandise, Isabella turned towards the stairs. It was time she righted their marriage.

At the top of the stairs, she opened the door and entered the room. Men stood in small groups. Waves of their excited chatter filled the space. Merchants and shipmates mingled with filled glasses in their hands. The scent of rum and sherry tickled the air. The floor was made rough by streaks of mud from the bottom of boots and the scrubbings from a wire-brush.

Isabella paused when the voices hushed. A smile ghosted the corners of her mouth, then quickly faded when the only other woman in the room turned. Their gazes held. Isabella's chest became heavy under the weight of her pounding heart. She'd heard whispers of women flocking to ships when they docked, but this woman didn't dress like the street walkers she'd seen around port.

The woman seemed to share in the camaraderie, yet she held herself apart. It was in the way she kept smoothing her skirts and glancing towards the office door.

The door at the end of the room opened. Isabella turned towards the new intrusion. It was Nicholas. His imposing figure stood in the doorway of his office. Tom, his accountant, stood at his side. This time when her heart drummed, it was in tune with her husband's.

"Good day, Mr. Jenkins," Isabella said.

"Lady Isabella." Tom smiled.

Over the past few weeks she'd come to know Tom and respected the man for his cleverness. He'd accomplished more than seeing to her accounts. He was a shrewd businessman, and knowing he favored their marriage and campaigned for the union, proved his devotion. It was with Tom's help that she intended to show Nicholas she intended to be more than his way into society.

"I trust all is in order?"

She touched his elbow. "Yes. Thank you, Mr. Jenkins."

Clearing his throat, Tom touched the brim of his hat before leaving them.

"I don't think I've seen Tom blush," Nicholas said as he stepped aside and allowed her entry into his office. "Don't tell me you've unleashed your charms on the man?"

"Hardly."

When the door closed, Isabella turned. Though subtle, she was struck by the evidence of his life at sea. His shoulders were broader beneath his white cotton shirt. His skin was also favored by the sun. The bones at his cheek were pronounced and the lines under his eyes spoke of a wariness that hadn't been there before.

"What are ye doing here?"

"I came to welcome you home."

He took a step towards her, closing the distance until they were only a breath apart. "Welcome me home, Isabella?"

"What's wrong with that?" Her chin tilted up.

Slowly, his hand touched her hair. A curl wrapped around his finger before he smoothed the wayward strand behind her ear. Isabella swayed closer. The tip of his finger caressed her cheek, running along her flesh until he held her tilted chin between two fingers.

"Everything." He snatched his hand away, burying it deep into his pockets.

Her heart thundered. Everywhere he touched was left heated. Searching his face, she realized he felt it too. The air had grown thick from their nearness. He'd not forgotten their night of passion. It was what she'd hoped.

"You needn't have come, Isabella." He faced the window overlooking the docks. "I haven't forgotten our arrangement. I'll have my belongings removed from the house tomorrow."

Her heart sank. He thought she'd come to remind him of their bargain. "There is no need…"

He turned. "Have you changed your mind?"

Yes! She wanted to shout as they stared at each other. What if he laughed? What if he still thought her the silly chit he'd sailed from months ago? She couldn't handle his rejection. Not now. The time for words had passed. She needed to show Nicholas she wanted their marriage.

"I didn't come to toss you from our home."

"Nae?"

"I came to congratulate my tenant on his return."

Those dark eyes narrowed.

"I've taken the liberty of acquiring the building next door. One of your warehouses, I believe."

"I've tried to get that building for years. How did you... Tom." He chuckled.

"Before you aim your musket, you should know he was only following my direction after I became aware the owner would not sell to you. The owner feared backlash from the more...favorable gentlemen who were also interested. A fair price was negotiated."

"Tom would not spend a shilling of my money if the investment was not sound."

"My funds," she corrected sweetly.

Nicholas tilted his head to the side. "Your dowry was to be used..."

"As I intended."

After a brief pause, he nodded. "It's prime real estate, Isabella. In a few years, you will have earned more than your investment."

Her stomach fluttered at his approval. "We."

He frowned.

"I have no doubt we will earn our investment with you overseeing our businesses."

His eyes closed, then opened. "What is it you want from me?"

Her breath stilled as she held his gaze. "I'm interested in a partnership, Nicholas."

With slow purpose, his eyes ran the length of her. "You no longer need me."

He was wrong. Still, she remained quiet, waiting for his answer. When he nodded, she wanted nothing more than to go to him. She resisted. She needed to do more than gain his respect—she needed to win his love.

"If that is what you truly seek, you shall have it."

"Splendid!" she said and hurried from the room. She had one more stop to make, and she couldn't allow the heat from his caress or his stormy eyes to drive her to distraction. Least not yet.

CHAPTER 26

*I*sabella moved from one glass case to another, examining the merchandise. The duchess's card had led her to the small, well-hidden shop.

Isabella looked more closely at the objects in the case. She would make him desire her as much as she did him. Persuade her husband to their marriage.

The next time she held her husband close, there would be no question as to her desires.

The shopkeeper chose that moment to enter the room. "Afternoon, my lady. My name is Maria."

She announced her name with such boldness Isabella lifted her head in surprise. Maria was plump, wide hipped, and her low neckline garnered the right amount of interest. She was attractive. Full features and the mysterious glint in her eyes hid her age. Her Spanish accent added to her air of intrigue.

Isabella smiled and wondered what other secrets the duchess kept to herself.

Her regular dressmaker normally hurried around her shop in a fluster of skirts at the beck of spoiled young ladies all wanting her attention. But not Maria: she was confident as she moved further into the room with no sense of urgency. And Isabella had a feeling the woman's skirts never rustled unless it was her intent.

Isabella frowned. How had she missed such a presence?

As if reading her thoughts, Maria said, "I like to give my visitors time to browse with all their senses. If they have not fled by the time I arrive, they are less likely to swoon at my suggestions."

No, her regular dress shops would certainly not do today.

Isabella cleared her throat, the action fortifying her courage as well. "I would... I mean, I was hoping..." Oh this was not a very good start. This woman would think her a ninny!

"Who do you wish to seduce?"

Isabella blushed. "How..."

Maria smiled. "This shop is for amour. My visitors come for romance."

"My husband."

Maria considered her for a moment, as if measuring Isabela's sincerity. She felt like a very small butterfly. The woman's narrowed eyes did nothing to ease her growing discomfort. And just when she decided the visit was a mistake, Maria's fingers snapped with assurance.

"Come, we have work to do. If a man such as yours is not tempted by your beauty, he must be *loco*."

Isabella said nothing when the woman sent a charming smile over her shoulder. She followed Maria to the back of the shop and into a small change room surrounded by tall mirrors.

"Tell me, señora, what do you know of seduction?" Maria asked as she tidied the small space, picking a few discarded items from the seat.

Isabella flushed. Nicholas was a worldly man. The little

knowledge she had would not do. Her beauty, as Maria said, had not held Emsley's attention, and she refused to suffer the same fate with her husband.

Looking up from her task, Maria smiled patiently. "A hint of innocence is a strong lure. *Dios mio*, a man likes to know his woman is not tutored in all things." She picked up the last forgotten garment and placed the pile on the seat. "Turn around."

Doing as she was told, Isabella offered Maria her back and felt efficient fingers loosen the laces of her dress. "Is this necessary?" Isabella moved just out of reach.

"It's a pretty dress, but your husband does not need a lady to warm the sheets. He needs wicked. Someone who will make him not seek expert courtesans."

Isabella swallowed. They stared at each other through the mirror. Maria's hands were on her generous hips. When Isabella had set out to entice Nicholas, she had only thought of a new fragrance, or perhaps an appetizing meal prepared from one of Miss Conley's special menus. She had even toyed with the notion of broaching the topic with Virginia— after all, she had been married once.

She felt her resolve slipping and crumbling into a million pieces. Once again, she offered her back. Her dress came loose, the sleeves sliding from her shoulders with lazy grace.

"That is how you undress for him, señora." The garment slid past her corset, the curve of her hips, to pool around her feet. Every uncovered part of her skin tingled from the exposure and boldness Maria suggested. "He must wait to taste your fruit, no?"

Each movement was filled with sensual purpose.

The reflection in the mirror held glimpses of a new woman. A woman she barely recognized. Never before had she felt desirable. For brief moments, maybe, perhaps a time or two in her youth. But never this pulsing boldness that overcame her now; never this desire to flirt with her image.

Nicholas was different. Almost cautious around her, as if holding himself at a distance. This was not the impulsive captain she desired. She wanted her brash Nicholas, the man who'd kissed and seduced her.

Had she pushed him too far? Was she fooling herself, thinking she could win his heart?

Isabella straightened her spine, she had changed too. Instead of fear, she yearned for the future the three of them might build. It had taken some doing, but she'd forgiven her father and was beginning to understand his shame—not in her, but of his own actions. She was also learning to trust again. She trusted Nicholas, she realized with a start.

He dared her to be more. Everything about him tested her in ways she never imagined. Though he spoke no words of love and honor, he inspired courage and passion.

She loved him. It bubbled like hot lava inside her.

Maria slipped from behind the curtain, startling Isabella. She had not noticed the other woman's disappearance.

Maria placed a few items on the chair, then held up a red lacy corset against Isabella's chest. "This will do," Maria said, helping her into the clothing.

Isabella's eyes quickly examined the other items. The fabrics demanded attention. Soft silks and lace. The under-garments—Isabella swallowed—hid nothing with their scandalous cuts and close fit.

The stockings were the first to slip into place. The garter belts came next, fastened from the top of the low stockings to the corset.

Isabella gasped.

Her breasts were barely concealed by the corset. The lace rubbed against her nipples, causing them to stiffen with movement. A blush washed over her neck. Despite the tension growing in her breasts, the material was soft. Isabella trailed her hand along her stomach, surprised when the material warmed under her touch. Red mesh lace covered the entire corset, offering glimpses of skin beneath.

Soft lace garters held the stockings high on her thighs and made her legs appear longer. Inviting. Isabella's fingers touched the small white bows tickling the top of each thigh. Maria's words came to mind. *Hint of innocence.*

"You like?"

She did. What would Nicholas think of his wife dressed so wantonly? It was not uncommon for men to seek their more randy pleasures elsewhere. She had always been told her place was to produce an heir and act as hostess. Isabella wanted a different marriage, however, and she was selfish enough not to want to share Nicholas's affection with another woman.

The bell chimed, signaling another customer. Maria gave her one last look of satisfied approval before dipping behind the curtain, leaving her to her own devices.

Provocative. That was the only word that described the reflection staring back at her.

It was too much. The lingerie, the fragrance, and for heaven's sake, what did Maria intend her to do with the rope?

Her breath hitched as a brazen thought came to mind.

She very much liked this game of seduction and the power coursing through her veins. With renewed confidence, she carefully removed the clothing, slipping back into her day dress. Taking a deep breath, Isabella placed her hands against her cheek. They were cool against her flaming skin. A few more adjustments and she righted her mussed hair, concealing the tangled strands set loose by Nicholas.

Sure not to leave any clothing behind, she moved the curtain aside and left the small dressing room.

Nearly to the front of the store, Isabella stopped. She hadn't expected to see the woman she'd seen earlier at Nicholas's warehouse again, least not so soon. Placing the items on the counter, she did her best to ignore the woman.

Maria quickly folded the corset and wrapped each item before placing them into a box, closing the lid. She was immensely grateful for the shopkeeper's efficiency. The woman she had recognized from the docks chose that precise moment to approach the counter.

Isabella braced herself.

The faint fragrance of sweet rose flooded her senses first. It was not overpowering. Almost inviting. Was that what intrigued Nicholas, Isabella wondered. The smell of a flower garden on a woman. Fresh. Sweet. Delicate, like the petals of a lily.

All at once she hated lilies. And roses for that matter!

Isabella wrinkled her nose. No, Nicholas did not desire delicate, that she knew of her husband.

The swish of skirts brushed Isabella's leg. This woman had no intention of fleeing, nor did she feel any shame, Isabella noted from the smug look on her face. The thought of meeting one of her husband's paramours never occurred to her, especially twice in one day.

"Thank you, Maria." Isabella reached for the box.

"For you, señora, it was my pleasure."

"Hope I haven't scared you away."

Isabella stared at the woman, surprised she actually had the gall to address her in public. Of course the woman spoke. Isabella mentally shook herself. That she chose to address Isabella directly was what shocked her.

Quickly stretching her lips into what Isabella hoped to be a pleasant smile, she said, "I wouldn't dare deprive you of Maria's full attention."

"I'm Judith, by the way."

That was not the name Isabella wanted to call her. Isabella nodded. She was positive the woman knew who she was, and likely all the gossip surrounding her marriage. In fact, she had the distinct feeling she'd been followed to the shop.

"Good day." Gathering her parcel, Isabella strode past Judith.

"Of all the days and nights Nicholas and I spent aboard, he never once mentioned a wife."

"And why would he entertain you in polite conversation?" Isabella asked in a casual tone that betrayed the tightening in her chest. She wanted to wipe the smug arch from Judith's brow. "Your services required but one use for your tongue."

"Don't you want to know what happened between us?"

Isabella paused. She raised her lashes to Judith's pinched lips. Judith's smug smile was replaced by anger. "I can guess your skill at entertainment, and I'm sure all aboard took pleasure in your presence."

Judith gasped.

Without a backwards glance, Isabella left the shop, the street noise drowning out everything but the image Judith had created of her husband.

CHAPTER 27

*D*oor ajar, Isabella stood outside Nicholas's bedchamber. Studying him without his knowledge rarely happened, except for brief moments of distraction.

The room was dark. A single candle lit the space from its perch on the vanity. His back faced her. The flicker of candlelight played across the room, never touching the eluded corners. Instead, it danced around him, afraid of being swallowed by the tension she felt.

Turning away from the window, he prowled his quarters. Stopping at the wash basin, both hands slipped beneath the cool water to splash his face. A growl escaped his lips when that didn't satisfy his purpose. Snatching a towel, he roughly dried his face.

Isabella bit back a gasp as he pulled his shirt over the broad planes of his back, then head, discarding it on the side chair. Muscles rippled in its wake. Licking her lips, she took a tentative step towards her husband, remembering too well the feel of those broad shoulders above her, strong arms wrapped around her waist, and the thrill of him cupping her sensitive breasts as he made love to her.

A shudder ran along her spine. Feeling self-conscious about what she'd chosen to wear, Isabella's fingers skimmed the material, and she wondered if she'd been too bold.

He was almost naked now, except for pants, which gaped at the waist. Her stomach clenched and unclenched.

Smoothing the thin silk nightgown that hugged her curves, a smile tugged the corners of her lips. Her fingers tingled from his nearness as excitement washed over her. She wanted him, this man who defied all others.

He had honored his vows. He'd proven that by coming home.

To their home.

In the past few weeks, she'd thought often of sharing a home with Nicholas. Now that he was home, she wanted nothing more than for him to remain here.

She loved him. And it no longer mattered if that love was returned. She loved enough for both of them. In time, when they were surrounded by their children and he found he could trust her with his heart…perhaps then, he would have discovered he'd loved her all along. Perhaps then, he would utter the words.

She needed their marriage. Too much was at stake. Cassie and any life they could have together would be ruined if their marriage did not work.

Joy swept through her. She'd have to make him see reason, show him that he, too, deserved more than a loveless marriage.

Isabella took another step towards the door, then froze. What if that was all he wanted: an empty marriage so long as Cassie remained happy? Her chest squeezed. No, she shook the condemning notion aside. There had to be more to marriage than this.

She must have made some sound. His movements stilled.

"Is something wrong?" he asked warily, his back still turned away. His thumbs tucked into the waistband of his pants, keeping them from sliding to the floor.

"No I…" She stood behind him.

"Is Cassie ill?"

"No. She missed you dearly. She thought… We all thought."

He didn't answer for a time. "I gave her my word, my captain's honor—"

"That no sea shall ever take you. Cassie reminded us often enough." Isabella sighed. He truly believed those words.

"She's right." His voice held true affection, whether from knowing his little girl missed him, or that she remembered their pact, Isabella didn't know. A bit of both, she suspected.

"I've missed you too," Isabella whispered.

The air grew thick with awareness.

In the shadows of light, she saw him rotate his shoulders as if the muscles there needed stretching. It seemed an eternity, rather than mere seconds. She wanted to scream, *"Look at me, say something, anything."*

"Did you?"

She stepped close, wanting to rid him of any doubt. Some of the hurt in his voice was her doing.

"Of course I missed you. You're my husband."

When he simply grunted, she took hold of his shoulders. He was stone beneath her touch. The muscles under her hand flexed and rippled.

"Leave," he growled, giving her ample warning.

"No." Shaking her head, she stood her ground. They needed to talk, or they would soon have no marriage.

Nicholas cursed. "I'm trying to hold fast to your wishes."

"I know." Her hand moved along his back.

"You're not making it easy."

She kissed his back and heard his swift intake of air. "I know."

His thumbs released their hold on his pants. Isabella's eyes widened when he faced her. Nicholas stood before her in all his male glory. She tried to take a step back, but his hand snaked around her waist.

"Oh no, wife, you had your chance to flee."

Isabella had no intention of leaving. Her gaze drew to his fully erect shaft and she flushed.

"Tell me, what else did you miss?"

He was being a rogue, baiting her into bedroom talk, knowing she wouldn't say what he wanted to hear.

"We should talk...agh!" He took her earlobe between his teeth and tugged, then moved to nibble on the side of her neck.

Isabella sucked in a shuddering breath and shut her eyes. He had never felt more delicious.

"Lost your tongue, wife?" He emphasized the title *wife* by firmly squeezing her buttocks in the palm of his hand. "Speak," he urged.

How could she? He was too close. Too intoxicating. And she wanted him exactly where he was.

This moment, here, now, had played a dozen times in her mind. Not once had it been like the unrestrained hunger coursing through her limbs. She wanted this. They needed this.

"I've missed you," she said, breathless.

"Hmm. So you've said."

His lips played over her skin. At times with the feather light whispers of a new lover, nibbling a slow trail of heat along the sensitive spots. Then he calmed the fire with the tease of his demanding tongue. She lost all thought in the arms of her husband. Her body responded, thighs squeezing together, begging for what only Nicholas could give.

When her limbs were no longer strong enough to hold her weight, he picked her up, holding her close until his cock pulsed at her core. They both gasped at the unexpected heat. With her legs wrapped around his trim waist, Nicholas growled when her hips bucked, seeking more of him. Hands on her bottom, he took them to the bed.

Expert fingers parted the thin vale separating them. "Beautiful." He cupped her breasts, first one then the other.

She arched into his touch.

"Look at me."

Isabella did as he commanded. When he licked the valley between her breasts, she shivered in anticipation. Watching Nicholas envelop one ripened peak, then the other into his mouth, was erotic, and each swipe fed the liquid fire at her core.

Time stood still. Nothing else mattered. Fingers buried deep into the strands of his hair, she held him close.

"I've missed you," she repeated, spurred by dark stormy eyes.

"Then welcome me home."

Knowing exactly what he wanted, Isabella reached between her legs and opened herself to him, her eyes never leaving his. His sharp intake of breath fired her wanton actions.

Wicked need surged in the depths of his eyes, and Isabella knew he couldn't resist for long. He kissed her knees. Her thighs. His tongue sent small jolts along her skin until he finally settled where he wanted to be.

Small, tender kisses were planted between her thighs. His lips settled where her fingers still held, and she arched towards him. Her hips bucked upward of their own accord, seeking the warmth of his mouth.

Her hands slipped away, giving him full access until he growled, stopping the glorious sensation. Panting, they stared at each other, his tongue licking along his lower lip.

"Give me what is mine, Isabella."

She swallowed.

Slowly her hands resumed their place.

She opened to his hunger.

Her hunger.

Her head tilted back against the pillows, eyes squeezed shut. "No," she cried when he stilled.

"Then look at me, lass."

She did. Watching him make love to her this way was the most erotic sight. She was bearing more than herself. She was bearing her soul.

There was no retreating from their love making. She didn't know it could be this delicious.

Had she ever known such colors, and bright sparks of light dancing before her eyes? No. Only Nicholas could give her that.

Familiar warmth started deep, spreading outwards until the only feeling that mattered was his touch. Isabella's eyelids grew heavy until they were slits. Her legs shook. The warmth shaking her body was hot and all consuming.

This... This was what she'd needed, what her body had demanded for weeks. Release.

Nothing else mattered. Not that he'd forced her hand in marriage. That she'd sent him away. That she'd lied that night. It didn't matter that they didn't love the same.

Her toes dug into the bed as wave after wave rocked her body. "Nicholas," Isabella screamed as she fell over the edge.

Kissing his way up her body, his lips pressed against hers. She tasted herself and gasped.

As his tongue brushed the walls of her mouth, he thrust

deep, entering her with one long stroke. They both moaned at the sensation of him filling her.

It was spreading again. That consuming heat. Starting from where their bodies joined. He held still, paying dearly by the looks of his clenched jaw.

She needed him to move. Needed to feel the power of his deep strokes.

Feeling bold, Isabella flexed her hips.

Nicholas's fingers dug into her thighs, holding her still. Eyes closed, he panted. "Please, I don't want to hurt ye."

"You won't."

He searched her face, and she saw the doubt in his eyes. He also feared she'd come to regret their lovemaking.

"It's been too long...do you understand? Let me gather my..."

It must have been the devil, Isabella thought as her hips gyrated again, this time grinding firmly against his.

"Damn it, Isabella," he gasped, no longer afraid of hurting her. He surged forward, strokes growing longer and harder as they moved together. This was her Nicholas, free and wild as he let go of all control in her arms, demanding no less of her. The ruthless captain she fell in love with.

He'd showed her a glimpse of passion that first night, but that paled compared to what he showed her now. Fingers clenched in his thick hair, she wrapped her legs around his hips as he took them to the edge and over.

She wanted them to stay as they were. Tangled limbs.

Easing himself on his elbows, Nicholas stared at her. The back of his fingers brushed her cheek before he placed a gentle kiss against her lips.

Nicholas rolled onto his back. They didn't speak, the silence only interrupted by their breathing. Neither did they touch. There was none of the romantic notions she'd imagined in the aftermath of their passion. Suddenly she felt cold and bereft. Sighing at the turn of her thoughts, she rolled on her side, away from Nicholas.

Seeing the discarded nightgown on the floor, she moved towards the end of the bed. Whatever fueled her wanton behavior had fled. Before her feet touched the cold floor, Isabella found herself flat against Nicholas's chest.

"No, you don't. I like this new wife that comes to me willingly."

Isabella blushed and was sure he felt the warmth against his skin.

"Did I hurt you?"

Was that all he wanted to know? Did he feel guilty? Well she didn't want his guilt. She didn't want to taint what they'd just shared.

"Isabella?" he asked again.

His hand cupped her jaw, tilting her chin up.

"No." She shook her head. "You didn't hurt me."

He sighed. Hugging her closer against him, he said, "Good, because that was—Jesu, Isabella, you'll drive me to an early grave."

"Is it always like that?"

His arms tightened. "No, love."

She looked at him, brows arched.

"Never with anyone else has it been like that for me."

Oh, Nicholas.

"I was afraid you hadn't changed yer mind about keeping our marriage one of convenience. That you'd again come to regret my touch."

"I never wanted a convenient arrangement. Growing up, I had grand ideas of what I wanted, what I imagined my prince to be."

"I know." He swallowed. "You didn't want to marry me. I'm sorry, Isabella."

Such hurt. Virginia was right. Nicholas's eyes hid much from the world.

"No, Nicholas." She looked into his eyes, willing him to believe. To see that, while his held secrets, hers told him the truth. And the truth was that she chose him. "What I didn't want was a loveless marriage. A husband who could easily be sated in other vises destroyed my mother." A tear slid past her lashes.

"I'm not your father."

"I know," she whispered, and turned her cheek into his calloused hand, stroking the side of her face. She planted a kiss on his palm.

"I cursed every day we were aboard that bloody ship."

Isabella laughed, knowing she'd cursed him a time or two, too.

"I rode the men hard to make better time. Then there you were. I remember feeling whole for the first time in my life. I belonged." Nicholas squeezed his eyes closed. When he finally opened them again they were coal. "He was with you, holding your hand. That should have been me."

Gasping with understanding, she sought to quickly reassure him. "There is nothing other than friendship between Daniel and me."

"I know." Taking her face in both his hands, he smiled. "Virginia tried to tell me, but that didn't stop me from being good and vexed. I thought, if I gave you space, maybe you could hate me a little less. Maybe I would grow to tolerate your affections for Daniel."

"I don't hate you, Nicholas."

"I love you, Lady Isabella Ferguson."

Tears filled her eyes and she couldn't stop them from spilling over the corners. Her heart swelled at the wonder of his words. *He loved her.* "Oh, Nicholas. I love you, too."

Isabella rained kisses on his chest, his cheek, before she claimed his mouth. He loved her. Didn't he know she loved him, would always hold true to her vows? Well it was time he did.

"I want a true marriage, Nicholas—family, a home with you and Cassie," she paused, knowing this house was filled with people she'd grown to love.

"Do you, Isabella?"

"Oh yes! And children, I want lots of little brats, like their father." He'd be an excellent father, of that she had no doubt. Hadn't he proved that with Cassie?

"Impertinent wench." He swatted her bottom and they both laughed. Lying on their sides, he adjusted their positions until they were chest to chest. He brushed a few strands of hair from her forehead before tracing the outline of her face, her ear, and when his idle fingers reached the back of her ear, she began laughing. "Ye are ticklish."

"I am not!" she said with all the dignity being naked could afford.

To prove his point, he did it again and was delighted when she snuggled deeper against his chest, her laughter rumbling against his chest.

"Nicholas?"

"My love."

"It's just that…the hairs on your chest." Isabella bit her lip.

"What of it?"

How did one tell their husband that the rough hairs on his chest rubbing against her sensitive nipples were doing delightful things between her thighs? She blushed, not sure how to proceed.

"I see." He took one hardened nipple between his thumb and forefinger, then began massaging the bud until she nearly went mad.

She squirmed in his hold and they both gasped. "Do you think? I mean, could we…"

Groaning, he rolled them until she was firmly beneath him. "I belong to you, Isabella. Never forget that."

No, she wouldn't. Never again.

"Guide me, Isabella. Take me home."

CHAPTER 28

"Welcome back, gentlemen." Lord Eaton rose from his seat, taking first Nicholas's hand, then Harold's in a firm grip. "When word reached London of your troubles, I thought surely we'd be fishing you and my whiskey from the bottom of the sea."

Nicholas laughed, as did everyone in the room. Eaton valued liquor and friendships. In that order.

"Looks like you fellows started without us," Harold said, noting the tossed cards on the table as he made his rounds, greeting the four gentlemen in the back room of Baker's.

"Nothing too serious, only a friendly game of twenty-card poker," Lord Richard assured.

Nicholas, too, circled the poker table, shaking each outstretched hand, and though Emsley nodded as they passed, Harold noticed the firm line of his lips and the cold set of his eyes.

Harold took a seat as the waiter added two more chairs to the table.

"I think you know most of the gentlemen here." Eaton nodded to the one man in the room they had not met. He also sat protectively close to the half-full bottle of alcohol. "Sir James Trudell has taken a liking to your rum. Mr. Ferguson and Mr. Duncan are to be members at Baker's. I trust we can all be friends?"

There was a stillness in the room, as if waiting for Emsley to object to their membership.

But it was Lord Richard who raised his glass and spoke. "To friendship."

"Not if my wife has anything to say on the matter." Nicholas smiled. "She considers you to be family."

"And what does she consider you, Nicholas?" Richard asked.

"She has nae decided," Harold teased.

"Smart woman!" Eaton said.

"So she insists on reminding me."

Richard laughed.

"A fresh deck, will you?" When the waiter placed a deck of cards into Lord Eaton's hand, he broke the seal before them. Each time he passed the cards, the crisp shuffle of a new deck echoed around them. "Since there are now six of us, the game is 52-card draw poker." Looking at Nicholas and Harold, he asked, "Any questions?"

Over the next hour the tension grew with each new round, and the size of the wagers kept increasing. It was what Harold wanted. Nicholas had lost most of his coin, adding to Harold's chips. Emsley grew bold, losing a great deal of his chips, but Harold could tell Emsley did not notice so long as Nicholas lost as well.

With all of Nicholas's chips in, it was Emsley's turn to call his bet. He raised the stakes, adding three more chips to the pile.

Nicholas kicked his chair back and stood. "That's it for me, gentlemen. I'm all out."

While the others bid good eve, Harold watched Emsley's

eyes widen in surprise and anger as Nicholas picked his coat from the wall, leaving them to finish their game.

Sir James folded next, abandoning his cards on the smooth surface of the table.

Lord Richard called, adding to the coin.

Lord Eaton shook his head, signaling he was out. That left three players.

Emsley flipped his hand. "Two pair, Aces and Queens!"

Richard groaned, tossing his cards onto the center of the table.

"Not so fast. Three of a kind." Harold revealed his hand.

Emsley's lips pinched as Harold started racking the chips. Harold was certain the man would accuse him of something outrageous, perhaps even cheating. What no one expected was Emsley's cold demand.

"Another round!"

They stared at the man. A sore loser if they ever saw one, coupled with the fact that no more of his chips remained.

"You owe me that much," Emsley said.

"I don't owe ye anything. I played a good hand and won. Yer out of chips, Emsley."

"I agree. Let's call it a night." Eaton pulled on the end of his cigar. "We are all members and can plan a rematch."

"One more game," Emsley insisted between clenched teeth.

Richard twisted in his seat.

Eaton released a slow breath of smoke. "Lord Emsley. You've already increased your debt to Baker's once. Maybe you should stop now."

"I know what I'm doing."

Lord Eaton paused, then said, "One more game, if you agree to my rules, and if Harold does not object, of course."

Harold nodded. So far, he'd known Lord Eaton to be a reasonable mon. "I agree, on one condition. Should ye lose, you will put to right the rumors of Lady Isabella's reputation."

Emsley's face grew red with anger.

After a lengthy pause, Emsley nodded. Lord Eaton dealt, giving a hand to each man. Whether he knew it or not, Emsley had already showed his hand. He was desperate. Desperate men made foolish mistakes.

With each new shuffle and deal, the pot grew and the wages increased.

The lines around Emsley's mouth deepened with the smallest curving of his lips.

"I didn't figure the captain the type to send another to do his bidding," Emsley taunted.

Harold chuckled. "The mon is newly married and spent weeks away from his bonnie wife. He is bound to seek her favors over yours."

Emsley bristled. His lips thinned. When he did manage to part his lips with a laugh, the sound was raspy and lacked humor. "She's an enchanting wife whose favors have kept better men up at night." He raised his glass.

Judging from the man's air of jealousy and clipped tones, Harold doubted Lady Isabella shared her favors with anyone, and least of all with Emsley. In fact, he was beginning to believe Emsley started the rumors of her adventurous spirit to keep her at his side. It had nearly worked. Isolated from her peers, and with other suitors driven away by rumors, he had only to wait for the right moment.

Men like Emsley were dangerous, he reminded himself before drawing a new card.

"I'm out," Lord Richard said, allowing Sir Trudell to refill his glass.

Emsley's eyes rounded.

Two more rounds came and went. Cigar smoke hovered just out of reach. On another occasion, in a game where

Isabella's reputation was not at stake, Harold would have enjoyed a game in such a grand establishment. The room boasted privacy, secluded at the end of a short hallway and far from the patrons that only desired casual drink and chatter. Yet it was not spared elegance. The lush carpeting, upholstered furnishings, every stitch made to foster comfort. Easing further into the cushion of his chair, he braced himself for the end of his little game.

Emsley smirked, then laid his hand on the soft red surface of the table. "A straight."

Harold's eyes moved to the cards. His chest tightened. "Not good enough," he said, laying his hand in plain view. "Full house, Kings and Sevens." From where he sat, he felt the other man's rage.

"I thought you were having beginner's luck." Emsley's face twisted.

"So ye planned on easy pickings?" He collected his chips, stacking them with new grace borne from outwitting the now-angry Lord Emsley. "At sea, we have nothing but time to hone our skills. 52-card poker is a merchant's game."

Lord Richard chuckled.

Lord Emsley's frosty eyes narrowed on a blessedly foxed Lord Richard before focusing on him again. "How is it you're related to the captain?"

Harold shrugged. So the man sought to embarrass him before his peers. As pieced together as they may be, he was proud of his family. "Cousins," he said as way of explanation. "Our mothers, God rest their souls, were sisters."

"Yes, but—" Emsley began.

"That reminds me." Lord Eaton took a sip of his drink. "Nicholas must pay a visit so I can thank him for the case of scotch. It is truly the best I've had in years."

Thanking the men for an entertaining evening, Harold stood to leave. When Emsley did the same, Harold stilled.

Eaton cleared his throat. "Emsley, if I may have a word regarding your debt to Baker's." Not waiting for a response, he turned to Harold. "We must do this again."

Harold nodded his thanks before taking his coat. At the door, he paused, holding Emsley's gaze. "On your honor, Lord Emsley, I expect the gossip ye've started to be put to bed."

Emsley paled.

Signaling the hack parked along the curb, Harold directed the driver home.

He chuckled. By the time Emsley realized he'd been lured into the card game, the man had already lost more than he could afford. Nicholas had pegged the man perfectly, and now they had gained far more than what Isabella's father had lost. Her father's judgment and wounded pride, however, could only be fixed between father and daughter.

Harold handed over his coat and hat to the weary-eyed butler before running his fingers through smoke-filled hair. He hadn't expected to be greeted at the door, especially at such an hour.

"Shall I see to a late supper, sir?"

Thoughts of food reminded him of the brandy burning in his stomach. "Don't trouble yourself. A bath is all I want."

"Very well, sir. The master said you'd be wanting to wash, so I've taken the liberty of drawing a hot bath in the kitchen."

Remembering that Nicholas had left the club hours ago, he said. "I'll see to warming it."

"No need, sir," the butler said. "It sits on heated bricks."

"Thank you."

The man nodded. "After you, sir."

"To bed with you," Harold scowled. "I can wash my own back."

"But…"

"Off with you."

Harold smirked when the man turned on his heels and fled the room with all the air of an earl. The Berths' presence, especially Pashkin, had turned Winston's demeanor far more proper than they were accustomed.

After eight rounds of brandy, a night of cards proved a greater success than he could have hoped. Weeks of luring Emsley into a game at Baker's, and weeks of planning to regain Isabella's inheritance, had finally paid off. He'd even managed to win a few hands for himself.

Nicholas, on the other hand, would not have stopped until Emsley left the table with nothing more than the clothes on his back. Harold chuckled at the memory of Emsley hurling threats at each player. The more he lost, the greedier he became, watching the chips stack on the table. Lord Eaton kept the glasses filled, attributing his good mood to his free case of scotch.

Certain that Winston had gone to bed and wouldn't attempt to wash, dry, and powder his bottom, Harold headed for the kitchen, intent on privacy and a hot bath. The man was too efficient, he thought, reminding himself it was high time Winston visited his family in the country. Loosening the knot at his neck, Harold shook his head.

The last time the butler visited his family, he'd returned two days early demanding to resume his duties. He'd mumbled for days about the insolence of women. It seemed his wife didn't take kindly to talk about man's duty and a woman's place, especially when she performed both duties while he played housekeeper.

Slowing his stride, his good humor slowly drained the closer he came to the end of the hall.

It was the sound of humming that shattered his hopes for solitude. Hand sprawled against the wooden door, he pushed. He was not alone.

Taking a sharp intake of air to steady his quickening

pulse, Harold stood just inside the kitchen. Not wanting to rattle her, he drank in the sight she made.

Closing his eyes, he allowed the memory of Virginia soaking in his bath to be locked away for eternity.

He imagined the softness of her skin beneath the soapy water. Her breasts full, rounded by the warmth. The petals of her mounds reaching for something beyond her own touch.

Harold groaned.

With a final tug, the cloth fell from his neck to the floor. The buttons on the front of his shirt were freed. Still she hadn't noticed him in the candle-lit room as he firmly jerked the shirt from the waist of his pants.

Moving fully into the room, he approached her. She startled, splashing soapy water onto the floor.

Her wide eyes told him exactly how he looked. Harold shrugged. He was never one for formalities, or modesty for that matter.

"Is that cinnamon I smell?"

Virginia licked her lips. "I... I hope you don't mind?"

"Mind?" Harold chuckled, before tossing the remains of his clothing aside.

"Your bath water... I thought you were out."

"Mm..." By the time he stood before Virginia, she'd already leapt from the tub like a frightened lamb, a towel clutched to her chest.

"I don't mind, as long as Miss Conley doesn't have your head for sampling her spices." He let his fingers follow the trail of water droplets sprinkling her arm, delighting in the quickening of her breath. "Tell me, love, does all of you taste as good as you smell?"

And before she had a chance to respond, he claimed her mouth. Gently their lips brushed against each other. Virginia's shoulders relaxed, giving into the tenderness of their kiss. Oh how he wished he could make this moment last forever—the smell, the feel of her softness against years of hard labor, to be wrapped in the safety of her arms. But tonight, he needed so much more. He needed her. He'd fought his hunger for her and lost. Tonight, he wanted to revel in it. Tonight, he wanted to be consumed.

His tongue slid along her lower lip, more a demand than a caress, until he held the tender flesh between his teeth. He bit down until she gasped, opening for him like no other could. Harold groaned as his tongue explored the depths of her mouth.

He released her mouth. And while she gasped for air, he kissed the line along her jaw, her throat, all while backing her against the counter.

"Harold...not here," she demanded breathlessly.

"I plan to have you here. Each time you enter these walls, I want you to remember us."

He unclenched one of her hands from the towel, wrapping her warm fingers around his engorged manhood.

"See what you do to me, Virginia?" he whispered in her ear. Fingers around her waist, his hands moved lower until he held her bottom, molding her closer to him.

Her breath quickened at his crude words, breasts swelling against his chest.

With swiftness she had not expected, Harold spun her around.

"I suggest you let go of the towel love, and take hold of the table."

When she resisted his suggestion, he leaned her forward until she had no choice but to obey. Only then did he allow himself to enjoy the softness of her flesh. He dipped his fingers between the sweetness of her thighs and almost lost his seed at her readiness.

Her back arched. Her thighs opened to him.

When he finally removed his hands from her folds to cup her breasts, she was moaning in his arms.

Thrusting his hips forward, Harold entered her.

They both moaned.

Harold gritted his teeth, resting his head against her shoulder and allowing her to adjust to him.

It was only when he felt her walls clutching him that he started to move with long, powerful strokes.

This was the Virginia he loved, the part of her not afraid to be free. The part that embraced passion. The Virginia that did not fear him when he was crazed with hunger. She moved with him, matching his every stroke. There was nothing more magical than the sounds of her cries.

But this time he wanted more. He desired her soul.

God help him, but he wanted all of her.

He needed to taste the sweetness of her fire on his tongue.

His muscles flexed from denying his release. Turning Virginia around, he sat her onto the edge of the table. He was not prepared when she ran her nails along his arms, his chest, and the rippling muscles of his stomach. Harold closed his eyes, savoring the sensation of her bold touch.

Harold sucked in a sharp breath as she cupped the weight of his sack in one hand and wrapped the other around the length of him. It was the thought of being buried in her moist heat that kept him from losing himself like a youth.

"Let me taste you." He eased her down until her back lay against the table.

His tongue danced across the soft flesh of her stomach, kissing a path to her inner thighs. Harold teased until her back arched. Her fingers dug into his hair, sent him deeper into her folds. She was sweeter than he imagined.

Her thighs trembled against him. He wanted more than

knowing he'd brought her release. He wanted to feel her shatter around him.

Harold positioned himself between her thighs, and with one long thrust, he buried himself inside of her warmth.

Virginia's cries filled his ear. Her hips bucked, driving him deeper.

His lips crushed hers, letting her taste his heaven and hell.

She stilled for a moment before the wave crashed, engulfing them in its madness. They rode the storm together. Hard. Fast. Until there was nothing left but tangled limbs.

Still panting, they held each other.

"Marry me," he whispered against her cheek, voicing the desires that had plagued him for months.

Virginia gasped.

Their breaths mingled. The air was charged with the magic of what they had just created, what they had always created. They were two lost souls.

He kissed her shoulder, her neck. "Marry me, Virginia." Feeling her stiffen in his arms, Harold raised his head until he was looking into her chestnut eyes. Only then did he see the despair there.

"Oh Harold, I… I can't."

Harold clenched his jaw to tame his own anger. "Why?"

What a fool he'd been. He searched her wide eyes for the truth he was finally ready to accept.

"Answer me, damn it!"

"Harold…" her voice was barely a whisper.

"Nicholas." Fingers clamped around her arms, Harold shook her. Furious, he ignored her pleas.

Shaking her head, Virginia said, "No, I don't love him, not that way and you know it. I never did."

"Then why?"

How could she admit to him what she'd only not long ago admitted to herself? When a man married it was because he wanted a family, children. For a time, she'd blamed herself for her husband's drinking. Three years of marriage had given them no children. Pellian had made sure she knew her only duty to him that remained. How could she marry Harold knowing she was barren?

She'd chosen Nicholas not because of love, but because he had Cassie and would demand nothing from her.

Looking into Harold's angry face, she had to tell him.

"I can't give you children, Harold. I can't give you the one thing you want."

He searched her face. He'd met families without children. And though many doctors and husbands readily blamed the wife, he suspected the husband's weak seed to be the cause. But this was not the time to convince her of that.

"What of love, Virginia? Is that of any value?"

She pushed at his chest in response. Harold wrapped his fingers into her hair until she had no choice but to look at him, his free hand buried between her thighs until she was once again panting. "Wife or mistress, Virginia, you decide. Because the next time I'm inside your warmth, I won't deny myself release."

"I never asked you to!" The words escaped in a choked whisper.

"No." His eyes darkened. "No you didn't."

With effort, he untangled himself and gathered his discarded clothing before leaving the kitchen.

He never heard her sob, or saw her arms wrap around her body to restore the warmth that had departed with him.

CHAPTER 29

*N*icholas roused to the sound of his wife's gentle breathing. Wild strays of hair fanned his shoulder and soft breaths tickled his chest. She shifted, nestling her head further into the crook of his arm. Tightening his hold, he held her close.

Usually he'd wake from a night of restless sleep and vivid dreams. Not today. Last night he'd found peace in Isabella's arms.

Thoughts of his mother no longer caused him pain, nor did he feel ashamed or pity her. As for his father, Nicholas did not hate him.

Kissing the top of Isabella's head, he knew she was the source of his peace.

Though he'd never forgive his father, and he'd never understand how a man could so easily turn his back on family, Nicholas understood the man's fear. A fear his mother, Harold, he, and for a time Isabella, shared and lived. Lord Jeffery Ferguson, his father, cowered at having nothing. No coin or grand home. No influence. And in the midst of his panic, he'd forgotten the power of family. He'd turned his back. He was faithless. Nicholas would never forgive him that.

For years, he'd blamed his mother for not fighting harder, not demanding his father take responsibility. Mayhap even shaming him before the ton. After years of navigating the streets of London, he now understood that even in heartbreak, his mother thought to keep them safe from a man who might easily snuff them out.

Isabella snuggled closer at his side.

"Did I wake you?"

"No. What occupies your thoughts?"

"My mother. She would have adored you."

"You think so?"

"Aye. She would have liked your spirit."

"If she is anything like her son, we would not have gotten on," she teased.

Nicholas chuckled.

Isabella looked at him. "You did not have a bad dream?"

He frowned.

"That night, our wedding night, I heard you from the sitting room. You were…restless."

"Ye said naught."

"You would not have welcomed my interference, not after our cruel exchange."

"I'm sorry, lass." His whispered words were hoarse.

"Tell me of your dream."

There was a short pause before he answered. "It's of my mother's death."

"But you weren't there."

"What if I had been? Mayhap I could have helped her, prevented it."

"Nicholas…"

"For some time I knew. I think we both did. Feeding both of us could not go on forever. My mother never said a word.

She thought I never saw the portions of food on her plate each night lessen. The molded ends of bread she'd keep for herself."

"I'm sorry."

Nicholas squeezed her arm, needing her warmth as he never had before. "Soon after, Harold and his mother arrived. Do you know he is heir to land in the Highlands? Because of greed, they fled from an uncle who wanted the clan and lands for himself. They ran for weeks…

"Mother shared what little we had. Her sister…" Nicholas closed his eyes. "While Harold laid unconscious in bed from a badly healing broken leg, his mother died."

Isabella gasped.

"His screams are what haunt me at night. He was seven, and while he cried for his mother, I remember feeling…relief."

She shook her head. "You were only a boy."

"Even then, I knew her death meant one less mouth to feed. And though guilt came quick on the heels of my relief, there were still too many of us to support."

"That's why you left?"

"Aye."

"As to not lose any more family."

"She died anyway."

"Only this time, Harold was there for your mother the way you were there for his mother years earlier." She soothed his guilt.

"Yer a smart woman, Isabella."

"You say that as if you chanced upon it in the dailies."

"Impertinent wench." He chuckled.

Her hand covered his chest. "It's not your fault your mother died. Last night—"

"No." Adjusting their position, Nicholas cupped her cheeks in his hands. "You've lit every dark corner of my dreams, Lady Isabella." He kissed her. A long, lingering kiss that professed his love and gratitude. "I have a gift for you." The back of his fingers stroked her cheek, her ear, before letting strands of her hair curl around his finger.

Throwing the covers from around his waist, he swung from the bed, feet landing on the cold floor. He opened the dresser and took out a slender box adorned with a white silk ribbon. It was a simple gesture, a peace offering of sorts. He wanted her to know he had not taken her for granted or made light of the strength it took to commit to their marriage. He walked back to the bed and handed her the box.

"What's this?"

"It doesn't replace what was taken from ye."

She looked at him. The ribbon unraveled after a gentle tug. Holding his breath, he watched her lift the cover.

Trembling fingers ran along the necklace. "It's beautiful. The stones... I didn't think I'd ever see that shade of blue again."

"That night, at the ball, you were hurting. Had I looked past my own needs, I would have seen your tears. On the balcony, you weren't crying for the loss of Emsley, were you?"

"No." She looked at him.

"Your mother's gift to you, a necklace, was stolen. You were in pain and I added to that. I'm sorry."

"You gave as much as you took that night, Nicholas."

His chest squeezed. Catching her fingers in his, he stilled her hand when she reached for him. "There's no need to be gentle, Isabella, I was less than kind."

Isabella smiled. "It was not kindness that made me accept your offer of marriage. Truth, I've never forgotten our first meeting under that wretched boat. Nor did I forget how I felt that afternoon. I wanted you, too, Nicholas, but those feelings frightened me."

"Is that true?"

"I thought to hide my feelings behind marriage to Emsley."

"My brave lass."

Shaking her head, she said, "I wasn't brave then, and my father would never have approved. Then I saw you again and I had to be sure I hadn't imagined your touch."

"Was it as you remembered?" Nicholas swallowed.

"Yes," she whispered as his fingers touched her flushed cheek.

Setting the box aside, he held her, circling his arms around her slender waist. Closing his eyes, he listened to their beating hearts, certain their love was matched.

"How did you know about the necklace?"

"Pashkin told me how much it meant to you."

Isabella gasped, her grip tightening on his arm. He glanced down at her upturned face and kissed the tip of her nose. They held each other for a time. Needing no words.

"If I stay in bed any longer, I'll miss my appointment at the agency."

"Cassie doesn't fair well with governesses," he said.

"I'm not hiring a governess," she said and almost laughed at the look of relief that crossed his face. "I intend to teach music."

"Wife, have ye heard Cassie sing?"

Her chin angled up.

Nicholas sighed. "The child lives to torment me and no doubt has rallied you to aid her."

"Nonsense. Cassie loves you. In time she will improve."

"Not before I lose my ear."

"I don't intend to solely teach Cassie, Nicholas," she said before he interrupted again. "I mean to be a tutor, and for that I need students. Students the agency can supply."

He looked at his wife, finally understanding her intent. It

was hopeless trying to convince her she needn't worry about money. He suspected it was more than that. She found joy in music and, like him, Isabella had sampled freedom and found it to her liking.

His fingers stroked her cheek. She defied him at every turn, his Isabella, when no one else dared. "It's an ungodly hour to seek students."

"And the break of dawn is not?" Blushing, she spoke of their morning play. Still her chin tilted upward, their eyes locking.

He shifted, their limbs tangling. Her boldness was inviting. "I could think of other ways to spend your time."

"You promised I could carry on with my affairs." Her fingers combed his hair. "You promised not to interfere." Her free hand trailed down his stomach until she cupped him. "Do you plan to go back on your word, sir?"

If he wasn't already lying down, he would have swooned like a maiden having her skirts lifted for the first time. Closing his eyes, Nicholas savored her warm stokes. When he'd promised she could carry on with her affairs, he'd meant with her lovers. She'd been so reluctant to marry him that he'd thought her hesitation due to another man. But hadn't she proven her virtue on their wedding night? What a fool he had been. There was no doubt she'd kept faithful to their vows. Him. Placing his hand beneath her chin, he tilted it up until they were a mere breath apart. Knowing he was his wife's only lover made him possessive, reckless, as he covered her mouth with his.

Her breath hitched, and he swallowed the startled sound between his parted lips.

She was his, always his.

The tightness in his chest eased, replaced by an entirely new feeling. Belonging, or was it happiness? Was this how it felt to be truly happy? Heavens, he wanted to explore this sensation forever. He gathered her closer. Their breaths mingled. The scent of their lovemaking flooded his senses. Fully intending to ravish her, Nicholas shifted his hold, giving him greater access to the sweetness of her mouth. His tongue licked across her lower lip, nipped, until she welcomed him in.

This moment had evaded him for far too long. From Africa to China, weeks and months at sea, all his exploring and plunder had not found him such treasures. Yet here she was, holding the key to his very happiness, ignorant to the crumbling walls around his heart. No other woman had ever affected him so.

He was lost in the sensation. Hungry for her touch. This woman, his wife, he would show her that she was more than vows said before a priest. He would show her that they were bonded.

Nicholas eased away from their embrace. "Does that answer your question, wife?"

She smiled wickedly up at him. "No."

Nicholas's grin widened as he reached for her again, but Isabella placed a finger on his lips. "But it tells me that your thoughts have wandered elsewhere."

Nicholas laughed.

CHAPTER 30

$\mathcal{N}$icholas couldn't remember a time when he was more pleased.

Cassie had embraced and accepted Isabella. She had also taken to learning with the same spirit she showed aboard his ship. Mature beyond her years, the child now acted and played more like the little girl he had seen start to disappear while at sea. He was to blame for the loss of her innocence. Five years ago, he hadn't known what to do with a child, much less a lass. He'd treated her as he would a lad, taking her on voyages and having her at his heels when she should have been playing with other little girls.

Now he returned home to a wife and a marriage. Isabella surprised him. She'd fought for him—for them—even when he was prepared to grant her wishes of freedom. Isabella had set aside her fears. She had not doubted his faithfulness, and when they loved, they were equal. A position he was eager to implement in every aspect of their marriage.

It no longer mattered that he was not her peer or that she was abandoned by society. She loved him.

Closing his eyes, Nicholas recalled her whispered words

of love. Those words gained entrance to every fiber of his being. He'd never felt more whole, more complete than when he was in Isabella's arms.

With one last glance, he put Emsley's notes into his desk. Harold had done well, winning not only what was owed to Isabella, but also to her father.

Isabella's father would be repaid, but first, he'd see the money not gambled, but instead used to restore Lord Carolus Pennington's property and coffers. Family was important. A strong one, more so. With Isabella as his wife, her father and sister were now an extension of his family, and he'd see them thrive.

Closing the drawer, he moved from behind the writing desk and lifted Cassie from the chesterfield and into his arms. He held her close. For the past two days, Cassie had only allowed him brief moments of solitude. He did not mind. He had missed her too.

"Let's find your mother, shall we?"

"Papa, are we a family now?"

"Aye, lassie."

Cassie hugged him. "You, me, Mama, Uncle Harold and Aunt Virginia?"

He nodded. "You have a grandpa too, sweetheart."

She looked at him, wide eyed.

"Would you like to meet him?"

"Oh yes, Papa." She frowned. "What if he doesn't like me?"

"I think you'll be his perfect second chance." He tapped her nose.

"Papa? What's wrong with Uncle Harold?"

He chuckled at the unexpected change in discussion. Harold suffered from the same ills he did. "He's in love."

She made a disgusted groan. "I'm never falling in love."

Nicholas laughed and kissed her on the cheek. When they

entered the music room, they found Isabella looking out the window.

"Isabella?"

Turning, she offered a weak smile, her eyes watering with unshed tears.

Setting Cassie on her feet, he said, "Why don't you ask Miss Conley and Mrs. Berths to prepare a lunch?"

"With chocolate cake?"

"Aye lass, with chocolate cake." When she skipped from the room, he waited a moment longer before turning to Isabella. "What's wrong?"

Isabella wiped her cheek.

"Lass?" He moved until they faced each other.

When her fist moved along her skirt, only then did he notice the paper she held. Taking the letter, his eyes remained on her.

If this was another scandal in the dailies or another message uninviting her to an event, so help him, he'd see someone pay for hurting her. It was enough knowing *he'd* caused her pain.

"What's this?"

"A letter from my father."

He read the note once, twice, but couldn't find the cause for her unhappiness. Then it dawned. "You mean he's not paid you a visit?" The edge of the paper crumpled under his grip. How could the man not inquire as to his daughter's well-being?

"I believe it's shame that keeps him away." Her lips quivered.

Nicholas shook his head. "I'm sorry, Isabella." She came willingly when he folded his arms around her.

"To think that all this time he couldn't forgive himself. That he, too, was hurting."

Nicholas closed his eyes, holding her closer.

"Father wishes us happiness. He hopes in time I can forgive him." She looked at him. "How can I?"

"Isabella."

Pushing out of his arms, she shook her head and pointed to the letter. "He's put my dowry into an account."

Cursing under his breath, he ran his fingers through his hair.

"He's had it all along! How different would my life be? Father could have asked me not to marry Emsley instead of lying to me. Instead, I've had nothing but scandal."

"Would you have listened Isabella?"

She turned away.

"If your father had pointed out Emsley's flaws, would you have listened?"

"He led me to believe—he led all of London to believe he'd lost my inheritance when in fact he'd chosen to deny... Father watched me struggle. How could I forgive that?"

He couldn't let her go on hating her father, not when he was to blame. He'd lost his own father. Nicholas wouldn't let Isabella lose hers, even if that meant everything they'd shared since his return would now be gone.

"Do you regret it, Isabella, not marrying him?"

"No!"

He cupped her face in both hands while he searched for the truth. Certain she no longer cared for the other man, Nicholas released her. His hands dug deep into his pockets. "Your father told the truth. Your dowry came from me."

She gasped. "You paid for my hand?"

"We both know that's not true." His jaw clenched.

"I don't understand."

"We'd already come to an understanding when I visited your father. It was important to me that your independence be restored. In my own selfish way, *I* wanted to be the reason you chose my bed."

"Oh, Nicholas."

"I didn't want coin or dependents to be the reasons you stayed. Can you understand that?" He looked at her. "I wouldn't stand in your way should you choose to leave."

"Leave? I love you, Nicholas." Her arms circled his waist.

Eyes closed, he held her. "I love you too, lass. Isabella, I only wanted you to have the means to…"

"I know. Thank you."

"You'll make amends with your father?" He rested his forehead against hers, relieved that there were no more secrets between them.

"I would very much like that."

"You're not angry?"

A hiccupped laugh passed her lips. "That the mighty captain attended to my needs before his own? No, I'm not angry." Joy, that's what she felt as she rubbed her cheek against his chest. "Who knew you were this…tender."

"I'm nae tender, lass."

Isabella looked up and smiled. "You're thoughtful, kind, and generous."

Nicholas grumbled.

"And I love you," she said.

"And?" he teased.

"Knowledge of your softer character will never leave this room."

"I would hate to have my wife walk the plank." Lowering his head, he whispered, "I love you," before brushing his lips with hers. When she groaned impatiently, he deepened their kiss, giving his wife exactly what she sought.

CHAPTER 31

*I*sabella slipped out the kitchen door with her bonnet and gloves in hand and walked the stone path to the garden. With Cassie off for an afternoon stroll with Virginia, she had an hour before sunset and Nicholas's return home. She looked up at the late afternoon sun, which cast a warm orange glow across the sky.

She preferred the early morning hours, with the smell of roses and the fluttering of birds for company. But six months of marriage and Nicholas still kept them in bed past any respectable hour. She laughed. By the time their limbs were untangled, the sun would be high, and it would be too hot for outdoor work.

He did it on purpose. By starting her work at a late hour, he guaranteed she'd be where he wanted her. *In bed.* He'd stated as much without a trace of remorse.

She'd seen quite enough of dawn. Isabella smothered a yawn, promising to halt her husband's insatiable lust. Or at least to regain one night's sleep. None of her excuses or pretend ailments had worked. The man had a cure for everything, and she found herself, against her better judgment, enjoying his discovery of what ailed her.

Securing the wild curls of her hair under the bonnet, she pulled her work gloves on each hand and opened the door to the playhouse Harold built for Cassie. Smiling, she gathered the small box from the corner, tucking it under her arm. Isabella remembered the special pirate's permission she'd received from Cassie to store her tools in the corner of the doll house. She was also warned against crossing the threshold with anything as frivolous as knitting, or, heaven forbid, embroidery.

She had laughed until the child had added a bit to the ceremony about being tossed overboard. She shivered, and wondered if Nicholas had ever tossed anyone into the sea.

Setting the box down, she quickly got to work pulling the weeds. Pashkin had wrinkled his nose at her request to help tend the garden, but she had insisted. Much to his displeasure, he relented, giving her a plot of soil at the far end of the garden. They'd worked side by side on many evenings—which she'd learned was the best time to avoid the heat—slowly gaining his approval.

Isabella straightened her shoulders when a shadow blocked the decreasing sunlight. "You're incorrigible, Nicholas. Surely it's not time yet. If you're in need of my company, you'll have to take a turn at pulling weeds."

"As my mistress, there would be no need to play in the dirt."

Isabella stiffened. The miniature shovel fell from her grip.

"I'll see you in the style you're accustomed."

Gathering her skirts, Isabella stood, then turned. "But I'm not your mistress, Lord Emsley."

"A technicality, one I would see corrected."

"What do you want?" He was scaring her. "I have nothing else to say to you."

"I came to have words with your bastard husband, but found you instead." He shrugged. "You'll do."

He took a step towards her and she retreated with one of her own.

"Wait, Emsley," she said, and was grateful when he halted. "What do you want with Nicholas?" Her brows drew together. Other than Nicholas marrying her when Emsley had other plans for her future, Isabella couldn't see a reason why he sought her husband.

"Don't play naive!" His mouth pressed into a thin hard line. "Innocence wouldn't work now that all of London knows you are that bastard's whore."

Isabella shivered.

"He took a great deal from me."

"I don't understand."

His lips twisted into a grimace.

"Nicholas had nothing to do with us, Emsley. It was your choice. You chose someone else, and now we're both happier for it."

"No matter. He'll pay for taking what's mine."

Dear God, why wouldn't he stop rambling?

This was not the Emsley she remembered—the doting fiancé who indulged her childhood dreams and planned a future. This man's eyes burned with lust and greed. And he'd lost weight, drawing out the bones on his face.

"Your captain acted too hastily. My wife's estate is mine in name only, least until after the birth of my first heir." His smile was mocking. "But he holds my purse. I mean to have it back."

What on earth was he talking about?

He advanced again, forcing her to retreat further down the slope. She glanced towards the back of the house. With luck, someone had seen Emsley or would come looking for her.

Isabella shook her head as Emsley continued to ramble about the money Nicholas had stolen from him. The man did not make sense. Nicholas had a thriving business. He didn't need Emsley's coin. Then she remembered Nicholas's promise to see her return to society, and there was the dowry.

Her stomach dropped. If she was right, then Emsley might be much more dangerous than she had first thought.

"Think of your wife," she said, trying to reason with him. "This is madness."

"She's a cunning little gem." His head tilted. "She's the one who suggested making you my mistress."

Her brows rose. The first beads of sweat pooled along her spine.

"She devised a plan to make sure you were dependent on my support, and to secure your inheritance from your father as well. I wasn't sure at first, I really wanted you. Still do." His eyes raked along the length of her. "Such a nice girl you were. Untouched."

She pressed the back of her hand against her lips, suppressing a strangled cry. Her back came against the rough bark of an oak tree, and Isabella knew she'd retreated too far to be seen from the house.

"You're no better than the rest of them," he snickered, regaining her attention. "Not even a year and you were lifting your skirts."

"He's my husband."

"He wouldn't want you after I have a turn."

"You're wrong!"

She briefly thought of running, but his fingers closed around her upper arm.

He drew a gun from the breast pocket of his coat. Isabella whimpered. Suddenly she feared being rescued. What if someone got injured, what if it was little Cassie? Tears clouded her vision.

Emsley was mad.

Did he think she would welcome him after he married someone else? How had she not seen this side of him? Pressing her back further against the tree, she prayed for distance.

"I didn't know you had plans for us."

"Of course I did," he said, as though she was dense. "I was coming for you that very night. My wife thought a public show of sympathy and our offer of friendship would…" He shook his head as if disagreeing with his wife's reasoning.

"Think about what you're doing… Your wife couldn't have approved of this." To her horror, even as she said the words, they did not hold conviction.

He shrugged. "My wife only cares for wealth and has taken lovers of her own."

Truly, they were insane. "How did you know my father would act as you wished?"

A spark grew, softening his dark eyes. "He is a bad hand at cards. Once I called in my debt, and you were disgraced… he no longer had an enticing dowry. It was not my intention to disgrace you, Isabella."

Isabella spread her arms. "Yet, here we are."

"I needed to show you I was your only way. What difference would it have made if the ton thought we were lovers? You were going to be mine in the end."

Penniless and soiled, her father no longer had a daughter to repair his coffers and he had one more to marry off—her younger sister. And it had all been part of Emsley's plan. Emsley and his wife sought to bend her to their will. A wave of nausea curled in her stomach.

"You have everything," she said, unable to suppress a gasp

when his body pinned her to the tree. "Surely you can find others."

"I still want you as my mistress."

Isabella flinched.

The gun pressed against her side, Emsley released her arm. He hiked her skirts.

"Please no!"

"You've already lifted them for that bastard when it should have been me. You'll like me better between your thighs."

His mouth crashed against hers with punishing assurance. Isabella pushed his chest, fists beating against his shoulders with little damage, until one of her wild blows connected with his ear.

He would not have this. She would not let him!

"Stop," he grunted, bringing the gun fully between them.

Isabella screamed as his hand clutched her undergarments. He tugged roughly. The sound of ripping fabric pierced the quiet evening.

Shock stilled her. Her eyes squeezed shut. "I'll never forgive you."

"In time…"

"Never! Nicholas will see you dead." She looked at him. "And I," she leaned forward, "hope to hear you beg when he does so."

Wildly, she struck his face, again and again, until he released her skirts.

He backhanded her.

She fell to the hard ground, tears smearing down her cheeks. Slowly her hand covered the smarting flesh.

"See what you made me do."

He towered over her as she tried to push away. He would kill her and no one would know. She covered her face as he raised his hand to strike again. The blow never came.

The gun fired.

Isabella screamed, waiting for the pain.

When she opened her eyes Nicholas was there, lunging forward, his weight knocking Emsley to the grass. The men rolled, exchanging blows.

Hope surged when Nicholas straddled Emsley. Nicholas's fist raising high before smashing against Emsley's jaw.

Nicholas stood, dragging the dazed man up and handing him over to Pashkin and Chambers. "Take him to Bow Street...to the runners." He picked up the gun, tucking it into Chambers' pocket. "I intend to press charges," he said for Emsley's benefit.

The men were halfway up the slope when Nicholas knelt beside her. "Isabella? Did he..."

She followed his gaze to her shredded dress. "No," she shook her head. "He didn't." Isabella swallowed. Nicholas gathered her in his arms then grunted in protest. "You're shot!"

"Nae more than a graze."

Isabella searched his face, tears running down her cheeks. His hands cupped her face. "I should have killed him for what he did." His thumb caressed the swelling flesh. "I can't lose ye, lass." He kissed her hair, her closed eyes. And with the lightest touch, his lips brushed hers.

"Oh, Nicholas." Isabella buried her face against his chest. "I love you."

He held her as she cried, stroking her back in lazy circles. For a long time they held each other, basking in the pleasure of the other's embrace. His need for reassurance matched her own.

"How did you find us?"

He smiled. "I found Pashkin cleaning your tools and grumbling about never understanding women. It is not like you to abandon yer precious flowers."

She nodded, grateful it was him and not Cassie that came looking for her. He grunted again, reminding her of his injured shoulder. "We need a doctor," she said, shifting in his hold. "And rags. Hot water. And—"

"And there'll be no more gardening alone for a time."

Her brows rose. "But...why?" Emsley was no longer a threat.

His eyes darkened. "I didn't protect you today."

She gripped his uninjured arm. "Emsley's behavior was not your fault."

Nicholas ignored her reasoning. She'd seen that determined scowl before and knew no amount of reassurance would change his mind.

"You couldn't have known."

He stepped out of her reach. "I should have known he was dangerous. That he would not simply be embarrassed or accept his loss and move on. He could have killed you."

"But he didn't."

"What good am I if I can't protect you?" He tucked a loose strand of hair behind her ear. "I've brought ye nothing but trouble."

Her heart squeezed. Going to him, she circled her arms around his waist. "No, Nicholas. You've brought me happiness."

He didn't answer.

She tilted her chin, looking at him. "Nicholas?"

He didn't look at her.

"He'd gone because of you." She touched his chin until his gaze held hers and she saw that he'd been frightened. She saw her own fear reflected in his eyes. They had only just found each other and so much could have been taken from them. But it hadn't been, they were whole.

"What if I were not here in time?"

She smoothed his trembling lower lip with her thumb.

"But you were, my love." Her arms circled his waist again. "Are we to let him interrupt the rest of our lives?"

It took a moment as she watched him wrestle with his emotions—his belief that he'd placed her in danger at war with his need to be at her side—before he growled and lowered his mouth to hers. "Nae." He kissed her then, gently at first, before deepening their embrace to one of hunger and need. The need to reassure each other that they were alive. She welcomed the feel of his tongue moving against hers and knew he was reveled in knowing she was safe.

"Now come, husband. I'm an excellent nurse maid."

Nicholas grunted. "Are ye now?"

"Aye," she teased.

CHAPTER 32

"*I*an." He clapped the lad lightly on his back.

"Aye, Captain."

Captain. It was his first journey without Nicholas at the helm. Harold swiped his long fingers through his hair, his only show of nervousness and excitement. He was ready, more than ready to sail.

"Inform the second, we leave in ten."

"Aye, Captain." Ian finished securing the remaining rope around the hook, then dashed off in the direction that would take him below deck.

Holding onto the rails, his eyes roamed the shores of London. It was just as he remembered—the call of the ocean, the stillness of the coming morning. Harold closed his eyes and savored all of it. He did not need eyes to see the thinning fog blanketing the Thames. He inhaled, dragging fresh sea air into his lungs.

A slow tingle started at his nape; the fine hairs along his neck stood. Dawn rapidly approached. He wanted the sun to greet him at sea. It had always been that way between Nicholas and him, starting their day—their journey—

without the stench of the city trailing after them. At sea, little touched them.

His eyes opened with renewed anticipation. A few of the crew said their goodbyes to their families, lovers and lads who would one day sail aboard his ship. Harold turned away, leaving them to their privacy. He reached for the bridge, their only connection to the docks, and tugged the strip of wood.

A swirl of skirts filled his vision. Harold paused as one slipper-clad foot, then another, stepped onto the plank of wood.

Every muscle in his back flexed. The last thing he needed was a woman begging for passage.

Harold grunted. "You'd best wait to board the Constantine," he said without sparing a glance.

He expected pleading or a harsh rebuke delivered from a delicate voice. He received neither. And when those soft feet did not move or retreat, he followed the trail of fabric.

Harold froze. *Virginia.*

He straightened, their gazes holding. Only then did she take a tentative step in his direction.

"Will you not let me aboard your ship?"

"What are you doing here?" His eyes moved beyond her.

She didn't answer.

He looked at her again. "What is it?" Had something happened to Cassie, Nicholas, Isabella?

Her fingers tightened around her bag's handle as she looked from one shipmate to another. Following her gaze, he cursed. The entire crew stared at them with mixtures of amusement and curiosity. Gripping her elbow, he guided them towards his quarters, then closed the door.

"What brought you to the docks alone, Virginia? At such an hour?"

"You."

Harold paused. His eyes narrowed. A week ago, she would not have him. Refused to be with him, and now she expected…what? His grip on her arm tightened. "Is this a game for you?"

"What…?" Her eyes widened.

"Tell me, Virginia. Is this how you plan to lead me on a merry chase?"

"No!"

"Do you think—"

"I love you."

They stared at each other. Him unable to believe her rushed words.

"I love you," she said again.

The words were a balm for his soul. He inhaled, filling his lungs with them.

"I want to marry you, Harold. I don't want to be afraid anymore. Afraid of my past." Her long lashes lowered. "I'm barren. You should know before we go any further, so there is no chance…" She swallowed. "I couldn't take it if you left or grew resentful."

"God dammit, woman."

She gasped when he shook her. Taking a steadying breath, he loosened his hold on her arm.

"Do you think I wanted you for the number of bairns you could produce?" He ran weary fingers through her hair. "Virginia," he said impatiently. "When I'm with you, I'm home. Do ye understand that? You take me as I am. You meet me halfway, and that's more than a mon like me expects."

"Then you wouldn't send me back?"

"I should. This is no short trip. We sail for Scotland." His lips brushed hers in a gentle caress.

"Scotland?" Her eyes widened.

"You'll do as I say, when I say, and not put yourself in danger."

"No... I mean, yes!"

He smiled and kissed the corner of her mouth. "With you by my side, I have a reason to reclaim my lands."

"You'll have me?" Her eyes closed in wonder.

"What better way to test your theory than as my wife." His hand moved to her stomach, fingers spreading wide to cradle all of her softness. Then his lips claimed hers for a kiss that took them beyond boundaries, beyond oceans and time.

EPILOGUE

*N*icholas woke his wife with tender kisses on her shoulder.

"You'll miss your voyage," she sighed.

"I'm not going on this trip."

Her eyes shot open. "Do you mean it?"

He chuckled.

When her hands cupped his face, he sucked one of her fingers into his mouth, sucking it gently before releasing it. "Harold is more than capable of captaining the ship, and he deserves the chance to spread his wings. He has proven that this past week."

"You're not staying because of me, then? To protect me, I mean?"

"Can't a mon want to be with his wife?"

She gasped when his hand smoothed over her stomach. "I don't want you to relinquish what you love, Nicholas. Captaining is the best part of you."

"Nae love, you're the best part of me." Nicholas smiled when she stared at him through half-closed eyelids.

"Harold won your dowry from Emsley, Isabella."

Her arms closed around his narrow waist. "Remind me to thank him."

"I'd rather you thanked me." His grin broadened. "If you agree, I will give a sum to your father to repair his debts and restore his lands to their previous glory."

"I'm not sure he deserves your sympathy."

Smoothing the frown lines along her mouth, he said, "I'm not doing it for your father, love, but to save your sister from the same fate ye experienced."

"I love you, Captain Nicholas Ferguson."

He rolled her over until she was flat on her back. His hips deliciously wedged against her core. "And I you, Lady Isabella Ferguson, and I you. Now…about our unfulfilled part of the bargain." He rocked back and forth. "Let's see what we could do about my request for brats."

"You're incorrigible." She laughed. "No respectable husband is interested in his wife long past honeymoon."

"There lie your problems," he said. "We haven't had a honeymoon."

"And what's my other problem?" Isabella moaned as he parted her folds, finding her slick, ready.

"I'm nae respectable."

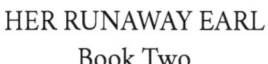

HER RUNAWAY EARL
Book Two

London, England
Mid-Summer

Lady Catherine Pennington stared at the drop of jam gingerly running down her first finger. Today should be a happy day, a cause for celebration. Instead, her thoughts kept returning to the threatening letter she received after confronting the gallery owner about the forgeries hanging on his wall.

Catherine grimaced as she thought of confronting the gallery owner again later today. It was a miracle the man hadn't thrown her out, or worse: canceled her noon opening.

Bringing her finger to her lips, she licked the droplet, intending to savor her breakfast, then cringed when the front door flung open, a loud thud echoing down the hall as the brass knob hit the plastered wall.

"I am here to see my grandfather," Cassie shouted, hurrying across the foyer.

Catherine turned in her chair as her niece reached the banister leading to the second floor a hair before the butler.

"But, mademoiselle, it is quite early," the butler groaned.

"Never mind that, Thornwell. Grandda is expecting me."

It was comical, Thornwell's reaction to Cassie's early morning visits, though she'd been paying them unexpected calls since she discovered she had a grandfather. Catherine slapped a hand over her mouth to stifle her laugh, least she give the child any encouragement. She eyed her strawberry-jam toast one last time and sighed before placing it back onto her plate.

Pushing back her chair, she brushed the crumbs off the skirt of her muslin dress. No doubt, the child had enough wit to out-maneuver the butler.

Cat sighed. She should intercept Cassie at the stairs—if only to give her father the grace of donning pants. The earl had likely heard the commotion and suspected his granddaughter was afoot. When she entered the foyer, Cassie was already halfway up the stairs.

"Lady Cassie," Catherine said, looking up from the foot of the stairs. "Is it not too early to call?"

Cassie paused for a senior's heartbeat, then turned, bestowing one of her many *why...I-don't-know-what-you-mean* smiles. "Good morning, Auntie."

Catherine frowned. Cassie refused all formality, and for that, Catherine blamed Nicholas, the child's father, for that slight in the girl's upbringing. Their family was considered the black sheep of the ton, but that was no excuse to prove the high society correct. "Why don't we have breakfast while Thornwell readies the earl?"

The child looked from the butler's stern face then back to her.

Catherine thought of nudging Thornwell into a reassuring smile as Cassie hesitated before starting to step down onto the stair below. One jewel-covered slipper peeking out from under her pale-yellow dress held suspended, as if waiting for the puppeteer to lower his string. Catherine held her breath, wondering if the child would retreat.

"You can tell me the reason for your urgency; mayhap I can help."

Cassie's descent halted, and she blushed. "Sorry, Aunt

Catherine!" Turning, she raced up the remaining stairs to her grandfather's rooms.

Catherine shook her head and sighed, intending to resume eating her jam toast. She had done her job, having given her father an entire ten minutes to button his shirt this time.

"I think our best course is not to answer the door, my lady."

Catherine considered Thornwell's proposition. "And yet, she is not beyond climbing the roses," she chuckled. "I don't want her getting hurt. Can you imagine? If Nicholas's wrath was not enough, Isabella would cut every hair on my head!" During one of their disagreeable moments as children, Isabella had shaved her head, calling it "airing out her thoughts." Catherine had no intention of being bald again. This time, it was the butler's time to sigh. "I shall answer her calls promptly, my lady."

Neither had moved from their position at the foot of the stairs. Usually, Cassie's impromptu visits were a moment of amusement. Cassie enjoyed having family and two households to scurry between. And despite her reservations about Cassie's early morning visits, Catherine and her father were also enjoying the disruption to their lives. If anything, the child's arrival had been a blessing. But something about *this* visit made her pause.

Thornwell cleared his throat. "I don't suppose you know what she's about, my lady?"

"Not the faintest clue, Thornwell."

"She was exceedingly determined today, my lady."

Catherine's eyes narrowed. "Quite true. I didn't even receive so much as a kiss or hug."

Thornwell nodded. "It was as if she came in on that new steam engine."

"And did you see? She had blushed, Thornwell...*blushed*."

"*Exactement a droite*. Precisely."

Catherine's eyes narrowed even further. She didn't like it one bit. One last look at Thornwell's face compelled her forward. The smooth bottoms of her slippers provided little grip as she hurried up the stairs after her niece.

Taking a lesson from Cassie, she pushed open the door to her father's room without knocking. When she entered, they both turned to stare. Catherine ignored the pinch of guilt she felt from barging into the room when she saw Cassie's cheeks were still flushed.

The unease that had chased her up the stairs after Cassie settled in the pit of her stomach. Taking a seat in the reading chair positioned in the corner of the room, she faced them, frowning when the pair said nothing. Instead they kept glancing her way, their heads coming together in hushed whispers.

Lord Carolus sat hunched forward, his back against the headboard in a manner unbecoming of an earl of his status. His nightshirt was carelessly thrown over the dressing bench. She guessed he'd had time to change into proper attire before sneaking back under the covers—thank goodness for that.

Cassie perched on the edge of the bed.

"Does your mother know you're here?"

Cassie turned and blinked twice before answering. "Aunt Catherine, would I not leave her word of my departure?"

Catherine smiled at the sly evasion. That was precisely what Cassie would do—and she had done it—cleverly and often.

"Chambers drove me," Cassie went on, her lashes downcast.

If it were anyone else, Catherine would think the girl showed a twinge of remorse. But this was Cassie, and the child proved naught but determined once she got her hooks into an idea. That persistence—and the fact Cassie sought Lord Carolus's council—confirmed her suspicions.

Cassie was indeed up to mischief.

"We do not want any harm to come to you. If we couldn't find you…it would worry us, especially your parents," the earl said sternly. "We have only just gained so much; let's not test the saints, shall we?"

Cassie's shoulders slumped, but she nodded, long strings of curls bouncing on her shoulders.

Catherine huffed. "Couldn't you have spoken to the earl at the gallery opening, Cassie?"

Cassie looked at the earl.

"Oh no, this was all your idea." The earl crossed his arms.

Cassie scrunched her nose and squirmed. "Well, since Uncle Harold came back from Scotland, and with Mama having the new baby, I started a family chart."

Catherine nodded. That made sense. Cassie had more family than previously, and she was the curious sort. It was natural she would want to know her parents' history.

It was also plausible she would need the earl's help. Catherine drummed her fingers against her skirt. Maybe she could persuade Aunt Megan to assist Cassie. After all, who knew more about their family than Aunt Megan? And as an added benefit, the distraction might even allow her to slip away from her chaperone to visit the little gift shop on Bond Street to purchase her new novel.

She had waited an entire month for the new installment, and this was her first opportunity to retrieve the item without the watchful gaze of her aunt.

"When Emmitt visited, he told me he has one too—a family chart."

"Yes, Emmitt comes from a long line," Catherine said. "They are ridiculously numerous."

Emmitt and Cassie became fast friends this past year, and the two got along well when they were not competing for one thing or the other. Even then, Catherine thought the two enjoyed the sport of besting each other.

Cassie linked her fingers together, her mouth stretching into a mischievous smile, and Catherine knew this was one of those times her niece sought to best her friend.

"I see." Catherine frowned. She was not convinced that wanting a chart was reason enough for Cassie's behavior.

"Let the child finish," the earl chuckled. "You haven't long to wait."

"Emmitt's is as big as the map on Da's ship, Devil's Pearl." Cassie's eyes widened, holding Catherine's. "His family chart has cousins...*cousins!*"

"Of course it does." Raising from the chair to sit at the edge of the bed, she took Cassie's small hand.
The earl groaned. "Catherine, you ought to hear the child out—"

Catherine waved her father's warning aside, choosing to reassure her niece. "Emmitt comes from a large family and an even longer line. But we'll all help with your family chart. Once completed, I'll make a painting of it. I bet Emmitt does not own a painting of his chart."

"But surely..." The child's smile broadened, reminding Catherine of the Thames under the glow of first light. "Surely, I, too, can have cousins?"

Catherine gave Cassie a wan smile. "I'm afraid the only way you can have cousins is if I..." Startling, Catherine looked from the child—whose face held all the excitement of gaining a new pet—and to her father. He had the grace to restrain his embarrassment along with the twitch hovering at the corners of his mouth. "Surely you don't expect..." she said, turning back to Cassie.

Cassie jumped off the bed so fast Catherine thought her legs would tangle in the sheets, but she landed on the floor with the swiftness of a cat into its second life. "I'll tell Aunt Megan!"

Catherine groaned. Aunt Megan would like nothing more than to find her a husband, even if that meant using her great niece's family chart as the reason. "Cassie, wait!" When Cassie faced them, eyes bright with excitement, Catherine couldn't bear to tell the child she had no intention of marrying. Father had just granted permission to display her paintings, and she planned to make great use of the gallery and the slice of freedom she had been allotted.

"You said you'd help!"

This time it was Catherine's turn to blush. She did not mean to *help* bear a cousin, as if a babe could be ordered with a new gown and fascinator from Paris. Whatever she had thought to sway the child would have to wait as Cassie sprinted from the room. Maybe it would be easier to persuade Isabella to let the child board Devil's Pearl. She blamed Nicholas's indulgence for Cassie's constant search for new adventures. Facing the earl, she intended to gain his support. "Father—"

"Don't look at me, I was roused the same as you." He pointed his finger in her direction. "I warned you to let her finish before offering your...*services*."
Catherine groaned.

The earl chuckled.

"What am I to do?" Catherine swallowed. As much as she hated disappointing Cassie, there was no other alternative.

She had long ago lost her heart and had no intention of giving what remained of herself to another.

"About what?" Isabella asked from the doorway, the captain standing behind her.

Since her sister announced she was with child, Nicholas had hardly left her side, no doubt another reason for Cassie's increased freedom. She looked at Isabella's rounded midsection and smiled. They were right together, Nicholas and Isabella. Seeing her sister made Cassie's innocent request more painful.

Catherine could marry, but that wouldn't stop her heart from being lonely. All because she had foolishly fallen in love with a man who was no longer in England, and she had fallen in love long before recognizing the emotion or having time to stop it from happening. Adding to her pain was his distance following the night his mother drowned in the lake. *Their lake.*

She swallowed, determined not to relive memories that still caused her nightmares and restless sleep.
Isabella shifted, rubbing her lower back. All her weight rested at her center, not a stitch gained anywhere else. If one stood on the nose behind Isabella, one could not tell she was pregnant.

"Am I to have no peace today?" the earl questioned, smiling nonetheless.

"I thought we were meeting at the gallery?" Catherine said. Excitement and a rush of nerves gushed through her as she remembered today was her opening. The first showing of her paintings.

"So did we, until Chambers told us of Cassie's escape," Isabella said.

"You shouldn't encourage her, you know." Catherine jabbed a finger towards the earl from her position at the edge of the bed. She supposed she ought to thank Cassie for the distraction, then shook her head.

"My one grandchild?" The earl slapped a hand over his chest in feigned affront.

"What happens when there are more? You can't indulge all your grandchildren, Father," Isabella said.
"You worry about giving me grandchildren. I'll worry about spoiling them."

"God's teeth, tell us what's going on?" Nicholas bellowed.

Poor Nicholas. He was having trouble keeping pace with Cassie. Added to that was a temperamental babe that had yet to be born. The thought of more children was surely adding to his graying mop of hair. She almost felt sorry for her brother-in-law.

Almost.

Catherine tapped her fingers against the red-and-gold duvet. "Your daughter…" Catherine smiled a small victory when Nicholas and Isabella groaned in unison. Any sentence beginning with Cassie did not bode well. That, they all agreed on. "Insists on having cousins for her family chart."

BUY HER RUNAWAY EARL

NEWSLETTER

Join Robecca's historical newsletter.
Link to Newsletter

The Social loop...

Facebook: https://www.facebook.com/
groups/robeccaaustin/
Website: https://www.robeccaaustin.com

Other Book by Robecca

Ladies in Scandal Series
The Captain's Lady (Nicholas and Isabella)
https://www.amazon.com/dp/B0886KD16Q

Her Runaway Earl (Jerr and Catherine)
https://www.amazon.com/dp/B08M65CG1T

Her Wicked Viscount (Ava and Daniel)
https://www.amazon.com/dp/B09FBVZHZ4

Briefs – *short stories with sizzle*
Champion of the Isles (Rand and Cathia) –Historical
Naughty Pleasure (Isa and Duncan) –Historical

Thank You

Thank you to my awesome readers!
If you help promote or read my books, thank you! Or if you

enjoyed this book or scooped it in a promo, consider leaving a review.

Meet the Author

ROBECCA AUSTIN IS the author of happy ever after romance stories. She enjoys crafting tales of sassy heroines and alpha heroes that have a soft center.

You can find her outside enjoying nature and lots of sunshine when there are no bugs. When she's not writing her next novel, she's busy battling Cystic Fibrosis and hugging family. She lives and works in Canada.

21701351R00169